Stubborn. Willful. Independent. Alone.

Each label he applied to her struck a responsive chord in himself. Suddenly, despite all sense, he wanted to know Jo Spencer better.

"Have dinner with me," he said impulsively. "Anywhere you like."

Jo shook her head and stepped into the elevator. As she pushed the button, he placed both palms against the doors to hold them apart. "Why not?"

"I have an engagement at seven," she said evenly.

"Break it."

"Why?"

He stared unsmilingly at her as the doors bucked under his hands. "Because you want to. Because, if you refuse, you'll always wonder. You say you want to know who I am. Have dinner with me. I guarantee that by the end of the evening you'll know *exactly* who I am."

Dear Reader,

Welcome to another month of top-notch reading from Silhouette Intimate Moments. Our American Hero title this month is called *Keeper,* and you can bet this book will be one of *your* keepers. Written by one of your favorite authors, Patricia Gardner Evans, it's a book that will involve you from the first page and refuse to let you go until you've finished every word.

Our Romantic Traditions miniseries is still going strong. This month's offering, Carla Cassidy's *Try To Remember,* is an amnesia story—but you won't forget it once you're done! The rest of the month features gems by Maura Seger, Laura Parker (back at Silhouette after a too-long absence), Rebecca Daniels and new author Laurie Walker. I think you'll enjoy them all.

And in months to come, you can expect more equally wonderful books by more equally wonderful authors—including Dallas Schulze and Rachel Lee. Here at Silhouette Intimate Moments, the loving just gets better and better every month.

Happy reading!

Leslie Wainger
Senior Editor and Editorial Coordinator

Please address questions and book requests to:
Reader Service
U.S.: P.O. Box 1325, Buffalo, NY 14269
Canadian: P.O. Box 1050, Niagara Falls, Ont. L2E 7G7

STRANGER IN TOWN

Laura Parker

Silhouette® ™
INTIMATE MOMENTS®
Published by Silhouette Books
America's Publisher of Contemporary Romance

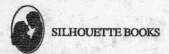 SILHOUETTE BOOKS

ISBN 0-373-07562-6

STRANGER IN TOWN

Books by Laura Parker

Silhouette Intimate Moments

Stranger in Town #562

Silhouette Special Edition

Perfect Choice #637
Dangerous Company #703

LAURA PARKER

is delighted to again be writing contemporary romance for Silhouette. By drawing on her experience
growing up along the Arkansas River, she feels a special closeness to both the characters and the places
depicted in *Stranger in Town*. "There's a sensual
quality to life in the South that is unique, immediate
and everlasting."

A Texas native, Laura recently made a "major" re-
location. Her office is now on the third floor of a turn-
of-the-century Colonial house in northern New Jer-
sey, where she lives with her husband and three children. Laura is often told that she must have the best
career around. "After all, my hours are my own. I
don't have to get up, dress and commute to work. I'm
available if my children need me. I can even play
hooky when the mood strikes. Best of all, I get to live
in my imagination—where anything is possible."

For Howard, David, Diane, Melvin and Richie of
United Van Lines—who packed my computer last.

Chapter 1

He watched the two women arguing, feeling a distinct sense of detachment. They had yet to realize that he stood on the rise above the cemetery. They were shouting at one another. Though his distance prevented him from hearing the substance of their encounter, he knew that the taller willowy blonde was being read the riot act by the shorter redhead.

He weighed the gestures between the pair, how the redhead kept pressing as the blonde retreated one graceful step at a time. Poor lady, he thought impassively. She didn't know how to defend herself. He admired her effortless grace, but it seemed her finishing-school manners had not equipped her for life in the real world.

On the other hand, he suspected that the redhead had had plenty of opportunities to learn how to deal with the real world. Even though he could not see her face clearly, he guessed her expression was as determined as her physical stance. With the impartial interest of a passerby, his attention remained on her.

There was strength of character in every line and curve of her body. It was a nice body, if a bit shorter and more rounded than the blonde's. Even from a distance, the red-

head's zest for life was obvious. He envied her that lust for
life. He'd lost his taste for it more than a year ago. Living
had become what he did to fill up the hours between rising
and sleeping each night.

He didn't know how long he might have gone on watching them circling like dancers in a postmodern ballet. Maybe
until the inevitable occurred.

The taller one looked up first and saw him. Her reaction
was theatrically exaggerated. One hand flew to her heart
while she stumbled backward two full steps. After an initial start of her own, the redhead came straight at him.

He watched her climb the incline of the levee as though it
was level ground. The breeze molded her cotton sundress
against her until the imprint of her breasts and thighs was
clearly revealed. Outlined against the vivid blue of the
summer sky, her tawny hair seemed to crackle with life. But
it was her expression that intrigued him. He had never seen
a pretty woman look more enraged.

When she was within arm's reach of him she suddenly
stopped, her lips drawn back in a snarl. "You son of a
bitch!"

She struck so quickly that her slap caught him full in the
face. He heard her swear in pain even as his face flamed
from the strength of the contact. For one vivid instant he felt
as if he had just been wakened, however crudely, from a
long sleep.

He didn't stop to think about what he was doing. He just
reached for her and dragged her close by the arm she had
raised to strike him. He had the sudden impulse to kiss her
and stared into her wide eyes for one long, silent moment.

Surprised by the intensity of his reaction, he let the redhead go, even as she jerked free of his grasp. Breathing hard,
she fell back a step. "This is all our little melodrama
needed!" She wiped her mouth with her hand, looking as
though she'd been licked by a dog.

"Jo!" the blond woman cried as she reached them. "Jo,
what are you doing?"

The woman called Jo swung around toward the other
woman. "Did you know he was back, Adelle?"

The blonde who turned to face him was so pale that he wondered if she was going to faint. "No...no I didn't." She stared at him as though she'd encountered a ghost. Her mouth formed the word twice before her breath gave it sound. "Brett?"

In view of the tension humming in the air between the three of them, he knew his reply would be anticlimactic. He chose the most direct route. "Sorry. The name's Gus Thornton."

"Liar!" Jo stepped forward again, her chin thrust out. "You're Brett Ashwood. I'd know you if you were ninety and bald."

His gaze swept dispassionately over her, taking in her cotton sundress, bare legs and sandals. Then he rubbed his cheek. "If that's your way of introducing yourself, I'd have preferred that we remained strangers."

He saw the look of confusion enter both women's expressions as he spoke. His Australian accent drew an inordinate amount of attention wherever he went in the States.

"Your voice, it's different," Adelle said, bewilderment etching a few faint lines in her porcelain complexion.

"It's just a trick," Jo countered, her face full of skepticism, "another Brett Ashwood trick."

Deciding to focus on the one in doubt, he smiled at the blonde. "Who's Brett Ashwood?"

"He ... he's someone I used—" Adelle glanced again at Jo. "I think we've made a mistake." When her gaze returned to him, her expression was doubtful. "I apologize for my cousin's behavior. It's just that you do look so much like Brett."

"Oh, for the love of Mike!" Jo burst out. "You're not going to pretend he's not Brett? You were married to him, for God's sake. It's him! The same expression, the arrogant stance. It's him, all right." Her cinnamon brown eyes reflected red glints of rage as they focused in challenge on him. "What I want to know is what you're doing here?"

"I'm just passing through, Miss—?"

She laughed unpleasantly. "That's right, you're not Brett, you're a stranger, right?"

"Right," he supplied simply.

"Well, if that's the case," she answered, disbelief coloring every syllable, "I've nothing more to say to you."

"Not even, 'I'm sorry'?" He touched his cheek for emphasis.

He saw her gaze shift to the place where her fingers had left their imprint. "No. If I'm wrong—and I doubt it—you deserve whatever you get for having the ill luck to resemble Brett Ashwood." She turned and began stalking back down the slope. She had covered several yards before she turned back, a scowl marring her pretty face. "Aren't you coming?"

Adelle shook her head so that her long blond hair flagged out across her shoulders. "In a minute. I'll meet you at the car in a minute."

"It's your funeral." Jo turned abruptly away.

Jo Spencer didn't slow her pace until she had reached the bottom of the levee, but fury and disbelief continued to dog her every step.

Brett Ashwood was back in town!

She couldn't have been more shocked, or more certain. Oh, he looked different. He was bigger and broader than she remembered, and surprisingly gray. Thick veins of silver ran from his temples into the dense growth of his mahogany hair. She had never thought of him as curly headed. The waves were too thick, too stiff. And his face was now creased by weathered lines. The old Brett had been a bit vain about his face. Eighteen and handsome in a rough, bad boy kind of way, he had liked to boast that he had a special way of shaving that avoided nicks and burns. "Smooth as a baby's ass," he'd once said to her, daring her to rub his cheek for comparison. When she'd reached out to touch him, he had whipped his head around and caught her finger in his teeth. The raw sexuality in his laughter had been too blatant for a fifteen-year-old to ignore, so she'd run from him.

Today she had slapped the face she had once been too intimidated to touch.

Jo sucked in a quick angry breath, physically shaken by the fury of her emotions as she remembered how he had held her in check while staring into her eyes.

Had he remembered her worshipful devotion to him when she was too young to know the kind of person he really was? Had he guessed that despite twelve years and a lifetime of regret, he still occupied a secret shameful corner of her heart?

No one knew the emotional impact seeing Zachary's grave had had on her already bruised psyche. It had stripped her of every defense, left her all live wires and exposed nerves . . . and vulnerable, much too vulnerable.

For a few agonizing seconds she had once again been a girl of sixteen staring into a narrow grave, trying to extract from it the meaning of the end of a life not yet fully sensate. Adelle's thoughtless remark, forgotten in the moments following, had sent her into a tirade. Then she had seen him—Brett—and there was only the hurting inside her and his remembered part in it, and the terrible, terrible guilt.

Jo clenched her right fist. Her palm still ached from the contact with his face, yet she itched to slap him again. In fact, she wished she possessed a body to match his six-foot frame so that she could beat him to a bloody pulp.

Many times during the first year after Brett had walked out of her cousin's life—and hers—she had had nightmares about this day. In the beginning she was certain she would take down one of her uncle's hunting guns and shoot him if he showed up again. It was only right that he should suffer, after what he had done. No court of law was going to do what was necessary. He'd been granted a divorce without even having had to appear in court. He'd gotten off scot-free while others had had to live with the results of his actions. The official cause of Zachary's death had been accidental. Yet she knew what no one else knew, where Brett had been and who he'd been with the night his two-month-old son died.

Now, after twelve years, he was back. He wanted something, that was certain. The old Brett had never been reluctant to make known his intentions, or to dare anyone to try to stop him. But what could he want after all this time?

Jo glanced back up the hill, her anger spurred by the fact that Adelle continued to talk with him. Fool, she thought. Adelle had remarried six years ago. She and Steven had two children and what seemed to be a scandal-free comfortable life. The sudden appearance of Brett Ashwood was bound to stir up memories best left in the grave. She had walked away from him. She only wished her cousin had been as brave.

With a whispered curse, Jo again turned away from them and looked out over the neat green lawn spread between the thick trunks of the oak and pecan trees that sheltered Cedar Bayou Cemetery. The cedar trees had passed into local history at the turn of the past century when the Arkansas River had taken a sudden detour away from the levee and left the land below it high and dry. The verdant growth that rose naturally from rich delta soil had gradually dried up the swamp and made it habitable.

Fifty years ago her grandfather had bought the property for a cemetery to augment his funeral business. He was buried here, beneath the huge white marble edifice of the Archangel Gabriel, as were her grandmother, two aunts and parents. And little Zachary Ashwood.

Jo walked over to the white headstone where minutes earlier she had placed a small wreath of white carnations and blue ribbons. The condition of the headstone had been the cause of the argument with Adelle. It was etched with lichen and green in places with mildew. It was obvious that no one regularly looked after it. She bent and began pulling away the tall blades of grass that the caretakers had been too lazy to trim. If Adelle could let go, why couldn't she?

Maybe, Jo thought sadly, the mistake had been hers in coming home on the anniversary of the worst day of her life. But recent events had crowded in on her and she wanted, desperately, to get away and think. As the past weeks of her life played back through her mind, she gave in to the hurt she had been avoiding since she'd left Baltimore yesterday afternoon.

Peter had walked out of her life a month ago. Or maybe she had sent him packing. The relationship wasn't going anywhere. As he had grown increasingly demanding, she had grown equally remote. She didn't love him, yet he couldn't understand why she was unwilling to move in and try to make it happen. The end result was that she was once more as she most often preferred to be, alone. Then yesterday, the rumor that half her department at East Coast Airlines was being laid off became fact. She was in the half given pink slips. She had simply gone straight to the ticket counter and, using her soon-to-be-revoked pass privilege, had caught the first flight heading west. She was in Memphis before she decided to come here, to come home.

She was looking for something, some part of herself that she had lost a long time ago. If only she knew how to find it. That was why she had come to the cemetery. The small marble headstone seemed to mark the beginning of her loss.

The ache at the back of her throat became tears as she stared out across the park. They gathered in her eyes until she could no longer distinguish shapes, only the dazzling green and blue shades of the day. Then one by one they silently rolled down her cheeks.

"Are you ready?"

Jo jumped at the sound of her cousin's voice so close by. She lifted a hand to wipe away the telltale tears and then blinked up into the sunlight. "You took long enough."

Adelle primmed her mouth as she always did whenever Jo was being ungracious. "We made a dreadful mistake. That wasn't Brett Ashwood."

Jo rose to her feet before replying. "Don't deceive yourself. It was Brett." She pretended to dust the grass from her skirt while covertly scanning the levee. He had disappeared. "I don't doubt he's ashamed to have been found skulking around his son's grave after all these years. He should have thought better of coming back to Cedar Bluff in the first place." She glanced back sharply at her cousin. "You did tell him to go away?"

Adelle stared at her. "It must be the heat. Didn't you hear me? The man's name is Gus Thornton. He's Australian. Isn't it amazing that a man from a place so far away looks so much like my ex-husband?"

Jo took her cousin by the shoulders. "Look at me, Adelle. Are you telling me you believe him? That wasn't Brett?"

Adelle shrugged under her cousin's hands. "Oh, for Pete's sake! Of course he isn't Brett. What's wrong with you?"

Jo let her cousin's conviction sink in. "He persuaded you? Completely?"

In a characteristic gesture, Adelle swung the hair from her face with a graceful movement of her head. "Okay, so he did spook me at first. The resemblance *is* startling, until you notice the small details."

"What small details?"

"Oh, that he must be five, even ten years older than Brett. Mr. Thornton looks about forty, and Brett would be just thirty-one."

"Hard times can age a man," Jo said, unconvinced that Adelle really meant what she was saying. The man she'd just encountered didn't look or act at all decrepit. In fact, he seemed much more virile than Adelle's thirty-something husband. No, for a hard-living man, Brett looked just about right.

" . . . and his limp."

Jo registered late the tag line of the statement she'd not fully paid attention to. "He limps?"

"You might have noticed if you hadn't stalked away," Adelle admonished in a peevish tone. "Jo, you're awful!"

"A lot can happen in twelve years," Jo replied, not about to be drawn off the subject. "He could have had an accident that caused a leg injury."

"And the accent?" Adelle's laughter sounded a shade forced. "When did you ever hear an Arkansan, even one who's been to Harvard, sound like him?"

"Could be faked. Brett liked to mimic everybody from Sylvester Stallone to William F. Buckley. Don't you remember, or don't you want to?"

Adelle's expression lost all its humor. "I think you've insulted me enough for one day. As for the poor man you accosted, well, I'm just glad he's not staying in Cedar Bluff. Imagine if he were to tell somebody one of the Spencer girls struck a complete stranger." Adelle turned away and began walking toward the shady spot where she'd parked her car.

Ignoring the appallingly outdated reference to herself as one of "the Spencer girls," Jo hurried after her. "Just a minute. How do you know he's not staying in town?"

Adelle turned but merely folded her arms and stared sphinxlike at her cousin.

Jo glanced once more toward the levee, half expecting to find him there again but he seemed to have disappeared for the present. "If you don't tell me, I'll just have to go after him and ask myself."

Adelle's expression altered to one of alarm. "Don't you dare! He told me he's staying at the Holiday Inn at the airport in Little Rock. In case you wanted to send him an apology, he said."

Jo eyed her skeptically. "Did he invite you to come see him?"

Adelle shook her head.

"Did he say what he was doing sneaking about this cemetery on the anniversary of his son's death?"

Her cousin's expression crumbled at the mention of Zachary. "I do believe living in the East has made you hard, Jo. Just why are you here? Is it to make the rest of us as miserable as you are?"

The question struck closer to home than Jo was ready to admit, and she thrust away the pain it caused, afraid of it. Her expression wary, she said, "I needed to be near family, but maybe that was a mistake."

"Oh, Jo!" Adelle reached out and threw her arms about her cousin. "Damn you! Nobody else can get my goat the way you do. Of course you're welcome here. Always."

Jo let Adelle kiss her cheek, then backed out of her embrace, embarrassed by her cousin's sentimental reaction. "Next time I'll even pack first." She tugged at the too-tight bodice of her dress. "You and I have never been the same size."

Adelle smiled. "Let's go home."

Linking arms, the cousins turned and headed toward Adelle's sleek new silver Cadillac with cream leather upholstery, a recent birthday gift from her husband.

"It was a strange coincidence, wasn't it?" Adelle ventured after they reached the car.

"Yes." *If it was coincidence,* Jo added in her own thoughts.

Adelle turned the key in the ignition. "I'd feel very foolish if anyone learned about what happened here today. Perhaps we shouldn't say anything about it to anyone."

Jo noticed the tension in her cousin's profile and wondered at its cause. Was she simply embarrassed or was she feeling the same strange thrill of fear that Jo was experiencing? "You're positive he's not Brett?"

Adelle blushed. "Really, Jo. A woman's not likely to forget a man she once thought she loved."

"No," Jo agreed softly. "She's not."

Chapter 2

The entire family was assembled for the noon meal because lunch was often the only meal Adelle's busy husband could manage to share with his young family. Jo watched her cousin spoon a mouthful of mashed peas into her four-month-old son's mouth and smiled as Steve, Jr., made a face worth capturing on film.

The boy was nothing like Zachary, she thought with a little pang of relief. She wondered if she would be able to look at him if he had been more like his half brother. Zachary's hair had been dark and his eyes navy blue, an indication, said her aunt, that they would have turned tawny brown like Brett's. Stevie was towheaded with a clear gem-bright aquamarine gaze. Like his father's.

Jo smiled as she met Steve Lawson's eye. He had just forked another mouthful of his salad into his mouth and couldn't speak. Having met him only once before, at the wedding six years earlier, she had almost forgotten what he looked like. Adelle's annual professionally airbrushed family Christmas photos failed to convey how the lines about his eyes and mouth had carved a more masculine attractiveness from what was an ordinary face. No doubt the changes were due to the hard work that had landed him a junior partnership in one of the state's largest law firms. He seemed a nice man, a good steady provider, just the sort of man Adelle's parents had always envisioned her marrying.

Because of him, Adelle's life was safe, ordered and predictable. Like the four previous generations before them, the newest generation of Spencers—even if the surname was Lawson—was firmly ensconced in the family residence. Uncle Robert and Aunt Della had moved into a town house to give their daughter the space her young family needed. Yet everywhere one looked, family history and tradition snagged the eye. The white-columned house, built before the First World War, boasted two parlors and the formal, French-doored dining room in which they now ate. The antebellum mahogany table, which Great-aunt Mary had carted up the Mississippi from Lafayette at the turn of the century, was covered in Great-grandmother Hershey's hand-crocheted cloth. The roses drooping from Aunt Celia's cut-crystal bowl were from Grandfather Spencer's rose arbor at the back of the spacious garden. The silver and china were a collection from assorted relatives.

Jo dropped her gaze into her lap, feeling a little dazed by the memories slip-sliding through her mind. Once she had lived in this house as a member of the family, the orphan cousin who had had the good fortune to have rich relatives. Unlike Cinderella, she had not been mistreated or reminded to feel grateful for the luxury that surrounded her. She was one of "the Spencer girls." That single phrase had given her a tacit acceptance and privilege that few people who had not grown up in a small Southern town could ever understand, let alone appreciate. The Spencer girls had led charmed lives. Adelle still lived a charmed life.

Jo glanced again at her cousin. She retained the ethereal beauty that had once made her the most sought after girl in Cedar Bluff. To look at her, one would never guess that she had ever known a moment's pain or unhappiness. Her life was full. It seemed perfect.

Jo looked away, amazed by the feeling sweeping through her. It was envy, nothing less. Good old-fashioned green-eyed envy. Not because Adelle had things she didn't but because Adelle accepted her life, lived in it, not despite it.

Unlike me, thought Jo. The phantoms that shaded the edges of her life were of her own making. Secrets she'd never dared share with another living soul. Ones that exacted a price and left her alone and lonely even in the midst of others' joy.

For as long as she could remember, she had struggled with the world.

"Poor little Jo," Aunt Nora liked to say. "Even at six months she was an aggressive little thing. One afternoon I came in to fetch her from her nap, and there she was, hanging on to the top rail of her crib. Now she couldn't even crawl, but after that there was no stopping her. She was determined to walk. She'd pull on just about anything and stand there until her tiny little legs just gave out. Never did learn to crawl, but Dr. Childress said to leave her alone. Some children have their own ideas about how to do things, even if it seems the hard way."

Here I am again, Jo mused, *living my life the hard way.*

She picked up her fork and sank the tines into the plump body of a freshly steamed shrimp. Some people might consider her situation—manless and jobless—pitiable. She didn't want anyone's pity, least of all Adelle's. That's why she hadn't told her cousin the real reason behind her visit. She just couldn't say the words "I've been fired" to someone who had everything. The layoff wasn't her fault; she wasn't the only one affected by it. Yet it seemed to her she'd be whining if she said she'd come home to be with family while she nursed her ego. The real truth was that she'd come home because she had grown tired of running away.

"It's really a shame you chose to come home when Mother and Daddy were on vacation." Adelle's voice broke in on Jo's thoughts, snagging her back. "They ask about you all the time."

"I'm sure they're finding their Alaskan cruise more interesting than anything I'd have to tell them." Jo smiled. "At least I don't have to explain my sudden appearance."

"Speaking of sudden appearances," Steve said between mouthfuls of his lunch salad, "how'd it feel to run into a stranger who looked so much like Brett Ashwood?"

Jo nearly choked as her gaze swung to her cousin. As their eyes met across the width of the table, Adelle turned the color of the chilled shrimp she had just speared with her fork. "Steve called soon after we got back, so of course I mentioned it," she said defensively and sent her husband a swift reassuring smile. "It was such an odd thing to happen, even if it was a case of mistaken identity."

Steve nodded. "I'll bet. I never knew Ashwood, but I've heard the stories."

"What stories?" Jo demanded.

"Oh, about his wild high school years," Steve said matter-of-factly. "Adelle told me you insisted that she visit the cemetery with you today." He reached out and patted his wife's hand. "You should know that we've put that behind us. Adelle has nothing to be ashamed of. If anyone's to blame for past misery, it's Brett Ashwood."

"Who's Brett?" chimed in five-year-old Sarah, swinging a curious gaze between her parents.

"One of your mother's old boyfriends," her father answered, before forking a last bit of salad into his mouth.

"Mama, you had a boyfriend?" Sarah's eyes were as wide as pansies.

"It was long time ago," Adelle replied, and picked up her napkin to wipe a smear of salad dressing from the corner of her daughter's mouth. "I expect you'll have lots of boyfriends one day."

Sarah, already a two-time Little Miss beauty-pageant winner, smiled in satisfaction. Then she looked at Jo. "Does Cousin Jo have lots of boyfriends?"

"No," Jo answered. Hearing the churlishness in her tone, she smiled at the child. She didn't mean to be unpleasant, she just wasn't comfortable with children. "It's because I didn't eat my lettuce when I was your age. Boys expect girls to be pretty and healthy these days."

Sarah tilted her head to one side, a look of skepticism in her blue eyes. "You're pretty, Cousin Jo. You got freckles, but your boobs are nice. Are they real?"

"Sarah!" Adelle laughed as she admonished her precocious daughter. "Mind your manners."

"You see?" Steve frowned at his wife. "I told you she'd pick up all kinds of unsavory things by being in a ballet class with older girls."

"You're just being a prude," Adelle answered. "Girls have always talked about breasts."

"Not in front of their fathers." Steve wiped his mouth and then pushed back from the table. "I've got a few minutes before I need to head back to the office." He rolled his eyes in his daughter's direction. "Now what do you suppose I should do?"

"Push me in the swing!" Sarah cried, and bounded from her chair while her napkin sailed from her lap onto the floor.

"Steve's good with kids," Jo observed a little later as she helped Adelle clean up after the meal. Her gaze kept straying to Stevie, who was chewing on a toy with the tenacity of someone who hadn't consumed two jars of baby food for lunch.

"He's absolutely wonderful. More tea?" Adelle lifted the pitcher she was about to put in the refrigerator.

Jo shook her head and deliberately swung her gaze away from the baby. As she scraped the first plate into the disposable, she said evenly, "I thought we agreed not to tell anyone about what happened at the cemetery?"

"I didn't tell *anyone*. I told Steve," Adelle replied as she covered the remaining salad with cellophane wrap. "You can't expect me to keep secrets from my husband."

"I see."

Adelle gave the cellophane a hard tug to seal the edges. "If I hadn't said anything and then it popped out of my mouth next week or next month, well, it would've seemed strange not to have mentioned it before." She opened the refrigerator and shoved the salad inside. "You see that, don't you?"

What Jo realized was that her cousin was very anxious not to do anything that would upset her husband. As Adelle moved to the sink and turned on the water to wash the luncheon things, Jo wondered what Steve would do if Brett showed up. Her own reaction had shaken her composure completely. "Do you ever think about him?"

"Who?" Adelle looked up from the sink and blushed as she saw Jo's expression. "Oh, you mean Brett. Honestly? No."

Jo wandered over to pluck a dish towel from its peg, her gaze straying again to Stevie. "You were married to him, so you must have felt something for him."

Adelle squirted liquid soap into the hot water. "He was my first summer love."

"But you got caught," Jo finished for her.

Adelle withdrew her hands from the water and turned, propping one soapy fist on each hip of her cotton dress. "Just what do you expect me to say? We were too young to be thinking about marriage. The sex was...well, exciting because it was the first time. I had nothing to compare it to."

Jo sought out her cousin's gaze. "And now that you do?"

"Jo Spencer!" Adelle turned away and began washing the salad bowl.

Jo hesitated, but she couldn't halt the litany of questions. "In all this time, you've never heard from Brett?"

Adelle sent her a perplexed look. "Of course not. What was there to say?"

Plenty, Jo thought. "Don't you think it was just a little too coincidental that someone who looks exactly like Brett was at the cemetery this morning?"

"It wasn't Brett."

"If it wasn't Brett, then what on earth was the man doing there?" Jo said in exasperation.

"Mr. Thornton said he was driving through town when he got lost," Adelle said tersely.

Surprised yet again, Jo caught her by the elbow. "You didn't tell me that."

Adelle primmed her mouth as she continued washing. "You weren't in a mood to hear anything I had to say, remember? With all the road signs down because of construction, it's easy for a stranger to make a mistake. Anyway, he said he'd picked up a nail on the levee road and was having his tire changed. You might not remember Caleb Gordon's auto shop is across from the cemetery. When he heard women arguing on the other side of the levee, curiosity drove him to climb it to see what was going on." She glanced at Jo. "What *are* you doing?"

Jo looked up guiltily as Stevie began to wail. She held up a rubber ring toy with handle attached. "I didn't think he should have this. He was cramming it so far down his throat that he was gagging."

"Don't be silly." Adelle held out her hand for the object. As she turned to rinse it under the tap, she said, "It's a teething ring, Jo. He's supposed to exercise his gums with it." She handed it back to her pouting son with a smile. "No harm done."

"Sorry." Jo unconsciously retreated a step from the child and took the salad bowl Adelle handed her to dry. "Motherhood becomes you."

"You sound surprised."

Jo didn't look up. "I just thought you might be apprehensive. After Zachary."

Adelle nodded as she continued washing. "I was with Sarah. I don't think I slept a single night the first month after we brought her home from the hospital. Finally I realized that I wasn't being rational. The doctor said the chances of crib death occurring in a second child were extremely remote. I didn't do anything to Zachary. It wasn't my fault."

Jo envied her cousin that easy conscience. She longed desperately to know if her cousin blamed anyone else for Zachary's death, but as had been the case for twelve years, she couldn't get the words past the fear lodged in her throat. "Why do you suppose Brett wanted to see his son's grave?"

"It wasn't Brett, Jo," Adelle replied, her words laced with annoyance. "Even if it was—which it wasn't—his reappearance wouldn't bother me. Brett left my thoughts the day my divorce came through. Anything he does these days is his own business." She stared at Jo, daring her to contradict her.

Jo backed off, wanting to believe her cousin was right. If it wasn't Brett, then who? "What do you think happened to him?"

"I imagine he's married with a passel of kids." Adelle turned back to her washing, relief evident in her tone. "His father seems to think he's straightened out."

"When did you talk to his father?"

Adelle passed a dripping platter to her. "It was a few years after Brett disappeared. You'd already left for college. He came by the house to see me."

"Uncle Robert must have loved that," Jo said dryly.

"Just because Daddy refused to ever again speak to the Ashwoods after Brett left doesn't mean I felt the same. I never held Mr. Ashwood responsible for his son's actions. I suppose I should say Congressman Ashwood, because he'd just won his first term in the House of Representatives. He was moving more or less permanently to Washington and wanted me to know that if I ever needed anything he'd be willing to help. I'd already met Steve by then and told him I didn't think his help would be necessary. Naturally, I asked about Brett."

"And?" Jo prompted, when her cousin paused to scour a spot on the bottom of a copper pot.

"He seemed almost relieved I asked. He said Brett was occasionally in touch with them and that he'd joined the merchant marines."

"So the truth is, no one knows exactly what has happened to Brett or even where he is." Jo was willing to bet she knew exactly where he was, in a hotel in Little Rock. "I think I'll go out. I need some things." She didn't meet her cousin's eye. "Can I borrow your car?"

"Certainly." Adelle sounded suddenly cheerful. "Mangle's is having their Fourth of July sale this week. They have the cutest swimsuits and shorts sets on sale."

Jo smiled. "I was thinking of buying something a little more practical." Like interview clothing, she mused ruefully. "In fact, I think I'll drive up to Little Rock and see what's new in the boutiques. It's been so long, I'm curious to compare local fashion with East Coast tastes."

Adelle gave her the fish-eye. "I see."

"Just what does that mean?" Jo asked carefully.

"Oh, nothing. Only I wouldn't advise you to go anywhere near the airport."

Color rushed into Jo's cheeks. "Look, if it's inconvenient, I can wait and go tomorrow, or even the next day. I'll just get some underwear and a toothbrush here in town."

"No, you go on to Little Rock. I've got three ballet classes to teach this afternoon. Lillian will be by any minute to pick me up and I've not yet changed." Adelle moved to the high chair and lifted Steve, Jr., into her arms. "There'll be nothing for you to do all afternoon but read magazines and watch the soaps. Unless you'd like to baby-sit Stevie." She thrust her son playfully toward Jo.

"No!" Jo blushed as her cousin gave her a strange look. "I mean, I don't think he'd like me. I'm not very good with children."

"That'll change the moment you have your own," Adelle assured her.

"Maybe," Jo mumbled. "In any case, I believe I will borrow your car."

"Try to be back by seven." Adelle headed toward the hall. "Steve wants to take us out to dinner at the country club. That is, if I can find a sitter on such short notice."

Jo lifted a hand in acknowledgment before Adelle turned the corner. The country club! She smiled. What a hoot it would be to her urban buddies to know she had relations who "dined" at the country club whenever the mood struck. She had forgotten in how many ways Cedar Bluff was a different world from her present life. Beauty pageants for toddlers, church socials and country-club suppers; she felt like a stranger in her own hometown. Yet Adelle was born for it. It would be awful if her happiness was wrecked by something, or someone—someone like Brett.

Jo's lids shuttered down over her eyes as she felt again the impact of her surprise on sighting him. Her fingers curled into the dish towel she held. The hot beat of anger had prompted her to slap his face. How warm his skin had been, and hard his bones. He had taken the force of her blow without flinching. It had been Brett! It must have been.

Adelle stuck her head back in the kitchen. "Here're the keys." She tossed them to Jo. "There's gas money in the honey jar on the second shelf behind you. Steve says the oil needs to be checked. Would you be a dear?"

Jo smiled, her decision made. "Not to worry. I'll take care of everything for you."

* * *

Jo checked her makeup in the rearview mirror and frowned. She wetted the tip of her little finger with her tongue and stroked it over each eyebrow to smooth the arch. Satisfied, she checked her watch. It was nearly 5:00 p.m. because she had taken the time to have her hair done, as well as buy makeup and new clothes before driving out to the airport. At least she no longer looked a full ten years younger than her twenty-eight years.

She closed her eyes and took a deep breath. Brett Ashwood had caught her unexpectedly that morning, without makeup and in a borrowed dress. Her looks plus her actions must have left him with the impression that she was nothing more than a bad-mannered hick. This time she would leave an utterly different impression.

Her vulnerability, too, had been bricked over as easily as she had traded Adelle's casual sundress for the sophisticated three-piece ivory silk suit she now wore. She was in control, with the aloof veneer of perfect grooming. He would know that he dealt with a sophisticated, self-assured adult.

When she stepped out of Adelle's luxuriously appointed, climate-controlled car into the sweltering heat of the late-July afternoon, she remembered why Arkansans preferred the informality of sundresses and sandals during the summer. Her one concession to the heat had been to leave her tanned legs bare. She smoothed the line of her short skirt, adjusted her sunglasses and then walked briskly toward the hotel entrance. She felt as ready as she would ever be.

Once inside the door she looked for and found the house phone. "Brett Ashwood's room," she said when the operator came on.

After a moment's pause the young man answered, "I'm sorry but we don't have anybody by that name registered here."

"Then do you have a Thornton, Gus Thornton?" Jo inquired.

"Yes, ma'am. One moment, please."

Annoyance pricked Jo as the phone rang for the first time. Why had he gone to the trouble of registering under an assumed name? Did he really think he wouldn't be recognized?

It rang a second and third time before she heard someone fumble with the receiver and then heard a gruff, groggy, "Hello."

"Mr. Thornton?"

There was a pause. Finally she heard him make a soft sound like a yawn. "Who's this?"

"Jo Spencer." She held her breath during the next pause.

"You." She heard recognition and amusement in his tone. "The redhead with the right hook."

"I'd like to talk to you," she said shortly.

"Why?"

She could feel her patience slipping. Obviously, he wanted to play games. Even the phony Australian accent remained. "It's about this morning, Mr. Thornton. Or is it Ashwood?"

He was silent so long this time that she had about decided he must have hung up when he said, "When would you like to talk?"

"Now. I'm in the lobby. It's important," she added a little nervously.

"You promise not to get physical? No, scratch that." She heard him chuckle. "I'll take my chances. I'm in 234."

Jo put the receiver very carefully back on the hook. That last comment sounded very much like the old Brett. Perhaps she'd made a mistake in provoking him before they met. It was like tipping her hand to an opponent. At the very least she should have made him come down to her.

She lifted the receiver again before deciding against making that demand. It was too late. He would see her belated request as a sign of weakness. There was nothing to do but go through with it. She wasn't here to protect herself but to warn him away from Adelle. She let the receiver slip back into place.

As she stepped off the elevator onto the second floor, she was braced for any number of possible welcomes. Yet when he opened the door in answer to her knock, she discovered she had overlooked at least one possibility.

Chapter 3

He answered the door naked from the waist up.

He'd thrown a towel over his head and was rubbing vigorously with one hand. Jo's eyes widened as muscles rolled like sea swells beneath the skin of his bare torso and arms. If he thought she would be impressed, she was. And very resentful of the display.

An instant later she forgot resentment. Despite the masculine tangle of red-brown hair adorning the planes of his upper chest, it was impossible not to notice the series of smooth pink scars cutting obliquely across his torso from just above and below his right nipple down his flat abdomen to disappear into his waistband. Jo's stomach muscles contracted in empathy for the pain that must have accompanied such scarring.

He whipped the towel off his head after a moment and looked at her with a flat assessing gaze from whiskey brown eyes. "Sorry. I sometimes forget I'm a pretty ugly sight these days." The words were modest enough, but he didn't try to cover himself. In fact, he stood a moment longer, blocking the doorway with one hand braced on the frame and his hip jutted out. He looked wary but resolute, and thoroughly male.

Then she met his eyes and she forgot the scars and the fact that he was half dressed. Suddenly she was again sixteen, and the hammering of her heart found the rhythm of unrequited love.

This was Brett Ashwood. The shape of his face had haunted her adolescent dreams for years: the broad brow narrowing over sharp cheekbones to the chin squared off by a jawline that could only be called hard. There were tiny scars flecked across those weathered cheekbones and a thin jagged scar from the corner of his left eye into his hairline, but the mouth and eyes were exactly, achingly the same. Her gaze drifted southward from his face. He was bigger, filled out to man-size proportions. But the same.

"Seen enough?"

His words, spoken in the incongruous accent, jerked her gaze up. He was looking at her through slightly narrowed lids. "Have a passion for scars, do you?"

The rebuff triggered every instinct for self protection in Jo. A quick and reasonable fear gripped her. After Brett she had never again been attracted to forceful men, to charmers or to bad boys. Yet he was short-circuiting her protective armor by just his presence. Even with a half a dozen disfiguring scars, he was sexy as hell and he knew it. *Get a grip!* Her hand tightened on her purse in an unconscious gesture that matched her thoughts. "I'm Jo Spencer."

"Gus Thornton." He offered his hand. When she refused it, he shrugged. "Come in. I'm just clearing my head."

He ducked back into the bathroom, but he didn't shut the door as he finished drying off. "I developed this habit of dozing off at all hours while in hospital, and I can't seem to shake it."

Embarrassed by his casual intimacy, Jo moved on into the dim room whose drapes were drawn against the brilliance of the day. "What happened to you?"

"Plane crash. My fault."

Jo turned back toward the bathroom door. "You crashed a plane?"

He leaned out into the hall, his chest still bare. "Right crooked thing to do, eh? They say I'm lucky to be alive. Got splashed by burning petrol." He spread a hand over his chest and grinned. "I don't toss live shrimp on the barbie anymore."

"Dear God!" Jo whispered, moved despite her enmity toward the man. Burns were said to be the most painful injuries of all.

"I'll take it." He came into the room and reached for the black T-shirt he had left lying on the bed.

"Take what?" Jo demanded, her gaze drawn downward by his limp. Was this another souvenir of his accident? His thighs were loosely encased in denim, his calves and feet in scarred Western boots.

"Your concern. It balances the slap." As his head popped through the neck of his shirt, he said, "You're a rash woman, aren't you?"

Jo's chin came up. The comment stung because it was true. "I don't want you to excuse my behavior. I meant every moment of the morning."

His gaze was considering. "I take it you didn't care much for Brett."

"No." She folded her arms. "I don't like *you*."

He unsnapped his waistband and reached for his zipper. Jo didn't make a sound, but her absolute stillness seemed to make him think better of the gesture and he simply shoved his shirttail into the loosened waistband. After he resnapped, he moved to the dresser, where he picked up a brush and began dragging it through the stiff waves of his hair.

A single drop of water flew back and struck Jo on the cheek. As she reached up to wipe it away, his gaze met hers via the mirror. "How long has it been since you last saw Brett?" he asked.

"Twelve years."

"Yet you were certain enough of your memory to crack me across the face without even a word." His eyes, dark as plums in the half light, remained trained on her face. "He must have left one hell of an impression on you."

"You did," Jo answered, annoyed that he persisted in the pretense. She was ready to cut to the chase. "You got my cousin pregnant."

He didn't react as she expected. He simply put his brush down, continuing to regard her reflected image. "Twelve years ago you couldn't have been more than . . . what?"

"Sixteen," Jo supplied, annoyed that he didn't remember. "But I didn't come here to reminisce. I came to tell you to leave Adelle alone."

"The cousin." He said it flatly. "She sent you?"

"No. She doesn't even believe you're Brett." Jo moved closer, holding the reflected image of his gaze. "But I do. And I want your promise that you'll leave her alone."

Instead of answering, he reached for a bottle of after-shave and shook a few drops into his palm. With maddening deliberation he rubbed his hands together and then patted his face. Jo's fingers tingled as she watched him stroke the cheek she had slapped. "What's any of this got to do with you?"

"Don't play with me." Anger spurted through Jo, hardening her tone. "You always took what you wanted. Because you were the mayor's son, you thought you could get away with everything short of murder. Valedictorian and football jock, you thought you were too good for the rest of us. You were going to Harvard. The rest of us hicks should have been grateful you spoke to us, I suppose. I was naive enough to think you were my friend, but you betrayed even me."

His brows rose incredulously as he turned to face her. "Brett seduced you, too?"

Jo's cheeks flamed. "Like hell! But you might as well have. Remember?"

He moved in close, as though the gloom in the room was obscuring something vital. When he was within touching distance of her, he crossed his arms, balancing with one foot slightly forward. "Refresh my memory."

Jo knew she shouldn't say any more. Yet, as she stared up into the mature face of old hurts, the bitterness of her memories demanded a hearing. She swallowed back the choking tightness of emotions pressing in on her, but she couldn't stop the words. "You used me. You even made me part of your seduction of Adelle. You got me to carry notes to her, sent me to fetch her when you sneaked off from work to see her. Sometimes you'd meet in the park over by the river. There was a dilapidated boathouse that no one used anymore."

He didn't move or speak as the words continued to pour out of her, her phrases from an age when those memories were laid down, making her sound young and defenseless. "I hated being part of all that sneaking around, but I did it for Adelle. To protect her."

She was looking at him, but her gaze was turned inward on memories and emotions as vivid and primitive as a child's crayon drawing. She looked away from him, forcing her voice back to maturity. "Of course, in the end, I hadn't protected her at all. Just the opposite."

Jo's gaze met his, hostility drawing the muscles of her face tight.

"Tell me something," he said quietly. "If you really hate Brett the way you say you do, why are you here?"

Jo smiled grimly. "To find out why you came back, and what you want."

He canted his head. "What could I possibly want?"

"That's what I'm here to find out."

Exasperation entered his expression. He turned and moved toward the drapes. "I suppose the fact that I've told you my name is Gus Thornton has no meaning for you."

"You could call yourself anything."

"I could," he agreed in a reasonable tone and jerked the cord. The drapes parted on a day still so bright that Jo flinched as her eyes struggled to readjust their focus. By the time she stopped blinking, he had pulled his wallet from his back pocket and flipped it open. "I'll make this simple for you."

She moved in close as he held it out. It contained a plastic window through which a Queensland, Australia, driver's license was visible. Beneath his picture was typed the name Augustus Thornton.

She shook her head and stepped back. "Fake IDs are easy to come by. I had one in college so that I could drink in bars on the weekend."

As a jet's engines roared overhead, filling the room with vibration and noise, she moved away from him, her gaze seeking out the other details of the small room. The room contained two beds. The first was unmade, the stacked pillows retaining the impression of his head. She moved over to where his suitcase lay open on the other. She didn't touch anything, but she looked it over very closely. There was a baggage tag marked Sydney and another with DFW on the handle. His personal tag had a Queensland address. She was aware that he was watching her, but he didn't move or say anything until she had completed her inspection.

"Satisfied?"

She glanced at him, searching for the boy inside the man's exterior. "You're Brett Ashwood. I'll find a way to prove it."

"You're welcome to try. For the time I'm in town."

The statement surprised her. "What does that mean?"

"It means I won't be here long. I'm just passing through."

"I don't believe you."

His brow furrowed in annoyance. "I couldn't care less about—"

She held up a silencing hand. "I don't want to hear it, I just don't."

She moved back toward the door, her shoulders hunched against her own thoughts. When she turned to him the strain to retain her composure was evident in her expression. "Look, I may be wrong... but I don't think so. So, as long as you're just passing through, why don't you do that passing sooner? Like tonight?"

He stood perfectly still, his weight balanced evenly between his feet. He was ready for anything. "Why should I?"

"Because there're lots of people around here who remember Brett like I do. He... you weren't popular with everyone."

"Why?"

"Because you were a spoiled and arrogant rich boy who drank too much, talked too much and could get any girl he wanted."

"Sounds like a guy I might have envied at eighteen."

"Yes, well, we all grow up and learn better, if we're lucky."

He didn't answer that, only continued to look at her with a slight frown between his brows.

His measured responses made her uneasy. One thing the old Brett had not been, and that was thoughtful. He'd always acted first and deliberated afterward, if at all. He'd once told her that his temper was the cause of most of his fights with his father. He was reckless and impetuous...just as she was.

For just a moment the thought whispered through her mind, *what if I am wrong?* She had done a lot of talking and posturing with a man who was possibly a stranger. He hadn't done or said anything that seemed to indicate that he was a danger to Adelle. He hadn't even conceded that he knew Adelle. So why was she drawn against reason to prove who he was?

But she knew the answer. Behind the enmity and the anger, and the old hurt, was this pulsing emotion as raw and intense as it had been on the last day she'd seen Brett. This man brought it all back, every aching agonizing moment. And it was the first time in twelve years she had felt this much alive.

"So where do we go from here?" he said, when she seemed permanently stuck in her own thoughts.

"What do you mean?"

"Do we just shake hands and retreat to our separate lives?"

Jo looked at him, seeking desperately to read in his face an answer to her question. "It is you, isn't it?"

He gave her an equally intense stare. "You want to know who I really am?"

"Yes." Her reply was little more than a whisper.

"Then spend the evening with me."

"Absolutely not!" Alarms went off inside her head as she backed up a step.

"What's the matter?" His temper was clearly getting the upper hand. "You're the one who started this. I'm not accustomed to being slapped by strangers." Traces of a not altogether friendly smile sketched his mouth. "Even my friends would think twice about that. You're so certain you're right, yet you're too afraid to find out. I wonder why?"

"I'm not interested in your analysis of my motives," Jo snapped. "If you'll give me your word that you'll do nothing to disturb Adelle and Steve, I'll go."

"Who's Steve?"

Jo hesitated. He didn't know. "Adelle remarried six years ago." She watched his face carefully but saw nothing in his expression to discourage her. "She has two children now, a son and daughter."

"Sounds like a nice little family."

"Yes. It's perfect."

Something in her tone made his expression quicken. "That must be hard for you."

The question surprised Jo. "I don't know what you mean."

"To see your cousin turn her life around while you—" He moved a little closer. His gaze seemed to seek entrance into her very thoughts. "I wonder what your story is."

"I have no story." Jo squared her shoulders. "I don't live here anymore. I've just come from Baltimore for a visit."

"Just another weary traveler? Well then, g'day, Ms. Spencer."

She met his dark gaze with equal parts of challenge and entreaty. "I hope it is goodbye."

As she turned away he felt almost sorry for her. From the moment he had first seen her in the cemetery, he had known she was willful and passionate. Now he knew other things about her. She was courageous and loyal, as well. Her cousin Adelle could not have chosen a better ally. But Jo Spencer's defensive posture was unnecessary. She had come looking for Brett Ashwood. All he had to offer her was Gus Thornton.

"That should be enough," he murmured, surprised by the dregs of disappointment that laced his words. No doubt about it, she had hooked in to something deep within him. He admired her courage, but he sensed that behind that tough exterior was a tender and lonely soul.

He understood loneliness. During the agonizingly painful months he had spent in the hospital crawling back from death into life, he had realized that no one would have truly mourned his death. Oh, he had friends, but no one special love.

Yes, he understood her wistful tone as she spoke of her cousin's life. He suspected she often was a spectator in the lives of others. He also suspected that most often she hid the shadows that he'd glimpsed in her eyes today. She said she no longer lived here. Was just passing through. Perhaps she, more than he, was the stranger in town.

Stubborn. Willful. Independent. Alone. Each label he applied to her struck a responsive chord in himself. Suddenly, despite all sense, he wanted to know Jo Spencer better.

Jo looked up at the sound of rapid footfalls in time to see him round the corner of the second-floor hallway at a jog.

The elevator doors whooshed open before her as he said, "Have dinner with me. Anywhere you like."

Jo shook her head and stepped into the elevator. As she pushed the first-floor button he slapped both palms against the doors to hold them apart. "Why not?"

"I have an engagement at seven in Cedar Bluff," she said evenly as the alarm for obstructed doors went off.

"Break it."

"Why?"

He stared unsmilingly at her as the doors bucked under his hands. "Because you want to. Because if you refuse you'll always wonder. You say you want to know who I am. Have dinner with me. I guarantee that by the end of the evening you'll know *exactly* who I am."

She knew he was trouble. She knew he was baiting her. She suspected strongly that he was Brett Ashwood.

As she looked into his liquor brown eyes, she thought she saw the ghost of the wild young man she had known a dozen years ago. Yet it was the vital force of the man facing her now that made her feel the impossible was possible. "The Excelsior Hotel."

He released the doors and smiled. "Seven. Reservation in the name Thornton."

Chapter 4

"That's right, an old college friend," Jo lied, crossing her fingers just like a child as she spoke by phone to Adelle. "I hope this doesn't mess up your plans for the country club. Oh, I see. No, this works out well. Honestly. Tell Steve I understand that business comes first. Don't wait up for me. Under the mat? Okay. See you later."

As she made her way from the public phones back to the club room of the Capitol Hotel, Jo wondered if she had made the wrong call. Perhaps she should have lied to Gus Thornton about having to go back to Cedar Bluff because of some sort of an emergency. She glanced at her watch. It was seven-twenty-five. She was standing him up. The Brett Ashwood she remembered would have stormed out of the restaurant in a rage by now.

She slid back into the booth she'd been occupying for more than an hour and picked up her mineral water. As she put the glass to her lips, her gaze met that of a young businessman at the bar. He had been sending speculative glances her way for most of an hour, but she hadn't allowed him into her line of vision before. Encouraged by the eye contact, he lifted his drink and raised an eyebrow in inquiry.

Jo shook her head and looked away. She'd had her fill of strangers for one day. Even if he did look as if he might be pleasant, she was way past pleasantries.

She drained her glass, the cool metallic taste of the liquid easing the tightness in her throat. She had rethought her decision to meet the man who called himself Gus Thornton a dozen times. There were good and reasonable arguments against it. No one would fault her if she just walked out to the parking lot, slid in behind the wheel of Adelle's Caddy and hightailed it back to Cedar Bluff. Better than that, no one would even know she had seen him.

She stuck a finger into her glass and began swirling an ice cube. By meeting him she was admitting to an interest in the man that went beyond what the situation required. He said he wasn't Brett. After talking to him again she was no longer certain who he was. By meeting him she ran the risk of encouraging him to think she was attracted to him. If he really was Gus Thornton, she had badgered a stranger. Which was thoroughly embarrassing. She should end it here. All good reasons. Solid rationale. She should go home.

Jo dried her fingers on her napkin, then pulled a generous tip from her purse to lay beside her glass. She scooped up her jacket and slung it over her arm as she walked slowly toward the exit. She felt justified, exonerated, relieved. Yet when she reached the street, she didn't turn toward the parking lot but toward the Excelsior Hotel.

There was only one good reason for meeting Gus Thornton, and it overrode all her practical considerations. From the moment she had first seen him, she was positive that he was Brett Ashwood. He had promised her the truth. She had to know.

"The truth," she repeated as she crossed Main and Markham to reach the Excelsior. Could she handle the truth?

A few minutes later she entered the lobby. Though she didn't acknowledge it, she was aware that she turned a few heads. Redheads usually did. The form-fitting sleeveless silk V-necked vest she wore beneath the jacket she had shed in deference to the heat drew admiring glances. She'd need every ounce of confidence to get her through the next hour.

She entered Josephine's, the Excelsior Hotel's famous restaurant, with a hurried step, a bit of pretense meant to illustrate to any who cared to notice that she was aware that she was late.

"Good evening," welcomed the hostess. "Do you have a reservation?"

"Yes, I do. That is, I did. It may have been canceled." Yet even as she finished, she saw him coming across the room. Bracing herself, she turned toward him slowly.

She noticed first that he wore a beautifully tailored pearl gray suit. He looked at home in a suit, all male and very appealing. She saw two young women at a nearby table lean out of their chairs to get a view after he passed them. Only his limp reminded her of the brutal scars hidden beneath his impeccable tailoring. Then she looked up and saw the features of Brett Ashwood. Her mouth went dry. Each time the similarity caught her unprepared.

He took the hand she automatically extended in greeting and covered it with both of his. His palms were rough and warm, his touch very personal as his fingers wrapped hers. "Did you get lost or did I misspeak the time?" He sounded like a concerned boyfriend, but the humor in his expression said he knew she'd almost chickened out on him. His gaze took her in friendly appraisal, lingering just a fraction of a second on the shadowy cleft revealed by her top. "You look great." She met his gaze skeptically but saw no trace of mockery in his face.

He turned a smile a foot wide on the hostess. "Trust an Aussie to get his compass wonked when he's talking to a beautiful woman. Ta." He applied the lightest of touches to the small of Jo's back to steer her into the dining room.

"There was no need to lie to the hostess for my sake." Jo slanted a look back at him as they crossed the room. "Or was it your pride you were protecting?"

"What difference does it make?" he asked amicably.

"Aren't you going to ask why I'm late?" she continued, provoked that he was taking her tardy appearance in stride.

He leaned forward to catch her eye, his eyes full of devilment. "Do you have a good excuse?"

"I don't trust you," she said simply.

"Good." He grinned at her surprise expression. "You're too impetuous. A little old-fashioned caution is good. Here we are."

He had a table by the windows. Beyond the glass, the late-afternoon sun laid down gold tracks on the rusty back of the Arkansas River. The sight was heartening, familiar. She took the chair he pulled out beside his, noting little details as she did so. There was already an open bottle of wine on the table. At his place, an appetizer sat half eaten. He'd not left, but he'd not waited for her, either. She glanced up at him as he sat down.

"Two things I never wait for," he said without regret. "One is a late passenger. And other is a meal."

He reached over and took the wine bottle out from under the hand of the waiter who had come forward to serve them. "Sorry, mate. The lady's in my keeping. But you can bring my guest one of these." He pointed to his plate.

"What is it?" Jo countered. His highhanded attitude was really too much. Nor did she like the fact that he had seated her next to him instead of across the table. He was taking up entirely too much of her space and prerogative.

"Pâté of duck," the waiter said.

Drat! She loved duck. She nodded. "Fine."

When the waiter retreated, she turned to her companion and met his grin with a frown as he splashed pale amber wine into the glass at her place. "I don't like pushy men. What if I didn't like what you were eating? I could have been allergic."

"To duck?" He moved to replenish his own glass. "By the look of you, I'd say you're an adventurous eater."

"What does that mean?" she asked defensively, thinking that he was referring to the fact that she was a little too voluptuous for today's esthetic.

He set the bottle down and turned, looking straight at her in a manner that demanded her full and total attention. "You meet the world with wide-open eyes. Devouring eyes. Right now you're staring at me like you want right inside my skin."

Jo flicked her gaze away. His words precisely matched her feelings about his own gaze. Despite his accent, when she looked at him she found it difficult to distrust the evidence of her own eyes. "Anything else?"

"You've a greedy mouth."

"What?" She gave in to the impulse to look at him. He was smiling as though at some private joke.

"Maybe greedy isn't the right word." His gaze skimmed her mouth. "More like generous, ripe, full of promise. You've a hunger for the world and its pleasures. Given the chance, I think Jo Spencer would eat life with a spoon."

Heat flashed through her body with a force like flame crossing a gasoline spill. "That's none of your business."

"If you say so." He picked up his glass and clicked it to the rim of her untouched one. "To beautiful, irrepressible women."

Jo turned her head toward the river as his quiet laughter moved through her lower regions. She had picked up on the subtle reference to "women" rather than "woman," which would have made the compliment exclusively hers. He was having fun at her expense and perhaps she deserved it. She had, after all, nearly stood him up. This date was going to be much more difficult to endure than she had supposed.

She noticed a barge passing through her line of vision, its wake disturbing the golden sheen of the river. As long as she didn't have the image of Brett Ashwood before her, she could maintain the impartiality required to judge this man who called himself Gus Thornton. It was looking at him that played tricks with her mind. "What do you do for a living, Mr. Thornton?"

"Don't." He said the word softly, but it brought her head around once more. This time she didn't meet his gaze. "I beg your pardon?"

"Don't give up so easily. This is a test for me, remember? Call me Brett or Gus or nothing, if you prefer. But don't hide from your reasons for being here."

Touché, Jo thought. "Okay, what have you been doing for the past twelve years?"

"That's better." She saw his lips form a smile. How could such a hard face have such a sensual mouth? "I own an independent air service in north Queensland."

"A passenger airline?"

"Passengers, cargo, medical supplies—just about anything that needs delivering."

Keep him talking, she thought. His accent distracted her. "Is there much call for that sort of thing?"

"Oz isn't the States. We don't have many roads. Those we do have are stretched between the cities. When you consider that more than ninety percent of the population is urban, that leaves a fair share of the country empty. The distances between settlements are often vast. My little empire is part bus, part truck and part emergency-vehicle service."

"Are you a one-man operation?"

"Hardly. There's Shep and Ringer and Molly and Rick and Coke."

Jo focused on the red taillights of late-evening traffic crossing the nearby Main Street Bridge. "How many planes do you have?"

"Three in regular service. Which means we play catch-up a lot."

"Why?" On the other side of the river lights were coming on one by one.

"We need four planes flying to keep our schedule. Since we lost one last year, it's been like running a relay race minus the fourth leg."

Jo's gaze drifted back toward him, drawn by the inflection in his tone. "You're referring to the plane you crashed." She met his eyes—*Lord, his lashes were longer and thicker than hers! Just like Brett's.* Her gaze skipped away. "Where'd you learn to fly?"

"I didn't, not according to my mechanic." His self-deprecating laughter did things to her breathing. "Actually, I picked it up when I went north. Next question."

Jo scooped up her wine and took a sip. The cool crisp fruity taste put her back in touch with her own reality. She took a second sip as she drank in the rose-gold tones of the sunset. He had taken control of this interview and she wanted it back.

She set down her glass carefully and looked directly into his face. "So, where were you born?"

He grinned like a schoolboy. "You'll want a notarized copy of my birth certificate to verify it."

"Try me."

"No." He looked away first, shaking his head. The retreat disconcerted her. Hadn't he just dared her to test him?

The moment did not have time to grow in implication because the waiter arrived with her appetizer and a menu. She was almost grateful for the interruption. She took the menu and focused for a moment on the lettering.

"At the risk of being overbearing again, I suggest the catfish."

A broad muscular hand moved into her line of vision as he pointed to an item on her menu. She saw a thin ragged scar crossing the width of the back. More pain. Inexplicably, it was all she could do to keep from touching it, as if the stroking of her finger would erase the memory of the injury. She set her jaw. Why were women such suckers for male suffering?

"You could at least say no."

"What?" Jo looked across to find a twinkle in his gaze. "I ate here last night." He tapped the menu again. "The catfish with pecan breading and sweet potato timbale is a wonder."

Jo looked up at the waiter. "A Caesar salad, thank you." "Is that all?"

Jo nodded and closed the menu. "I'm not very hungry."

She felt his gaze linger on her. "The lady wants a Caesar salad," he said smoothly. "I'll have the catfish. Ta."

When the menus had been gathered, he leaned forward and laid a hand near her arm, his fingers just missing skimming her skin. The fine hairs on her bare arm danced. "What would you do with the truth?" he asked.

She looked up, her gaze grazing his face before moving beyond it. "I don't understand."

He was sitting perfectly still, his expression unreadable. "Sure you do. You want—no, demand—to know who I am. You say your cousin has put the past behind her, is happily remarried with everything a woman could want. That leads me to conclude that this quest of yours is personal. What possible difference could it make to *you* if I were Brett?"

The question caught her unprepared. He had been listening more closely than she realized to everything she had said and had put two and two together with remarkable accuracy. Her mission was personal, very personal. Suddenly she realized that the answer to his question would leave her terribly embarrassed, and much more, appallingly vulnerable.

Before she could form an answer he went on. "Look at me."

Jo lifted her head, but her eyes remained unfocused.

"I said look *at* me," he repeated, his voice no louder but containing such force that she obeyed him automatically. "Do you expect Brett to remember you? You said you were cupid to his Romeo, but look what happened? Would he even want to remember the young girl he dragged into that kind of mess?"

Jo bit her lip, as his words struck blows to her self-possession. "Y-you don't know what you're talking about," she said hotly. "You don't know what happened, what shouldn't have happened. What—" Suddenly she realized she was embarrassingly near tears.

His hand moved a few scant inches until his fingers rested very lightly on her wrist. "Don't." He said it softly, quietly, but with enough urgency to remind her that they were in public.

Jo swallowed. "I'm sorry. I just need—" She rose from her chair but not before he shot to his feet to help her.

"The ladies' room is just there," he said gently, and nodded toward the front. As she turned away, he hooked two fingers into the crook of her elbow to detain her. "Come back," he said softly. "Promise me that."

Jo nodded and hurried away.

He watched her go with a slight frown gathering together his brows. Not that he didn't appreciate the view. Her short straight skirt hugged the slopes of her hips and suggestively cupped the rounded curve of her bottom with each step she took. A thin gold leather belt encircled her narrow waist, and as she turned to the right and her profile came into view, his gaze drifted to her bodice and remained. She was built more like Marilyn Monroe than Julia Roberts, and that suited him just fine. She was even more attractive than he'd first thought, but that wasn't the reason he continued to frown as he reached for his wine.

He'd seen a remarkable number of expressions on her face today, from shock and blind rage to aloofness and cold fury. Exasperation, irritation, frustration and wariness had also wandered in and loitered on her softly molded features. The one he liked best was her wide-eyed amazement. But it was her last expression, the one of hurt and misery that had nearly erupted into tears, that had moved him most strongly. He could feel it still, quivering in his gut.

Did he have the power to make her cry? Or was it Brett? When she looked at him, did she see only the past? Was that why her gaze kept slithering away from his? She was caught in some quicksand of emotion he wasn't at all certain he wanted any part of.

He gulped his wine. It wasn't often a woman struck him as novel. His roving days were long behind him. Even more rarely these days was he goaded into doing the unexpected. He didn't relish the thought of battling old ghosts, especially one that wore his face. So why was he sitting here waiting anxiously for her to return?

He'd come to the States to rest, to relax, to get his bearings. A year ago he'd been in constant agony from third-degree burns. There'd been more than one moment during those first weeks when he thought he would lose his mind, had wished to die. Several surgeries and skin grafts had finally patched him up. Then came the physical therapy. His leg had been crushed. Six months ago he hadn't known if he would ever walk again without crutches. Now his business was suffering during his absence. He had his own problems, dozens of them. He liked his solitude. He didn't need any more complications, certainly not a stubborn emotionally charged package named Jo Spencer.

She was ruining the first week of calm he'd known in more than a year. So why did he feel this connection with her? Was it her pain? He frowned harder. She'd trip-wired his temper, and the detonation had exploded his emotional barriers. Now he felt in every nuance of her expression an answering echo in himself. He had to know if it was real, this tremulous bond he felt with her.

When she returned to the table a little later, their entrées were already in place. She gave him an apologetic smile and slid into her chair and picked up her fork. Her eyes were just the slightest bit red, and the end of her nose pink. Otherwise, she looked powdered and lipsticked to perfection. He regretted upsetting her with his dose of rationality. He wouldn't make that mistake again.

Jo was grateful when he didn't return to the pursuit of the question she'd left hanging. In fact, he turned the conversation to talk of Australia, telling her, between consuming mouthfuls of his dinner, droll stories of his life. Little by little she began to relax under the crisp broad inflection of his voice. His accent was tailor-made for telling tall tales, as she suspected many of them were. Beneath every word was the wry self-deprecating humor that she had heard Aussies were famous for.

When dessert was offered, she was about to agree to the rare indulgence when he said, "No, thanks, mate. Just the check."

Jo suppressed the desire to tell him that he was being presumptuous again, but he must have seen her thoughts in her expression because he said, "I thought we'd go somewhere else for an after-dinner drink." He smiled. "If you'd like."

"Okay." She said it before she considered the implication of her agreement. She was saying she wanted to spend more time with him. "Only I'll pay this time."

He grinned at her. "Whatever you say." The expression in his eyes was more amused than the moment required. What was he thinking? No, she didn't dare wonder or she might not go with him.

When they reached the street, darkness had claimed the sky. Though the heat of the day had been nearly unbearable, the river was rapidly cooling the air. He held her jacket as she slid her arms into the unlined sleeves and then smoothed the thin fabric across her shoulders to remove any wrinkles.

"Just a moment," he said, when she turned to thank him. He reached out to unfold her turned-under collar. She felt the whisk of his fingers against her neck and it chased a shiver across her skin. When she felt his warm fingers against the nape of her neck, she automatically hunched her shoulders against the intimacy. "I can do that," she said a little brusquely and reached up.

He caught her hand, enfolding her fingertips in the palm of his. She looked up no farther than his mouth and saw amusement had lifted the corners. "I believe you can do many things. Why is it so important to constantly prove it?"

Jo shrugged and he freed her. This time he used both hands to turn her collar, his arms looping lightly around her neck as he worked. He moved slowly, untucking the collar inch by inch. She didn't dare look at him, but his presence crowded in on her just the same. The thick weave of his brilliantly colored tie was a foot from her eyes. The line of his chin cut off the upper limits of her vision. He smelled lightly of a citrus cologne and the darker purely human scent of clean skin.

When he was done he brushed her cheek with the knuckle of his forefinger. "So, Ms. Spencer, do you have wheels?"

She blinked. "A car? Yes. Why?"

"I thought we might change the scenery." He reached up and began jerking loose the knot of his tie. "You've seen my city manners, so I thought we could both relax."

"I'm driving Adelle's car. It's parked over there." She started across the street and he followed.

He slowed as she reached the car and gave an appreciative whistle. "Silver Caddy with gold trim. Your cousin's doing all right."

She glanced back at him. "What do you drive?"

"Land-Rover, mostly." He came up beside her. "Are you now going to prove what a wonderful driver you are?"

He was deliberately baiting her. She thought of several solid reasons why he shouldn't drive. She didn't know if he had a driver's—yes, she did know that. She *didn't* know if that license allowed him to drive in the States. She didn't know if her cousin's insurance would cover him. She didn't

know if he was sober, though he'd had little to drink. She
didn't know any of those things. What she did know was
that when she looked at him full face, she received all five
hundred watts of his charm, and she liked it.

She handed him the keys.

He smiled. "I like a woman who's strong enough not to
fear showing her vulnerable side."

Chapter 5

"Where are we going?"

"Upriver a bit." They were racing through the night, the golden cones of the Cadillac's headlights the only illumination in the blackness surrounding them. He lifted a finger off the steering wheel to point ahead. "There's a place not too far from here where you can drink beer and dance till dawn."

She frowned. "How do you know that?"

"I've already been out here. Last night."

"You certainly get around. Cemeteries and bars."

She saw his smile as a faint flash of teeth. "During the last year I missed a lot. Evenings in a pub used to be one of my favorite ways of relaxing."

"You won't find a pub in all of Arkansas," she answered with a little laugh.

"Want to bet?"

The rear of the Cadillac suddenly fishtailed while gravel spun out with a hissing sound as he, without warning, swung the huge car from the blacktop into an unpaved road.

"Careful!" Jo cried in alarm as she braced herself on the dashboard with both hands. "This isn't my car."

"And you don't want your cousin to accuse you of damaging the paint." He accelerated smoothly and the car shot off into the pitch-black canyon formed by thick woods. After a few seconds he turned off the air conditioner and then opened all the windows. "Too bad it's not a convertible. Then we could have some real fun."

As the sultry night air invaded the interior, he heard her groan in protest. "I'll be blown to bits." She reached to push Up on her window button.

"So what?" From his side he lowered the window she had just raised. "A little fresh air won't hurt you."

Jo folded her arms to resist the temptation to turn this into a battle of the dueling window buttons. It was the kind of game Brett loved to play. He always won because he didn't mind being wilder, going further than anyone else would dare. "This is a brand-new suit. I don't want it streaked with red river dust."

The window on her side zoomed up. "Don't you ever get out of line?"

"You're not going to find out," Jo answered shortly, though she knew she had been nothing but out of line since she agreed to meet him.

"A pity. You look like you'd enjoy joyriding."

She turned to him in the darkness. His dark profile was gilded by the backwash of the panel lights. "Churning up dust on country roads isn't my idea of fun."

"What *do* you do for fun?"

His tone made her feel like a spoilsport. "I don't waste my time. I work five days a week and some weekends, when I can get the overtime."

"I was asking about fun."

"I coach a girls' soccer team three evenings a week," Jo admitted.

"Soccer. That explains those great strong legs." He glanced sideways at her, his eyes gleaming faintly. "I've a liking for strong women. You need stamina to live west of the Great Dividing Range. Ah, here we are."

Ahead, Jo saw light from an unseen source spilling across the empty road. A few seconds later the tires again crunched gravel as they dug for traction. The next moment the car swooped off the road onto a dirt driveway.

She saw now that the lights came from two Night-watchers posted high on telephone posts. Below them in the pale blue-white light dozens of cars and pickup trucks filled the packed earth parking lot while dozens more were parked in the grass between the trees. Beyond the parking lot was a long low wooden structure with a row of windows each sporting a different neon beer sign. Above the door hung a huge illuminated sign that said River Bottom.

He pulled into a space near the driveway. The moment he turned off the engine, the sound of music reached out across the distance to greet them. As they slid out of the car, the rhythmic pulse of a bass line and the *thump, thump* of a drumbeat resounded in the air.

Jo turned to look at him across the width of the hood and saw that he was stripping off his jacket. He tossed it in the back seat, locked the door and then began working loose his button cuffs. She glanced again at the honky-tonk as a noisy crowd of patrons spilled out the door. One gave a rebel yell while the others roared with drunken laughter. She looked askance at her host. "I didn't know there were still places like this."

"That's a pity." His affection for dives was obvious. He had rolled up his sleeves and was casually unbuttoning his top two shirt buttons as he came around the car toward her. "The Outback's darted with pubs. They're often the only social life for hundreds of miles. Come on, then. I'll show you what *I* do for fun."

It was a country-and-Western club, complete with a live band and dozens of couples crowded onto a dance floor meant for half the number. The blast of frigid air that greeted them at the door dissipated ten feet into the room, overwhelmed by armpit-dampening body heat, tobacco smoke and the boozy breath of the company. The sheer din of amplified wailing guitars seemed to press the company to the walls. The rafters of the rustic tavern vibrated with sound.

Jo paused while he paid the entry charge, uncertain of what to do. The crowd was young, between twenty-one and thirty-five she gauged, and dressed in jeans. Most men wore T-shirts while the majority of the women seemed to have stripped down to their underwear. Bustiers and skimpy bralike halter tops abounded. She felt very much out of place in a silk suit, and wished she, too, had left her jacket in the car.

"Keep right behind me," he said as he came up next to her. "Get lost in this lot and we'll never find each other until closing."

She didn't get to answer, for he plunged into the crowd to their right. Afraid he would lose her, she grabbed a handful of his shirt back and was carried along in his wake.

He seemed undaunted by the press of people at the bar that ran the length of the wall. But with every step Jo took, people pressed in on her from both sides, making her feel slightly claustrophobic. It was impossible to pass someone without brushing with indecent familiarity against an arm or hip, breast or buttocks. The men in particular seemed to welcome the jostling. More than one man in boots and cowboy hat looked around as she skirted past to favor her with a smile. "Sorry," she mumbled repeatedly, keeping her head down.

Finally, she was shoved from behind just as she was squeezing past a knot of young men. Before she could brace herself, her chin collided with a hard shoulder. She heard a gruff exclamation as her teeth banged together painfully.

"Now looked what you done. Spilled—" The man swung around, blue eyes blazing.

"I'm so sorry," Jo said hurriedly as she spied the lake of beer foaming across the wooden bar. She tried to pull her shoulder purse free of the crush. "Let me buy you another."

But he only continued to stare at her a moment, taking in her hair, her face and then what he could see of her clothing. When his gaze came back to her, he was smiling. "You ain't a regular." Jo shook her head. "That's all right, then. A pretty gal can rub up against me anytime." He took her arm in a proprietary grip. "Let me buy *you* a drink or two."

"Sorry, mate, she's taken."

The young man's appraising gaze met Gus's easy grin and then moved down to the grip he had on the woman's other arm. "Right." He released her and tipped his hat. "He don't treat you right, you let me know." He winked at Jo and turned back to the bar.

"Come on, away from the music," Gus said near her ear. He directed her toward the back of the room with the subtle pressure of his fingers.

She was surprised by the quick rescue. Brett was notorious for his practical jokes and teasing. While she had never witnessed it first-hand, she'd heard the stories circulating around school. Once he'd tried to wager Angela Tucker, his date for the night, to a trucker he'd been playing poker with. Brett might have waited to see how far things would go before coming to her aid. This man had made it clear that she was with him. She liked him for that.

There must have been five hundred people in the place, Jo decided, and wondered with vague unease if they were not exceeding the fire ordinance. Yet, amazingly enough, they found an empty table near the back wall. "What would you like?" he said when she had taken a seat.

"Anything ice cold," she replied and began shucking off her jacket. And to think she had been worried about clay dust marks. She hung her jacket over the back of the chair. She'd be very lucky if it wasn't ruined by perspiration.

As he disappeared back into the bar crowd, she folded her arms and rested them on the table. The lighting was sparse, bare yellow bulbs in converted kerosene lanterns. Yet once out of the throng, she relaxed into the cheerful, insistent rhythm of the music, and it cheered her considerably. She fully expected to wait a long time for her drink. Even Adelle had sometimes complained that Brett often seemed to prefer anybody else's company to hers, unless they were "doing it."

When he returned after just a few minutes with two beers, he caught her swaying in her chair in time to the music. He set the bottles on the table and then inclined his head toward the crush on the floor. "Dance?"

She didn't look down at his legs, but she wondered if he could, with his limp. "I don't two-step," she said carefully. Let him make of that what he wished.

"Neither do I. Anymore." His ready smile eased over the moment. "Would you mind something slower?"

Jo smiled and took the hand he held out to her. As luck would have it, the band wound up a lively piece and swung without pause into a slower lilting waltz.

Jo juggled mixed emotions as she followed him onto the dance floor. A few hours ago she had been ready to stand him up. Now her quickened pulse told her the extent of her anticipation to be in his arms. He turned at the edge of the floor and reached for her. She moved readily into his embrace, already feeling the tempo of the music in her feet.

But once in his arms she suddenly remembered why she'd been so cautious earlier. He invaded her space in ways that had nothing to do with the physical. Her senses went on alert. Even in heels, she only reached his nose. That put her eyes on a level with his chin. As he drew her closer—admittedly because of the lack of room—she found her nose poking into the open front of his shirt. Bristling hair brushed the tip of her nose, tickling it. She snatched back her hand from his shoulder to rub away the sensation. As she turned her face away, she heard as well as felt his laughter. Guessing it was at her expense, she misstepped. *Concentrate,* she told herself. This wasn't an eighth-grade social. She'd danced with dozens of men, and more suggestively.

After a few more steps, he gathered her closer. His hand at her back rose up so that his fingers curled softly along her neck as he directed their movements with the force of his forearm slanted across her back. He brought their clasped hands in against his chest until the back of her hand rested on the skin bared by his open shirt.

"You like dancing. That's good," he said softly into her ear as he turned them into the crowd. The feathering breath of his words chased chills across her cheek. "I've always thought it was the most civilized form of seduction there is."

Jo smiled. She was accustomed to flirting. Man-woman sparring was more sophisticated in Baltimore than in Cedar Bluff. By now she recognized all the standard signals.

This was different. He hadn't said one really suggestive thing, yet her pulse was telling her that there was more involved in his communication than words and gestures. His manner was so easy, so casual, yet very aware.

She was aware of every move of his body, the shift of his thighs against hers, the occasional brush of his pelvis when the pressure of the crowd forced them closer. Despite his disability, he was graceful. He must have been something before the accident, she mused, and recalled the saying that a man who could dance well upright was bound to be a pleasure when horizontal.

It might have been her imagination, but his way of holding her felt different from any other man's touch. It was both protective and reassuring, making her feel less like a separate body being steered around the floor and more a part of him. She relaxed and let herself enjoy moving to the rhythm and the melody.

When one song melded into another, the mood between them changed again. Suddenly she was aware of everything again. His breath fanning her shoulder. The pressure of his chin and jaw along her upper cheek and brow. The faint drag upon her skin of his stubble, too fresh yet to be seen. The hand at the back of her neck was playing with the scattering of curls that had escaped. His heartbeat came faintly through the back of her hand. He smelled a little more strongly of cologne and his own pleasant body chemistry. And the heat. The sheer enveloping pleasure of his masculine body seemed to set the limits of her senses.

She began to feel a little dizzy. The lassitude carried her head naturally against his chest and she heard him sigh in approval, "Nice."

She wasn't certain of the exact moment she had stopped making comparisons. But suddenly she wasn't thinking of anything, or anyone, but Gus Thornton.

They danced three more dances, ignoring the changes in tempo and thereby gaining the smiling approval of those about them. She didn't want their partnering to end, and neither, it seemed, did he. They didn't talk. They didn't have to. Each moment was bringing them closer to some inevitable conclusion. Jo didn't want to think about what it was.

Finally, as if by mutual consent, they broke apart.

Jo moved quickly back to where she had left her coat, feeling as if she were walking on eggshells. The two beers he had left on the table had sweated great rings on the surface. She touched one. It was lukewarm. Not that she wanted it. Despite the heat, she felt as if she needed several strong cups of coffee to break through the misty drifting sense of ease and contentment lingering in her mind.

His touch surprised her. He wrapped one finger at a time about her upper arm, then leaned in to nuzzle her neck. "You ready to go?"

She half turned to him, not quite meeting his eyes. "Where?"

She saw his smile in the upper corner of her vision. "Joyriding."

She turned and walked toward the entrance without even thinking.

She shivered when she stepped outside, amazed that the night air was cooler than before. Then she realized that her skin was slick with perspiration. He dropped her jacket about her shoulders and hugged her gently. "Come on. We'll find a way to warm you."

Jo didn't dare ask him what he meant. She was afraid she knew, and didn't want him to see how much she hoped she was right.

They climbed into the Cadillac, and this time when he gunned the engine and spewed gravel from under the tires, she didn't say anything, just checked her seat belt. Leaning her head back against the leather, she closed her eyes as they shot off into the dark night.

A few miles down the road, he suddenly slowed the car and turned off the road onto the grass. Jo opened her eyes to see that he was pulling in under a huge oak. Twenty yards ahead in the headlights, she could see the oily black surface of the river. Then he turned off the engine and killed the lights.

For several moments neither of them spoke. When she turned her head toward him, she saw that he had angled his body toward her. One arm rested on the steering wheel, the other along the seat back. Her heart began to hammer as he reached over and unbuckled her safety harness. "Come here," he said softly, even as he slid over to meet her.

They moved slowly together, as if each was a little afraid of the other. His hand cupped her face, and she lifted her mouth to meet his. Their first kiss was tentative, a testing of a new partner. His lips were warm and tender, embracing hers in a gentle promise. The hand on her cheek firmed, urging her mouth more strongly against his as his lips parted. His tongue slid lightly over her lower lip, and she shivered. "Still cold?" he whispered.

Jo didn't reply. He dropped both hands to her shoulders and smoothed them repeatedly up and down her arms until the goose bumps disappeared from the friction. "Better?" he murmured against her mouth.

"Better," she whispered and lifted a hand to the opening into his shirt. Her fingers encountered springy hair as he moved to nibble her cheek and then her ear.

"You taste good."

"Mmm," she answered, arching her neck to kiss him eagerly as his mouth again found hers.

His hands were on her, pulling her closer and turning her until she was half lying in his lap. Time seemed to stop as one heavy, tonguing kiss followed another. And then the rhythm changed. They went at each other like teenagers, hungry, openmouthed, greedy for the taste of one another, as if French-kissing was an experience neither had ever before had.

After a while his hands went exploring. He found the shape of a breast through her clothing and began kneading it, fingers working until they found what they sought, the bud of a nipple. He unbuttoned her quickly, reaching inside the lace of her bra to bring the heat of his palm against her. As she arched against him with soft cries of encouragement, he squeezed a little harder, teasing the hard pebble of flesh with his thumb. And then he was reaching behind to unhook her. He stripped her vest and bra off quickly, lifting her to her knees on the seat so that he could reach the full roundness he had released.

As his lips surrounded the tip of one breast, Jo moaned and plowed her hands into his hair to steady herself. He drew her farther into his mouth, working the tender nipple with his tongue and teeth. When he had plumped it to his satisfaction, he turned to the other.

Jo bit her lip to keep from embarrassing herself with sighs, but he kept tugging so sweetly at her that finally little cries came from her in gasps. And then she was being lowered on her back on the wide seat as he trailed wet openmouthed kisses on her skin.

She tugged at his shirt to pull it from his shoulders, and he stopped to help her. When he bent to her again, she was embraced from shoulder to waist by the hot heavy wall of his bare chest.

He stretched out beside her and reached down to slide his hand along her leg, stopping to work the muscle of her calf with his fingers, an erotic message that both calmed and fed the mounting hunger in her.

She clung to his mouth with hers. With her hands she answered his stroking with long trailing caresses of her own. He felt wonderful, his skin smooth but more dense than her own. With her fingers she learned the contours and powerful cording of muscle in his back and shoulders, followed the curved ridges of his ribs until she encountered his belt buckle. He was strong and very human, and very sexy.

His hand slipped beneath her skirt, dragging it up as he moved until she felt his fingers graze the lower lace edge of her panties. She caught her breath, feeling as if she'd run a city block. Then his fingers were inside, stroking.

He groaned heavily as he encountered the warm drenching proof of her desire. She was so soft, impossibly warm and willing. Everything he'd ever desired.

When her hand slid inside the waistband of his trousers, he sucked in a breath to give her more room. He heard her tiny gasp of surprise as her fingers found him. He held that breath, wondering if his size frightened her. When she tentatively encompassed him, he bit down hard on his lip with a groan of pleasure. He'd been celibate a year. It would take precious little to cause him to embarrass himself.

Then it hit him. Jesus! Crap!

"Wait!" He caught her arm and dragged her hand up out of his pants. "Wait."

He groaned again and ground his hips suggestively against hers even as he slipped his hand out from under her skirt. "I'm...so...damn...sorry," he muttered, the short hot breaths of his laughter delivered directly into the well of her mouth.

"What's wrong?" she asked through throbbing lips.

She felt him sigh as if he'd been kicked in the stomach, her naked bosom receiving the pressured heave of his chest. "I didn't think—" He muttered something too low for her to hear. "You wouldn't want— I—I'm not prepared."

"Oh." She understood. He wasn't *prepared!*

Of course he wasn't, she told herself. He hadn't expected to make love tonight. Neither had she. She'd nearly left town without seeing him again. Lord! How had things gotten this far?

Acutely embarrassed, she pushed against him and he rose at once up off her. She told herself she should be pleased that he was a gentleman, that he'd been thinking of her. That he wasn't like so many overeager men, prepared even when they went out to buy a hamburger. Why did it seem like such a small consolation?

She brushed the hair from her eyes, wondering what had happened to all the pins. It was too dark to know. When she realized she was naked from the waist up, she instinctively covered her breasts with her hands. She felt like a teenager who'd just experienced her first heavy petting session.

He didn't seem in much better shape. Even in the dark she could hear his labored breathing and then saw the shadow of his arms as he raised his hands to rake them through his hair.

"Sorry." The shaky timbre in his voice made her tremble. "I shouldn't have let things get that far." She saw his profile angle toward her. "You don't—"

"No, of course not," she said hastily as she pushed her skirt back down over her thighs with a trembling hand.

"No, of course not," he repeated. He folded his arms across the top and leaned against the steering wheel. Damn! How had things gotten so far out of control so fast?

The blood roared in his ears and his body ached. His zipper dug into very inflamed and very frustrated flesh. As he had so many times in the hospital when the pain had gotten to be too much to bear, he willed himself apart from his body, forcing the clamoring hunger into another place.

"Well," he said huskily after a moment. "Now you can say you've been joyriding."

Jo was working to close the buttons of her vest, which she had found on the floor. "You don't mind if I reserve my thanks," she said carefully.

"Lady, I wouldn't be surprised if you shot me."

As he gunned the engine, neither said another word.

Chapter 6

No summer morning had ever felt better on Jo's skin. The sun laid warm fingers of heat against the back of her neck as she uncoiled the garden hose. When she bent to turn the faucet on, its rays caressed her midriff exposed by the tank top she had knotted below her breasts. As she padded barefoot across the lawn, chilly pearls of dew pushed between her toes. The gentle breeze tumbled the sassy ponytail of corkscrew curls atop her head and licked at her bare thighs as she dragged the hose toward the driveway.

She had awakened at six-thirty—alert, full of energy, and ready for the day to begin. Afraid she would wake the house if she tried to make coffee or listen to the radio, she had decided to try out the new running shoes she had bought the day before. She had run three miles in the neighborhood without even feeling that her feet touched the asphalt. It was only as she jogged past the corner privet hedge on her return and got a good look at Adelle's Cadillac sitting in the full glare of the morning sunshine that reality came thudding back. It halted her in midstride. Streaks and splatters of red mud marred the once-pristine silver surface like bloodstains at the scene of a crime.

She smiled wryly as she twisted the nozzle and sent water jetting against the side of the car. She might not have committed a crime, but she was as anxious as any felon to get rid of incriminating evidence. The last thing she wanted to do was explain that the car's condition was due to the fact that she'd been out joyriding with Gus Thornton.

Events of the night before quick-cut like a video montage before her mind's eye. The evening had begun with her accusations, disbeliefs and doubts. But once on the dance floor, and in his arms, she had stopped doubting, testing and comparing Gus to the memory of a man she never expected to see again. The last of her doubts had dried up within the heat of his embrace. The only doubt she had now was about falling so quickly and so hard for a stranger who reminded her of her painful past.

The ride back into town gave Jo plenty of time for second, third, even fourth thoughts. Each time she glanced with doubts mounting in his direction, he responded with a warmly intimate smile that the darkness couldn't disguise. If he shared her awkwardness in the aftershock of the passion that had erupted between them, he didn't show it. He drove with one hand draped lazily across the top of the steering wheel and the other stretched out along the seat behind her head.

Though he didn't touch her during the drive, once he parked in the lot outside his hotel he didn't seem in the least uncertain of himself as he turned to her. In the dim light, she saw him smile. "It's been quite a night. I wouldn't want to push my luck."

So, he wasn't going to ask her up to his room. She released a tiny sigh of relief. Or was it regret? "No, let's not spoil it."

She saw some hint of disappointment skim across his features, but it was gone in the moment it took him to lean forward and place his lips on hers.

She had thought to keep it light, a token closure to the evening. But the moment his mouth found hers she felt again that deep-down melting and couldn't resist the temptation to really kiss him back.

She lifted a hand, folding it on the column of his neck to hold his mouth on hers. Beneath her fingertips she felt heated skin and tensed tendons and realized he was debating the wisdom of their embrace. Then suddenly he scooped her into his lap, eliminating a quick retreat. She had no doubt then of his continuing interest. It pressed boldly against her. She'd said no, and she knew no was the right decision. Yet the outcome remained in doubt as the seconds piled up and his lips lingered so persuasively on hers. His argument was in his taste, his touch, and the potent tug of his attraction, something that she'd only begun to explore on the front seat of her cousin's car.

Jo pointed the nozzle skyward. The breeze raked the water, scattering rainbows in the air. Then it fell pelting her flushed upturned face. She'd come out of Gus Thornton's embrace with only one sure conclusion: never in all her life had she been so moved by a kiss. No one had ever made her just want to kiss and kiss and keep on kissing until she wore her lips out. Just the memory of it was enough to singe her eyelashes.

She couldn't really see the look in his eyes when the kiss was over but his voice was full of humor. "I've taken a helluva lot of cold showers lately. Guess one more won't kill me." Then he skimmed her lips with his thumb, pausing to press the fullness of her lower lip. "Anybody ever tell you what a sexy mouth you have?"

"Not really." Feeling confident once more, she spread her fingers across the expanse of bare skin revealed by his still-unbuttoned shirt. "Tell me more."

He chuckled deep in his throat as though something suppressed a few of the emotional chords within his amusement. "Lady, if I told you all the things I can imagine your lips doing, it'd scare you all the way back to Baltimore."

She had no comeback for that. She'd come out of his embrace, dazed and dazzled and humming with desire. Her skin was newly sensitized to the possibility of his touch, a touch he had just made her want very badly. But she wasn't nearly ready for what he offered. A slow grin spread across the shadowed contours of his lower face as he drew her hand up to his mouth. His eyes held hers as he rubbed the sensitive tips of her fingers against his lips, still moist from their kiss. "Go home, Jo Spencer," he said softly. And then she felt the sharp nip of his teeth on her middle finger. "Go home and think it over."

Jo shook her head, scattering water like a redheaded poodle. She'd taken his advice, slipped in behind the wheel without protest when he exited the car and floored the accelerator. If she'd not exactly run from Gus Thornton, she'd certainly made a strategic retreat. What had happened between them on the riverbank had been spontaneous and wonderful—and much too soon.

"Yoo-hoo! Jo!"

Jo looked up toward the house next door and smothered a curse. Fawn Gordon was waving at her from the back porch. It had been a cliché since junior high: in Cedar Bluff there were three forms of broadcast—telephone, television, and tell-a-Fawn.

"Jo Spencer! I thought that was you." Fawn came quickly down into the yard. It wasn't yet 8:00 a.m., yet she was fully dressed in a yellow halter dress and matching patent-leather sandals with sunburst beadwork on the toes. Every strand of blond hair had been lacquered into place, making her seem older than her thirty years. She paused out of range of the hose's splash but close enough to reveal the exact shade of her blue eye shadow. "What on earth are you doing here?"

Jo decided to be difficult. "Washing Adelle's car."

"Well, I can see that," Fawn said with a practiced runway smile. "I mean, Adelle didn't say nothing about expecting you when we ran into each other in the produce section of Piggly Wiggly's day before yesterday."

Jo sighed. Fawn was the kind of woman one skipped grocery aisles in order to avoid. She could always be counted on to turn a casual encounter into a tabloid session. Adelle's mother had once remarked, "It's a wonder that girl can keep a manicure, the way she digs after dirt."

Jo concentrated the hose on a rear tire. "I sprang myself on Adelle and Steve. Spur of the moment." No doubt Fawn would have it all over town by noon that Jo Spencer had *mysteriously* turned up. The insinuation subtle but clear: Jo had to be in some sort of difficulty.

Fawn's gaze followed the direction of the water, her eyes widening as she took in the condition of Adelle's car. "Did somebody have an accident? Looks like that car's been in a ditch."

"Nothing like that," Jo assured her. "Just a muddy road."

"Was that out by the cemetery?" Jo felt the hairs rising on her nape even before Fawn finished with, "Steve told me about Adelle's fright yesterday. How she thought she saw Brett Ashwood!"

The words settled like a chill on Jo's suddenly flushed skin. Chagrin and rage fought for dominance of her feelings. Adelle had sworn her to secrecy but now even "Foghorn" Fawn knew about the incident. Everyone in town would know about it by noon—if they didn't already. It wasn't fair, not when she hadn't yet sorted out her feelings about what had occurred.

"Did you see him, too?"

Jo swung about quickly, carrying the hose with her. The high-powered stream of water splashed over Fawn's yellow patent sandals. Fawn squealed and danced back out the way.

"Sorry," Jo said quickly, but there was more humor than regret in her voice.

Fawn glanced up from her dripping sandals, annoyed but undeterred. "You were with Adelle, weren't you? Did you see him?"

"I went over to Little Rock yesterday," Jo said, seething behind her deceptively mild tone. "If I were you, I'd go on and dry those sandals before they're ruined."

Fawn gazed down uncertainly at her damp footwear. "I suppose you're right. I paid an outrageous amount for them, even if I do own the shop. They're designer, you know, imported. Italian."

"I hope you kept the receipt. I read foreign goods aren't what they once were." Jo smiled sweetly. "It's the cheap glue."

"Really?" Fawn's eyes narrowed until her eyes were shaded by half-moon lids powdered robin's-egg blue. "Well, we'll just see about that!"

As Fawn hurried toward her house with a determined look on her face that boded ill for the wholesaler who had sold her boutique that line of shoes, Jo grinned in shameless satisfaction. At least she'd been able to divert Fawn from further nosing into her business—and Gus Thornton had definitely become her very own private business.

"Oh, there you are." Adelle appeared on the driveway from the rear of the house. "What on earth are you doing?"

"Washing your car," Jo answered sourly. Really, had it been declared Dumb Question Day?

"Oh." Adelle placed a hand visorlike over her eyes to shade the angle of the morning sun. "Is that river mud?"

"Top grade," Jo answered casually, aware that every window of Fawn's house was likely to be open a crack, just in case a snatch of gossip might drift in on the morning breeze. "Tell you about it over coffee."

"Then come on in. I've got about ten minutes before I need to start breakfast for the kids."

"Sure thing." Jo forced a cheerful smile in reply. "Just let me finish this part."

She turned quickly away from her cousin, gave the nozzle a vicious twist and aimed a narrowed blast of water at the right front tire. What was she supposed to say to her cousin? That she'd nearly made it on the front seat with a stranger because he kissed as if he had invented the art, with emotion and tenderness and the full intensity of his being? That she had never in her life been so sexually aroused? That for two cents and a dare she could right now be sharing morning-after coffee with a man whose real identity she still wasn't certain of?

As her toes curled in the soft damp grass, Jo squirmed inwardly. As teenagers, she and Adelle had shared every secret—but one. Yet time and distance and maturity had changed their way of relating to one another. The truth about the night before was too personal, and too raw, to share with anyone.

Jo shut off the hose and dropped it on the grass. She didn't have any answers. Besides, Adelle didn't deserve them if she had. Adelle couldn't even keep her own secrets anymore. Cedar Bluff already knew about the "Brett Ashwood" sighting. She'd have to find another way of dealing with her dilemma.

"You went dancing?" Adelle placed a Fitz and Floyd mug, its surface decorated in full-relief pink rosebuds, on the table before Jo.

"Yes." Jo reached for the matching rosebud creamer and poured a healthy stream into her cup. She hated lying, but she was stuck. "We were having so much fun I forgot about the time." She stirred her coffee slowly, wishing she hadn't started the explanation at all. But Adelle was asking questions. Short of being rude, she had to say something. "Sorry about the mud. I'll finish washing the car after breakfast."

"When we were first married, Steve and I used to go dancing all the time. But now, with the kids, we seldom find the time." Adelle sat down at the table, her eyes wide with vicarious pleasure. "So, where did you go?"

Jo decided to inject a little truth into the story. "A honkytonk called the River Bottom."

"The River Bottom?" Adelle looked faintly shocked. "Why, that's the old Murdoch place."

After the events of the past twenty-four hours, Jo was amazed that she could still be pricked by surprise. "Are you sure?"

"Well, I've never been out there, if that's what you mean. We were too young when it had a reputation for real wickedness. It was named Murdoch's River Bottom Saloon but everybody called it the River Bottom. Don't you remember? Sometimes they'd get raided because the fast crowd from high school used to sneak out there on weekends to drink beer."

"I remember," Jo said slowly, feeling as if the coffee in her stomach had turned into battery acid. *Brett used to*

drink there on the weekend. But he was never arrested because his father was the mayor and mayor's sons were above
the law, so he liked to boast.

"A few years ago it was shut down for a time after the
police discovered gambling in the back rooms." Adelle
passed a basket of blueberry muffins Jo's way. "I guess it
must be under new management."

Jo stared at the basket as though it contained snakes. Gus
Thornton, the Aussie, said he liked pubs, had found one
outside Little Rock. Was it just another coincidence he had
happened upon Brett's old drinking hole . . . or had he been
teasing her, playing cat's paws with her feelings? The dazzling memories of the night dimmed before the harsh glare
of this new possibility.

"You look a little flushed," Adelle said with a frown of
concern. "Maybe you shouldn't have gotten up so early.
You never were much of a drinker, but you must have had
a really good time last night."

"Yeah. Memorable," Jo muttered. What if he'd been
sandbagging her? She thought about the final kiss they had
shared. If she'd been one shade less wary she'd now be
sharing a hotel room with a man who could be a liar, a
cheat, a man she had hated for twelve long miserable years.

She jumped at the sound of the phone ringing. Simulta-
neously a hungry cry erupted from the baby monitor Adelle
kept on the kitchen counter.

"It's bottle time," Adelle said as she reached for the
phone with one hand and the refrigerator door with the
other. "Hello? Yes, just a moment." She passed the receiver on to Jo almost as she spoke.

Jo held it away from her. "Who is it?" she asked, though
she was certain she could guess.

Adelle shrugged and turned away to drop the bottle she
had retrieved from the refrigerator into the waiting bottle
warmer. She made a motion with a finger first toward the
monitor from which the sounds of Steve, Jr., cranking up
nicely could be heard and then toward the bottle as she
mouthed, "Back in a sec."

When she was gone Jo placed the receiver to her ear.
"Hello."

"Jo, love. How's my girl?"

The accent ripped it for her. If only he'd been honest. "Well, if it isn't Mr. Back-of-Beyond himself." She wrapped her hand around the mouthpiece and whispered furiously. "Go to hell!"

"A little remorse is only natural," she heard him say amicably. "You surprised yourself last night."

"I'll say!" Jo kept her voice as low as it was nasty.

"Never had the hots for a stranger? Never spent an hour in a motel only to regret it later?" His tone was gently teasing. "Sounds like your sex education has been neglected."

"I don't sleep around, and never with liars!" Jo banged down the phone so hard that she was afraid it might chip.

She'd come to Cedar Bluff for a pause in the emotional turmoil that seemed to rule her life. She'd needed peace and calm. Yet because of a man who reminded her of a past she'd rather forget, she'd run the gamut from malice to passion to mortification in less than twenty-four hours. Was this Brett? Coincidence was becoming too common to be easily believed.

She pressed shaking fingers to her lips to silence a groan of shame. That was what blistered her pride most. If he'd made a fool of her, it was only because she'd let him. She had thought she was smart enough to handle herself in deep water. In angling after the truth, she had even boasted to his face that she would catch him in a lie. Had she, instead, been the butt of his private joke.

She'd enjoyed it all; the dinner, the music, the dancing, even the romance because...because... "Face it!" Jo muttered between her fingers in annoyance as her mind skirted the tawdry label. She'd snapped up his Aussie charm hook, line and sinker because of the oldest craving in the world: lust.

She sank lower in her chair, propping her elbows on her knees and her chin in her fists. Never in her life had she been so ready to throw propriety—hell!—reason over for a hormonal urge. She'd been with attractive men before, entertained some pretty hot scenarios in her head on a first date, but had never ever acted on them. *You can't go to jail for what you're thinking* had been her motto. Lust in the heart seemed pretty tame compared to the dangers of the real thing in this day and age. But a pair of achingly familiar whiskey brown eyes in a face hauntingly aged by time and pain had made her forget to look for the hook in the lure.

When the phone rang again she made a grab for it. Just because Adelie hadn't recognized that phony Australian accent the first time, there was hardly a chance she wouldn't catch on the second time. "Hello?"

"Jo, I—"

She jabbed the button down and held it. What was she going to do? She gave the cord a considering look, but short of unplugging every phone in the house, she couldn't prevent him from calling back again and again. Sooner or later Adelle would either pick up or demand to know what was going on.

She released the button and very carefully lowered the receiver toward the cradle. It rang before it completely settled.

"Now listen—" she heard him begin with a definite edge in his voice. Then more uncertainly, "Jo! Jo?"

"Yes."

"Don't hang up."

"No. I can see that's pointless with you."

"Good. Now listen to me. You're upset. That means we need to talk."

"You promised not to cause trouble," Jo said shortly.

"Who am I troubling?"

"Me." She glanced at the empty doorway that led to the hall. Adelle would be down any moment with the baby. "No one knows I came to see you. If you keep calling, Adelle will recognize your voice. You swore you wouldn't cause her any more trouble."

"Then I guess you'll have to deal with me."

His voice was calm, even cajoling, but Jo couldn't trust it. "What do you want?"

"To see you again."

"Last night was a mistake."

"I don't like mistakes."

She believed him. However impulsive and reckless eighteen-year-old Brett Ashwood had been, this man didn't seem likely to take rash action or make errors in judgment.

After all, a snide little voice inside her head reminded her, *he had been the one to break up their lovemaking because he wasn't prepared.* She hadn't thought that far. Lord! She hadn't been able to think at all.

"You still on the line?"

"Yes." She didn't like giving him credit for anything that had occurred, but fairness demanded it. "Look, it was my mistake. I knew you were trouble the moment I saw you. Let's just forget the whole thing."

"Not a chance!"

Adelle appeared in the doorway to the kitchen at that moment with Steve, Jr., balanced on a hip and a question implicit in the two blond brows riding high on her forehead. No doubt about it, Jo thought sourly, the repeatedly ringing phone had not gone unnoted.

She didn't like giving in, but she knew she might as well be trying to extract burrs from cotton balls as dissuade the man on the phone from calling again if she hung up on him. "Where?"

"Thought you'd see it my way." His gloating tone turned her grip on the phone into a stranglehold. "Here. Noon."

"Can't."

"Why?"

"Transportation."

"Your problem."

Jo lowered her gaze before Adelle's curious expression as she sat opposite her to feed Steve, Jr., his bottle. A number of unfit-for-polite-company remarks graffitied her thoughts. "I'll think of something. Maybe. No promises."

"That's my girl."

She couldn't believe he hung up first. Nor was she prepared to answer the questions that were dancing in Adelle's eyes. She sprang to her feet and reached over to pat Stevie awkwardly on the head, making a funny face as she did so. Her expression drew a bubbled smile from him.

Avoiding her cousin's eye, she said, "Better finish the car before it gets hot. Think I'll take it to one of those do-it-yourself places. They've got all the brushes and stuff."

"Steve always has me take it to the detail shop over on Mulberry," Adelle said. "Because they guarantee to protect the paint," she added almost apologetically.

"No problem. My treat." Jo picked up her mug and downed the remaining coffee quickly. "Just let me get my wallet." She made herself move to the doorway before daring to ask the next question and hoped she sounded spontaneous as she turned about. "Oh, by the way. I've decided to rent a car. Can't keep borrowing yours. Any recommendations?"

"Devare's Cadillac has a rental service. I could ask Steve."

"No, that's fine. Fine," Jo repeated as she turned away. Her credit card had already had a healthy workout yesterday. If she stayed in town much longer, she wouldn't need a new job, she'd need to knock over a bank to meet the debts she was piling up.

Her sense of humor sobered as she climbed the stairs to her bedroom. There were all kinds of debts. For instance, what was last night's moment of weakness going to cost her?

Chapter 7

"I remember you, all right," said Caleb Gordon as he slid behind the wheel of his wrecker and adjusted his cap over a head of shoulder-length pale blond hair. "Must be six, seven years since I last laid eyes on you. Still, I knew. That redhead is one of the Spencer girls, I said to myself when I spied you standing by the road." He put in the clutch and shifted the truck into gear. "A lucky thing I was at the garage, ain't it?"

"Some kind of luck," Jo murmured, hanging on for dear life to the door handle as he hauled the wrecker, rent car in tow, off the shoulder onto the interstate.

Local wisdom said bad luck came in threes. If so, thought Jo grimly, then whoever was in charge of that department had lost count. The morning had been a disaster. First the detailer's automated system had refused her credit card. Then the auto dealer informed her that he had rented his last car five minutes before she arrived. Finally, the clunker that she had borrowed out of desperation from a repair shop had gone belly up on the interstate halfway between Cedar Bluff and Little Rock. That should have been the end of it. Three strikes and she was out. Yet, after a forty-five-minute wait in the pressure cooker her auto had become, she had spied

the wrecker pulling off the interstate with the words CE-
DAR BLUFF AUTO SHOP printed backward across the
hood, and had known that bad luck still dogged her. She
was being rescued by Fawn Gordon's husband, of all people.

"Where were you headed, anyhow?"

"Over to Little Rock," Jo answered shortly, wishing she
had specified that AAA send some other wrecker service.

"That so? I was going that direction myself when your
call came in. You need a lift, you got one."

"Thanks, but I've changed my mind." She was amazed
she sounded so calm. Inside, she felt frantic, like a squirrel
on one of those exercise wheels, spinning out of control but
going nowhere. She glanced down anxiously at her watch.
She was late and going to be later. Still, there was no way she
was going to ask Caleb Gordon to drop her off at the airport. If Fawn so much as suspected that anyone answering
Brett Ashwood's description was still in the area, she
wouldn't stop until she had ferreted him out. Yet what
would happen when she didn't show? Would he call Adelle?

"Funny how I recognized you right off," Caleb repeated
in his friendly drawl as he happily exceeded the speed limit.
"You married yet?"

The bald question would have seemed rude in the city but
in Cedar Bluff it was just small talk. Be polite, Jo told herself. "Not yet."

"So why not?" He gave her an up-and-down look, then
grinned. His crystal blue eyes crinkling upward at the corners reminded Jo why all the females in Cedar Bluff had at
one time or another had a crush on him. "Looks like all
your parts are still in order."

Jo smiled to herself. To the casual observer, Caleb Gordon seemed no more than a grease monkey. Yet when his
work cap was removed and the grease lava-soaped off, any
woman could tell you why Fawn Gordon, née Shibley, former Miss Sorghum and second runner-up to Miss Arkansas
1982, had married him. Caleb Gordon was six feet of easygoing, towheaded, all-American male. In a word he was
"gorgeous." Of course, there was a drawback. As Jennifer
Pevey once remarked after trying to teach him algebra in

trade for lessons in French-kissing, Caleb Gordon was "one heck of a biology experiment but dumb as a box of rocks."

That description might have detracted from his appeal if not for the "gift." Caleb loved cars: any kind, any condition, any age. While he couldn't retain the rules of long division, he could take apart and reassemble into working condition the engine of a car blindfolded. Word spread quickly. A high school dropout, Caleb was now one of the most sought after mechanics in racing circles worldwide. On any given weekend, he could be found in the chase car tailing a formula car across sand-strewn tracks south of Cairo or through the hairpin turns of southern Italy. The gift had made him wealthy and famous. Surprisingly, he always returned to his garage on Elm Street.

"So, you don't cotton to Yankee males?"

"What?" Jo hadn't realized her thoughts had drifted.

"Fawn always thought you would marry a Yankee, but I told her no self-respecting Cedar Bluff girl could stomach them quiche eaters." He favored her with another of his toothy sweet-potato-pie smiles and a wink. "You come home to look over the stable?"

Was this the rumor Fawn had fabricated about her, that Jo Spencer had come home to find a man? Jo inhaled slowly as she controlled her temper. "Actually, I'm home for a little R and R."

"Just as well. Ain't much to pick from these days. Now there is Carl Purvis. His missus up and left him for that biker from Idaho who came through last fall. Rode a beauty of a Harley. A 1964 classic. Don't see chrome like that anymore. I fiddled with the exhaust for him. Anyway, you wouldn't want Carl. He's fond of chewing tobacco and don't keep his autos up. Been three months since I told him his pickup needed a lube job."

"Thanks for the tip," Jo said less graciously than before.

Caleb slanted a speculative glance her way. "Heard how you thought you saw Brett Ashwood at the cemetery yesterday. You ever wonder what's become of him?"

The barest whisper of a sigh escaped Jo. Tell-a-Fawn was in perfect working order. No doubt she would later pump her husband for every word they exchanged. The conversation had become a mine field. "We saw a man who bore a passing resemblance to Brett," she said, keeping her voice neutral. "Turns out he was just a tourist driving through."

"A shame Ashwood never came back," Caleb remarked as he reached for a stick of gum from the package lying on the dash. "He was about the best friend I ever had."

Jo frowned. "You and Brett were best friends?"

"Kinda surprising, ain't it?"

Jo blushed. "I didn't mean—"

He grinned at her. "Know you didn't." He folded the gum in thirds before tucking it into his mouth. The silver paper he tossed back on the dash. "You wouldn't have known much about us, being as you was a few years younger. Brett mighta been valedictorian, but on the football field things was more equal between us. The friendship just naturally went on from there. Always liked that about him, that he made friends according to who he liked instead of hanging out with the 'right' crowd. His daddy sure hated it. But Brett was loyal once he made up his mind about something." He nodded to himself. "We weren't no angels. But we never hurt nobody. Brett always was a gentleman with the girls. She said no, he took her home. Damn shame about Adelle. I don't blame him for taking off. Shotgun weddings ain't any man's style."

Jo was amazed. She'd never heard Caleb string so many words together, even if he was misinformed. "Brett and Adelle were in love. If it hadn't been for the tragedy, they would've worked things out."

Caleb shook his head, blond hair whisking the collar of his denim shirt. "No way. Brett told me before it happened that it'd never stick."

Jo's head jerked around. "Brett said that?"

"He did. When he came back from Harvard for the wedding, he looked me up. Loyal." He winked at her. "Some of us threw him a stag party before the wedding at Murdoch's. Even got a gal to—" He grinned. "Well, you know. Anyway, that's where he said it. Just till the babe's born, he said, then he was getting on with his life."

"Brett loved Adelle," Jo maintained, feeling family loyalty demanded she respond

Caleb shrugged. "There's loving and then there's loving. Was plain they had the hots for one another them times they came out to the levee that summer."

"The levee?" The surprise in Jo's voice was genuine. The levee was notorious. Going there with a boy was tantamount to a girl's agreeing to go all the way. Adelle had told her many things, but never about going out to the levee.

"Adelle turned out to be a real good drinker." A smile of distant memory invaded Caleb's expression. "She could dance, too. Real dancing, not that tippy-toe stuff she learned in Memphis." His gaze again left the roadway to meet hers. "You ever get to the levee?"

Jo shook her head. "No."

Caleb shrugged. "Ain't surprised. Truth is, I kinda figured Brett was waiting to take you there himself."

Jo glanced down at her hands. Each revelation seemed to knock her further off balance. "Why would you think that?"

"Maybe because he warned me off you. Said you were too young. Till he said different, you were under his protection."

Jo felt her cheeks burn. To prevent him from asking another question, she quickly posed one of her own. "What, exactly, did you say was wrong with my car?"

"Could be the timing chain," Caleb answered, shifting conversational gears as easily as he did those of his wrecker. "Still, my guess would be the rocker arm..." As his explanation drifted off into the technical, Jo retreated into her thoughts.

Brett had once told Caleb Gordon that he considered her, Jo Spencer, under his protection! What she would have given to know that twelve years ago. It would have made her own secret longings easier to bear. She had believed that Brett and Adelle had loved one another in the beginning. Had she only been imposing her own desires on them?

She thought back to the tears she'd shed the day Adelle left Cedar Bluff, headed for boarding school in Memphis. She had worshiped Adelle for as long as she could remem-

ber. After the fatal car collision that had taken both her
parents' lives, the prospect of living with her beautiful older
cousin had been the only joy in her life. She'd thought she'd
die of loneliness when Adelle left. But then she'd met Brett
Ashwood, who had taken a part-time job in her uncle's law
office his senior year.

After all this time she could still remember every detail of
their meeting. He was crossing the lobby of the office suite
with a tray of mail balanced on his head for the amusement
of the secretary. He was doing a Carmen Miranda imita-
tion, with a sweater tied about his hips to accent his exaggerated movements. She couldn't help but recognize him,
though she'd never before been close to him. Because he'd
been quarterback and class president, his picture spent an
amazing amount of time on the pages of the *Cedar Bluff
Register.* Now here he was in the all-too-compelling flesh:
the brown eyes with golden halos around the irises, a razor-
sharp grin that forewarned friend and foe of a reckless
streak, and a swagger that was pure sexual confidence. If he
had glowed like a lava lamp she couldn't have been more
impressed.

The fact that he paused to speak to her seemed a miracle.
Later she learned he was like that, spreading his easy charm
around generously. While she was suffering through every
moment of an acutely self-conscious, hypersensitive fifteen, he at eighteen seemed invulnerable: cocksure, popular and smart.

They became friends after a fashion, though experience
would have told her not to take his attention too seriously.
She couldn't afford to harbor deep feelings for a young man
like him. It was like pinning her dreams on winning the lot-
tery. It would only break her heart. It did.

At the end of the school year, Adelle came home, newly
graduated and more beautiful than ever.

Of course, Brett fell for her. Seen side by side, they looked
as if they'd stepped off the cover of a romance novel, all
copper and ivory and destined for one another. Who could
resent Brett's attraction to Adelle? All Jo had to do was look
in the mirror for a reality check. Besides, she still adored her

cousin, wanted the best for her, and Brett Ashwood was the best.

Jo sighed as they whizzed past the exit sign for Cedar Bluff and took the exit ramp. She'd known Brett as anything but perfect. Rumors of his drinking and his reputation for taking girls out to the levee both repelled and fascinated her. But Cedar Bluff was a small town, and because he was the mayor's son, there had always been a net to catch him when he fell from grace, until Adelle Spencer got pregnant. This time Brett Ashwood crashed and burned. The socially prominent Spencers and Ashwoods could accept almost anything, except scandal. They insisted on a marriage.

Jo briefly closed her eyes. To think that he never loved Adelle seemed almost too cruel in the wake of what had subsequently occurred. Perhaps if she had stood silently by instead of reaching out to ease his fall with her own too-full heart, Zachary would still be alive. The devastation of her failure haunted her still.

The image of a permanently tanned face, slightly scarred but provocatively male, moved into Jo's inner line of vision. It was Gus Thornton's face. She fought the anticipation the image brought with it. She had believed him yesterday when he denied being Brett. Wanted to believe him still. But he would have to prove himself again.

The question she had been avoiding asking herself all morning came startlingly into focus: which did she want, to discover that he was Brett or that he wasn't?

The question disturbed her because, abruptly, she realized that she didn't know the answer. If her attraction to Gus was based solely on the fact that he reminded her of Brett, then last night was a sham. She had deceived herself as well as used a stranger to assuage old feelings for another man. Was she capable of that degree of self-deceit? Her skin felt suddenly chilled, exacting the slightest tremor.

"You cold?" Caleb punched the button on the air conditioner to switch it from full-blast frigid to medium arctic. "I boosted the standard output. Works right well, don't it?"

Jo nodded and stared out the front window at the heat shearing off in waves from the shiny black asphalt. It must be ninety-eight degrees in the shade, but she felt only a shiver of apprehension.

After she had paid the cab, Jo turned and walked slowly up the sidewalk toward the house. It had taken an hour to sort out her transportation problems. Thanks to Caleb's intervention, she'd come away not owing a cent. Even so, she'd had to wait until the paperwork was done. Caleb had offered to wait and drive her home, but she knew he had things to do. So she'd called a cab when she was done.

She wiped the perspiration draining between her brows with the back of her hand. Every ounce of her energy had been siphoned off by the heat. With each step her clothes clung damply to her back and legs. The sky had taken on a metallic shimmer. The weight of sunlight pressed upon the day. One heck of a thunderstorm was brewing. Today, tomorrow, the next day—the longer it simmered the worse it would be. In the meantime, she needed a little peace, and to be left alone to think through her dilemma. Yet she doubted she would get either.

She lifted her gaze warily toward the house, half expecting to find Adelle waiting for her. But the doorway was empty as was the columned porch that ran the length of the facade and then curved off to the right. In the turn trailing red roses climbed a trellis, shrouding the corner in deep cool shade. As a child she had liked to sit in the swing hung there in the shade and catch drifting rose petals as the breeze shook them free. The memory stirred others, those of Adelle and herself playing tag on the lawn in the summer. Even then she had often felt like a stranger in her hometown. She felt that way again. Why had she come home?

As she reached the top of the front steps, a movement at the far end of the porch near the rose trellis caught her eye. The porch swing was swaying slightly. The shape occupying it was long and lean and male.

She turned toward him with the fatalism of a prisoner facing a firing squad. Please, she prayed, let it be a quick demise.

He didn't say anything as she came toward him. Denim-clad legs were sprawled out in front of him, the squeaking movement of the swing directed by the rocking of his boot heels on the floorboards. One of his hands grasped the chain that held up one end of the swing while the other was stretched out along the wooden back. His white dress shirt was open at the throat, the long sleeves rolled back to reveal muscular forearms lightly dusted with silky dark hair. He looked at ease, as though his appearance was welcome. This was the man she'd kissed, nearly made love to the night before. Whoever he was, the feelings he brought roiling to life inside her now were real and fresh and very intense.

When she paused a few feet from him, he inclined his head to indicate the empty space beside him. The arrogance of his action revived a little of her natural feistiness. She folded her arms across her chest. "I prefer to stand."

"Did you think I was bluffing?" His voice sounded all the more unnerving for its quiet, level ease.

"No. Just tell me this." She paused, suddenly out of air, and sucked in her lower lip. The question had to be asked. "Does Adelle know?"

He didn't answer at first, only stopped the leisurely movement of his feet. "So we're back to that."

His accent was harsher than usual, as if he was reacting naturally to stress. And that made her furious. She didn't check the bitterness that leaked into her voice. "You knew I'd eventually figure out where we went last night. The old Murdoch place. Brett's old drinking hole. Guess the joke's on me."

Oddly enough, he smiled. "I understand it's always been a popular place, lots of local color. But that's not what's bothering you. You turn over enough rocks you're bound to find a snake. Question is, what are you looking for, Jo?"

The sound of her name from his lips moved her, as if he had reached out and actually touched her. She'd always thought it a blunt name but miles better than sappy Evangeline, which was her given name. But the way he said "Jo" as a little guttural whisper in the back of his throat made her think of his hands on her skin. All the old alarms jangled to life. "I don't owe you an explanation. But I'll say this, once bitten, twice shy."

She watched his smile stretch out until she glimpsed a row of white teeth. "I don't bite, at least not very hard. Come here and I'll prove it."

They heard the sound of high heels clicking on the drive at the same time. "Yoo-hoo! Jo? Adelle?"

The sound of Fawn's voice sent Jo spinning around. If Fawn found them, there'd be the devil to pay. In an act of pure desperation, Jo spread her arms in a protective gesture, as if her slender figure could shield her guest's broader frame from view. Then reason reasserted itself. She turned and grabbed him by the arm, drawing him to his feet at the same time as she put a finger to her lips for silence.

It was obvious that he didn't share her alarm. His look of amusement made her want to slug him, but she ignored the juvenile impulse. She gestured toward the side porch where they would be out of sight. It was only a few steps, but Jo felt adrenaline shift her heartbeat into overdrive. At the last instant she spotted the telltale movement of the deserted swing. As she reached back to still the action she felt the prick of thorns where her arm brushed against the rose trellis. She bit the inside of her lip, determined not to make a sound as she slipped back past the corner of the house.

"Yoo-hoo! Jo!"

Jo held her breath as she heard the rhythmic click of Fawn's heels climb the steps and cross the porch. Then the doorbell sounded its chimes from the entry hall.

"Easy." Hands framed her shoulders.

She tried to shrug off his touch, but he moved them toward her neck in a gentle massaging motion. "You're too tense," he murmured, leaning forward so that his words were delivered directly into the hollow of her right ear.

"Stop that!" she whispered urgently and again tried to shrug away his hands, but he only moved in closer.

Annoyed, she tried to nudge him away with her elbows, but he brought his arms forward and crossed them in front of her, locking her inside a muscular embrace of arms, chest and thighs. Trapped, she breathed in the tang of his light citrus cologne, vividly aware of the light caress of his body along the length of hers. The intimacy triggered a dangerous sensual memory of the contrast between the cool leather of Adelle's car seat and the blanketing heat of his body upon her bare skin. The memory set off flash points of heat throughout her body.

"I just have one question," he murmured, his lips now tasting the skin below her ear. "Why are we hiding?"

"You know," she said between gritted teeth. "Now shut up!"

"Okay."

His hands slid down her front, over the slope of her breasts, around and under to spread out across her flat abdomen. Jo bumped her hips against his pelvis in protest, but he chuckled and nudged her back, his metal belt buckle pressing coolly into the middle of her back through the sheer linen of her blouse.

Outraged, she nearly shouted in protest, but the renewed tap-tap of heels strangled the sound in her throat. As she held her breath she heard Fawn rap impatiently on one of the panes of beveled glass that flanked the front door. "Is anybody in there?"

Fawn paced farther along the front porch, stopping to knock at one of the windows. "I know you're in there, Jo Spencer. I saw you pay the cab!" She sounded so close that Jo jumped within Gus's embrace. She was just a few feet from the corner.

Jo didn't resist when Gus began waltzing her backward toward the far end of the porch. If she'd been free, she thought, she would have turned and fled. When they reached the side door into the house, he released her. She turned to tell him that she didn't have the key and saw that he had already thrown one leg over the banister. He winked at her, lifted the other leg and disappeared over the edge of the railing. Though it was an eight-foot drop, Jo followed without a second thought.

The impact, cushioned by the thick carpet of grass, was familiar. Many a time as a child, to her aunt's horror, she had vaulted over the banister when she was in too much of a hurry to walk around to the steps. With knees flexed, she still found it an easy exercise.

Gus nodded in approval as she straightened. "Good on you!"

She didn't hesitate when he reached for her hand. A moment later, they were racing across the back lawn like two children running from a well-deserved switching.

They didn't pause until they had ducked out of sight behind the trailing pale green drapery of the weeping willow that stood at the back of the property line. When they both stood facing one another, chests rising and falling a little rapidly with their exertions, he smiled at her. "You're not a bad runner, for a girl."

"Ha!" Jo sized up his boots and tight jeans with a sly smile. Compared to her espadrilles and shorts, his attire would be a handicap in a race. "Twenty dollars says I can outrun you within half a block." The moment she issued the challenge, she wanted to take it back. She had forgotten about his limp.

But if he read her thought in the change of her expression, he didn't respond to it. His grin turned wicked, the golden flecks in his dark eyes suddenly brighter. "You're on. My rental car's parked just in the next street."

The faintest jingle sounded on her internal warning system. "Why did you park out of sight?"

His knowing smile tugged her line a second time. "I didn't think you were ready to introduce me to the family *quite* yet."

That was an understatement. He was the very last person she wanted to introduce to anybody of her acquaintance. "Just where do you think I'm going to go with you?"

He rocked back on his heels as deep smile lines swallowed up the corners of his eyes. "Where else on a day like this? Fishing."

Chapter 8

Jo didn't say a word as he eased the car off the shoulder-less county road and onto the grassy slope of the embankment. Below them, shaded by a line of trees, ran an off-branch of the river. The area was laced with runoffs and tributaries that shrank into little more than swamps and mudholes after a spell of dry weather. Today the brackish water ran swiftly, a result of recent rains. Fishing would be good today.

Jo stepped out of the car as he did, and immediately an insect sang warningly in her ear as she wandered toward the rear of the car. He had opened the trunk to reveal a tackle box, ice chest, two cane poles and a pair of low-crowned flat-brimmed straw hats.

"You were serious," she said with a little laugh.

He nodded. "I'm on vacation, remember. What's more restful than fishing?"

Jo swatted at the insistent insect. "Okay, so where's the rods with reels?"

He chuckled as he bent in to retrieve the tackle. "What's the matter? You too much of a city girl to use a cane pole and floater?"

Jo tapped her chest with a finger. "You're talking to a former Quachita Girls' Camp cane-pole fishing champ."

"Then here you go." He passed a pole to her without looking back.

Jo smiled as the smooth- and knotty-sectioned pole slid between her fingers. It had been years since she'd thought of herself as a female Huckleberry Finn, scrambling along the banks of a stream with bait bucket and rod in hand. Her father had taught her to fish, had regularly taken her fishing from the age of five until his death just before her tenth birthday. After that, her only chance to fish came at summer camp. Her uncle had no patience with fishing, and Adelle hated the whole process: mud, live bait, slimy fish and all. Now that she thought about it, she would enjoy exercising her rusty skills. "Pass the bait box."

He straightened and held out a short-handled spade. "We're going native today."

Choked laughter erupted from Jo. "You're not serious?"

"Don't tell me. You never dug for bait."

"Sure. Lots of times. But that was before I had a manicure to worry about."

"Too messy for a city girl, huh?"

It wasn't his inflection—the Australian accent remained—it was his Southern phrasing. Suddenly Jo felt the world slide out of sync. Like a sharp image slipped out of focus, the cocky, smug features of Brett Ashwood overlaid for an instant the mature facade of Gus Thornton. Just as swiftly the suggestion of duality was gone.

"Well?" He waggled the trowel in front of her.

Jo blinked. "Right. Worms." She took the tool and reached for one of the two straw hats lying on the floor of the trunk. "What do I put them in?"

He handed her a metal container about the size of a large can of tomatoes. As she looked at it, she realized it was indeed a can with the lid removed. So much for fancy equipment.

"Don't forget to check the mud near the shallows for crawfish."

Suspicion nudged her as she watched him unbutton his shirt. "What would an Aussie know about crawfish?"

He stripped off his shirt and began folding it very neatly. "Let's see. Crayfish, crawfish, crawdads, mud bugs: any of a family of fresh-water decapod crustaceans resembling the lobster." He winked at her. "Read up on local color for the trip."

"I'm impressed," she said sourly, amazed at how unruffled he remained in all circumstances. What this man knew about self-possession should be taught for profit, she mused enviously. She could use a bit of it right now. Looking at his shirtless torso was undermining her equilibrium in a big way.

When he turned to put his shirt away, her gaze wandered freely. The skin of his back was smooth and golden, unmarred by the accident. She tried and failed to dismiss from her mind images of what had passed between them the night before. She could remember the exact texture and taste of his skin, recall the warmth and weight of his body on hers. They were strangers, yet she had been more intimate with him than with 99.9 percent of the men she'd ever known. The need to know more about him returned. Last night her conscience had been clear. The doubts had been gone. Now they were nudging back. She needed justification for her feelings, for the tug of desire he exerted simply by his presence.

As he retrieved a T-shirt she hadn't noticed before, she wondered if she would ever again touch him, or if she even wanted to. No, scratch that. Despite every common-sense reason to the contrary, she did want to touch him again, to kiss him and feel— Dammit, she thought a little desperately, she'd never lusted after a man before. Why him?

Something in her expression must have given away her thoughts because as he moved to pull the shirt over his head and paused to look at her, their gazes met and locked. In seeming slow motion she watched him put the shirt aside and straighten, their eyes never breaking contact. There was unfinished business between them, and they both knew it.

With an intensity that made her shiver despite the heat, she realized she hoped he would take the lead, come to her, take her in his arms and make love to her. Shock followed this silent admission. Her heart beat so loudly in her ears that she was certain he must hear it. She wanted him to take the decision from her, to remove the barriers, overpower her confusion and hesitation, her natural doubts in the face of possible disaster. She didn't want to be rational or realistic, or even right. She didn't care who he was, what he wanted. She wanted him to satisfy this very real and frightening hunger for him, which was demanding urgent release.

He came toward her slowly, arousing new emotions along nerve endings she thought were already in overload. *Please. Stop. Don't.* The words circled and circled in her head, chasing each other faster and faster until they formed phrases punctuated by her heartbeat: *Please stop, don't, stop, please don't, please, don't stop.*

She couldn't move, could scarcely breathe. He reached up to touch her face, skimmed his fingers over her brow, down her temple and over her cheek. She felt slick where he touched her, wondering a little foolishly if heat or excitement had made her damp with perspiration. And then she smelled it. Citronella oil. Bug repellent!

He drew back his hand and her eyes followed in hurt and confusion to see him pour a few drops from a bottle he held into his palm. "Bugs will eat up skin as tender as yours," she heard him say, his voice easy and matter-of-fact.

She flinched when he raised his hand to touch her again. Not like this! She'd rather he never touched her again than submit to this cool impersonal contact.

"I'm perfectly capable of doing that myself," she said harshly. "Give it to me."

She saw the humor ease from his expression. "Right, Ms. America." He slapped the bottle in her palm. "Now are you going to dig bait or watch?"

Jo turned away without comment. The pounding in her chest slowed, leaving a kind of spongy uncertainty in her legs, but she kept moving, castigating herself with very unladylike comments under her breath. She'd nearly made a fool of herself. That wouldn't happen again. The consolation prize was that he hadn't noticed. He hadn't felt a single degree of the hot jumble of emotions that had scorched her.

Gus stared after her as she walked away, wondering what the hell had just happened. When he had looked up from the car trunk and seen that raw needy look in her eyes, he could have whooped with delight. They were back where they'd been the night before, no questions asked, no answers needed. He'd wanted to scoop her up and set her in the damp grassy bank and finish what they'd started. He didn't care that they'd have been practically on view from the road. But he hadn't wanted to scare her. He'd wanted to be certain he was reading her right. The ruse of the repellent was meant to test the waters. But something had gone wrong.

As he walked back to the car, he reached up to rub the back of his neck where the sun stung the tender scars there. Nothing about Jo Spencer was easy. He'd realized that from the moment they'd met yesterday. Perhaps that was part of the attraction. But right about now he was beginning to wonder if she was worth the aggravation. She was harder to get a grasp on than a cactus. Had he been too subtle? Too slow? Too fast? Hell! How was he to guess the right combination of moves if she kept leaping away at every miscalculation? He needed some cooperation. Before the day was out, he meant to get it.

Gus was sitting on a blanket at the water's edge when she returned from her foray along the riverbank. She held up her can full of rich brown loamy earth like a trophy. "Mission accomplished."

He looked up and broke into laughter.

"What's so funny?" Jo demanded.

"Did you dig for worms with the spade or your nose?"

Jo wiped the tip of her nose with her palm but her hands were so mud caked that she was certain she was adding more to what must already have been there. "Do you have a towel?"

"Better than that." He picked up a cloth that had been lying on the blanket and rose to his feet. Moving to the edge of the water, he bent and dipped it in. "Come here," he said as he straightened while wringing out the cloth.

She approached and reached out for the cloth. For a moment she thought he might not give it to her. Then he chuckled and tossed it to her.

He watched, arms folded casually, as she scrubbed her nose. When she paused, brows lifted in inquiry, he pointed to his right cheek. She wiped hers. Then he pointed to his chin. Mud came away when she stroked her own. With each mime, his grin grew larger.

"Well?" she demanded when he finally shook his head.

"Looks like nothing short of a bath is going to set you to rights." He waved his hand toward the stream. "After you."

She set her can of worms down by her feet and slipped out of her espadrilles. The grass felt slick and tickled her insteps as she padded over to the water's edge. She was amazed by the water's chill as she stepped in. The next instant she realized that the river bottom was amazingly steep and treacherously slick. She yelped in alarm as the mud gave and her feet slipped out from under her.

He made a grab for her, catching her flailing arms by each wrist. Furiously embarrassed, Jo backpedled furiously, trying to regain her footing as he held her unceremoniously aloft. Finally, she dug first one heel and then the other into the mud and stood. "You can let me go now," she snapped, angry at herself.

He released her at once. Realizing how ungrateful she must have sounded, she turned to apologize but was checked by the look in his eyes. They were polished stones of tiger's eye between twin thickets of dark lashes: bright, wary and predatory. "If I'd known you were going to do a belly flop, I'd have suggested you go downstream. All that churning's probably queered the fish." He turned away and marched back to his blanket.

Feeling equal parts foolish and annoyed, Jo stooped in the shallows to wash the mud from her hands, arms and legs. When she finished that, she rinsed out the cloth he had given her and wiped her face thoroughly. Whatever makeup she had been wearing was now definitely gone. If she so much as stroked on a little lipstick he'd think she'd done it for him. The fact that it would be true fixed her decision not to do it.

Finally she glanced back at him. He was seated cross-legged on the blanket. He had removed his T-shirt and was rubbing sunscreen into his skin. He smoothed it on, palm flat, across first one shoulder and then the other. The action surprised her. Most men didn't bother with sunscreen. Then she remembered that his scars would be supersensitive to the sunlight and that he would need to protect them.

After he shook a few more sprinkles into his palm, he attacked his chest in a slow rubbing action. The intimacy of the act made her as conscious of him as anything so far this day. The oil left his skin gleaming as sunlight darted off hollows and planes and drew red highlights from his curling chest hair. As his hand moved down across his abdomen, her eyes followed like tracking radar. She remembered his self-deprecating stories about months of life in a hospital. That couldn't have been easy. Many men would have played up the pain, the isolation and the loneliness. His matter-of-fact tone impressed her. And that drew her sympathy.

When he turned his head in her direction, she glanced away, swallowing the inexplicable lump in her throat. Damn him, anyway, she thought miserably, for being so attractive. And for making her care.

"You plan to fish or just paddle in the water?"

She straightened at his taunt and started toward him. She was grateful he slipped into his shirt as she neared. When she lowered herself to her knees on the blanket beside him he held out the sunscreen. "You'll need to reapply it."

She did as he suggested, being extra generous about her ears and neck. As she screwed the cap back on the bottle, she noticed that he had readied his fishing line and said, "Pass me the other one."

"Anything the girl wants." He hoisted the pole and tossed it to her. "Need help tying the hook?"

Jo gazed across into those golden brown eyes regarding her with humor and said sweetly, "Thanks, but I know all about tying knots."

"I've got proof of that." A wolfish grin accompanied the remark. "Question is, how good are you at untying them?"

"Pass me the tackle box," she said evenly.

Leaning back leisurely on his elbows, he watched her choose a hook, snap swivel and lead weights, attach it all expertly and then add a red-and-white float to her line. When she was done, she looked around with a slight frown. "Where's the bait?"

He leaned forward and flipped open the lid on the smaller of two coolers at his feet. "Didn't want all your hard work to get away," he said as he reached in and withdrew the can of worms.

Sure enough, several worms had begun crawling down the side of the can. With a smirk, he flipped them back inside before handing the can to her. "Hope you aren't one of those who can't stand to harm any of nature's creatures."

"If you mean do I care about the environment," Jo replied coolly, "the answer's yes. If you mean am I a fanatic who's forgotten that life and death are irrefutable parts of the natural cycle, then no. I always bait my own hooks."

The smirk eased into a more friendly smile. "That's my girl."

Jo knew that she should resent his constant reference to her as a girl. It was patronizing, chauvinist and demeaning. Yet she suspected that worms weren't the only thing he was baiting. He wanted a rise from her that he wasn't going to get.

She dipped in and brought out three fingers of earth. Several wriggling worms dangled from the scoop. Aware that he watched her every move with the avid interest of a surgeon observing a new technique, she extracted a worm nearly four inches long and plopped the rest back in the can. Holding the bait in one hand and her hook in the other, she carefully secured the worm three times, leaving the barb embedded the final time. To be honest, this wasn't her favorite part of fishing, but she'd have eaten a can of mud before letting him know that the little creature squirming on her hook made her feel a bit like a sadist.

Avoiding her handiwork, she turned to him with a big smug smile. "Any questions?"

He nodded slowly, his expression suddenly serious. "What makes Jo Spencer run?"

"Big dogs and snakes in the grass," she answered glibly and rose to her feet before he could steer into murky waters.

He stood up and, though he didn't touch her, Jo felt the undeniable force of his stare. "Even long-distance runners get tired, Jo. What's your hurry?"

Keep it light, she told herself, don't give him an in. "Living in the rat race is what keeps me healthy."

"Too much exertion isn't good for your heart."

"Let's leave my heart out of this," she snapped, and turned away.

"You go on leaving out your heart, you'll end up very lonely."

She rounded on him. "Are you speaking from experience?"

"Why don't you slow down and find out?"

"Sorry, fresh out of sympathy here. Try the next counter."

"Some man hurt you very badly."

"Don't flatter yourself." She didn't want to spar with him any longer. Her feelings were much too volatile and fragile. She didn't trust him, and she didn't trust herself. She took a deep breath. "Just because I made a mistake last night doesn't mean I'm a sucker for a good line. I don't usually lose control."

"I can believe that." He watched her with absolute attention. "Which makes me more curious than ever. Why me, Jo?"

"Hormones. Insanity. A temporary lapse in moral fiber. Take your pick." She tucked her chin slightly toward her chest and glared at him. "Now, are you going to fish or cut bait?"

She chose a shady spot about fifty yards away from the road. In the dappled shade, the overhanging branches of cottonwoods and willows muffled the noise of cars whizzing past. Here the woods were full of birdsong and other natural sounds. She stood poised for a moment, rod in hand, listening and watching. Beneath the mirrored surface the water flashed green and brown, gurgling forth in bubbles where it ran past sunken tree branches and around protruding flat-topped stones. Gradually it came back to her that there, in the deep shade beyond the stones, was where fish were most likely gathered. With a flick of her wrist she sent her line angling out gracefully over the water upstream. The bait made a single soft *blip* as it broke the surface. She sat down on the bank, knees drawn up, and curled her toes in the moss. Smiling, she watched the red-and-white float ride the top of the current downstream and let her complicated feelings drift out and away across the serenity of the afternoon.

In his company she couldn't think straight. He charmed her with his Aussie accent and his fascinating stories. She wanted to believe him, but every other thing he did threw her off balance. Just looking at him was like gazing into a carnival mirror. She wasn't even certain why she was so attracted to him. All she knew was that she had crossed her own personal boundaries of good conduct because she had wanted to bask in the sexual heat in his eyes. He had gotten in under her guard once. Before he did so again, she wanted to be certain he would not hurt her.

He watched her from a vantage point farther upstream. He cast his bait in a halfhearted manner, uncaring where it landed. His interest was fully on the woman who'd just made it clear that she didn't want anything more romantically to do with him. An act of insanity! He didn't think so. No, not likely. Nor did he think it was a casual thing for her, an affair of the moment to be forgotten just as quickly. She had been too spontaneous, too natural. More than likely she was simply embarrassed. Another woman would have admitted it, asked for time, for him to slow down. But not the thin-skinned Ms. Spencer. She wanted to obliterate him from existence simply because . . .

"Because I remind her of someone else," Gus muttered under his breath. Well, he wasn't going to simply disappear for her sake, not when she'd made him feel things he hadn't felt in much too long. He knew about hard-won independence and how frightening it was to think of losing it. But she had barged in on his world, climbing that levee to slap his face. Now she'd have to live with the results, unless she was willing to turn tail and run back to Baltimore. Somehow, watching her, still but alert to every nuance of her fishing line, he doubted she would run in the face of adversity. He smiled slowly. That suited him just fine.

It was only moments before she got her first nibble and jumped to her feet, dancing like an excited child. He laughed with her, though she never turned to acknowledge him as she hauled in her catch. That was all right. He suddenly saw a parallel in the moment that pleased him. Jo was like a fish: bright, elusive, hiding in the dark shadows of her life. He might not know exactly what was going on under the surface, but like a good fisherman he could watch and wait and read the line. When she snapped at the hook again, he'd make certain he set it good and deep, just as she had with him.

Chapter 9

"That was quick," Adelle said, looking up as her cousin appeared at the top of the staircase.

Jo hurried down the carpeted steps, clutching heels in one hand and several pieces of gold jewelry in the other. "Sorry to keep everybody waiting."

"I'd say it was worth the wait," said Steve, clearly impressed that the same woman who had come flying through the front door thirty minutes ago smelling of citronella and streaked with mud now stood before them looking so poised and sexy. His eyes swept approvingly over the little black dress his cousin-in-law wore. Scoop-necked and midthigh, it hugged her curves like the peel on a banana.

The enthusiasm in his tone made Jo look up and then glance uncertainly at Adelle. "Is it too much?"

Adelle shook her head. "You look great."

"Yeah," Steve added. "Buy that at Fawn's?"

"Not a chance," Adelle chimed in. "Fawn thinks clothing made of lycra and spandex are fit only for exercise."

Steve's eyes lit up. "She may have a point there. I could work up a sweat just looking at a dress like that." He rolled his eyes toward his wife. "Why don't you buy one?"

Adelle gave her head a tiny shake, the movement scattering across her shoulders the few strands of hair she had left artfully loose from the smooth golden chignon at her nape. "I'm an old married lady with kids."

"And the greatest body in town," Steve and Jo chorused together and then laughed.

"Tell you what," Jo said as she slipped on her heels. "I'll leave the dress with you as payment for taking in a stray relative on such short notice."

"Really?" Adelle eyed the dress with renewed interest, then glanced at her husband for guidance. He nodded enthusiastically. "Okay. At least then I won't have to explain the purchase to Fawn. She takes it as an act of personal disloyalty whenever I buy my clothing elsewhere."

Jo clipped on the first of her earrings, a chandelier of golden geometric shapes and beads. Now was the time to begin the explanation they were both waiting for. "Did I tell you who rescued me this afternoon?"

"Caleb Gordon," Adelle supplied, a question in her eyes.

"Right the first time," Jo said with a carelessness she didn't feel. Fawn must have corralled Adelle the minute she got home from her dance school. It seemed equally obvious that Fawn hadn't seen her hightailing it across the yard with a man in tow. If she had, Adelle would have mentioned it first.

"Did you ever get to Little Rock?"

"No." Jo clipped on the second earring. "After Caleb towed me back to town I decided to entertain myself closer to home." She slipped several bangle bracelets up her arms. "I went fishing."

"You went fishing?" Steve's expression said he was clearly amazed. "Alone?"

Jo wondered what kind of penance these evasions were going to cost her. "I just sort of winged it, spur of the moment." She reached up to fluff her not-quite-dry curls. "Aren't we going to be late for our reservation?"

"Right." Steve reached for the keys in his pocket. "I'll pull the car around front."

As the door shut behind him, Jo met her cousin's puzzled gaze. "You look lovely, Adelle." She did. Her ivory lace dress, styled part Gypsy and part Edwardian, made the most of Adelle's fragile pale beauty.

"What's going on, Jo?"

"Going on? Oh, you mean the fishing?" Jo shrugged, avoiding eyes that might see too much. "I really should have left you a note. I'm sorry, really sorry, about that."

As Adelle approached her, Jo realized she had seen that exact expression a hundred times in her aunt's face when as a child she had done something beyond the bounds. The experiences of motherhood must have prompted Adelle's appropriation of it.

Adelle seemed to hesitate before she put a hand on Jo's arm. "Are you in trouble?"

"Heavens, no." Jo felt a too-bright smile stretch her face. "I'm fine, Adelle. Really."

"I know about the job." She sounded genuinely sorry as she spoke.

Jo felt her cheeks catch fire. "What do you mean?"

Adelle kept her voice low and level. "Your neighbor, Janet Mosley called. She said you all had a date for the theater last night."

"Rats! I forgot." Janet was her one close friend and yet she hadn't even thought to call her and tell her what had occurred.

"When you didn't answer her messages last night, she called you at work this morning. They told her you no longer worked there. When you still weren't answering your phone when she came in from work, she was worried and called here. She said you'd given her this number in case of an emergency."

Jo shrugged. "So now you know my secret." Feeling both foolish and thoughtless, she glanced toward the phone stand in the hall. "I'd better call her."

"Jo—" The sound of the car horn interrupted Adelle.

Jo turned toward the door. "That's Steve. Maybe we'd better go. I'll call later."

Adelle picked up her purse from the bench by the door. "I told Janet that you were okay." Her frown deepened. "I hope I was right."

"Of course you were right. Inconsiderateness isn't a crime, only a social faux pas."

"Isn't this just the most amazing fun!" Fawn Gordon perched on the edge of the chair a waiter had brought and placed beside Jo.

Yeah, like famine following a flood, Jo thought sourly, ignoring the silent plea for graciousness Adelle sent her way via a long-suffering smile. It seemed that since her arrival in town, every situation had been constructed for the sole purpose of running her back out. An evening with Fawn Gordon might just do the trick.

With her aqua blue strapless lace dress covered in iridescent sequins, fingers dripping with diamonds and hair teased to the size of a small bush, Fawn seemed a wicked caricature of the Southern socialite. "When Adelle mentioned this afternoon that ya'll would be dining at the country club, I thought to myself, why shouldn't Caleb and I do that?"

"'Cause I hate the damn—" Caleb paused and reddened under his wife's sudden glare. "The darn dress code," he finished weakly.

Jo had seen many men in suits in her life, but never one so uncomfortable as Caleb. His hair was freshly washed and blow-dried into an amazing pale gold fall, but she'd seen his work cap stuck in his trouser pocket before he sat down. His navy blue pinstripe suit fit a little too snugly across shoulders he kept hunching in response to some unseen stimulus. His gray silk shirt looked as if it had a stranglehold on his neck. As for the tie he wore, Jo doubted that particular combination of colors had ever before been seen outside a nightmare. If that weren't enough, it was fringed in purple. "Great tie," she murmured.

Caleb perked up, grabbing the end of his tie as he looked down at it. "Now there's a lady with taste." He cast a gloating look at his wife. "Told you."

Fawn gave a tiny shudder and looked away. "It's a shame we couldn't get a reservation of our own. Then I thought, why not wing it? Occasionally people with reservations don't show. I'd forgotten there was a band tonight."

"No need to explain. We'd have insisted you join us, in any case." Steve's gregarious nature was one of his assets as a successful attorney. "Glad to share our table with you." He signaled the waiter with a finger. "What will you ladies have to drink?"

"A martini," Jo said promptly. "A double." She smiled blandly at the table of astonished faces. If she had to endure an evening with Fawn she wasn't going to do it entirely sober.

"I love a sweet drink when I indulge, which isn't often." Fawn glanced purposefully in Jo's direction. "I guess that's why I never remember the names. Now what do they call that pretty little tropical drink with the umbrella?"

"Sex on the Beach?" Jo offered with a smirk.

Caleb erupted in a belly laugh as Steve said smoothly, "How about a strawberry daiquiri, Fawn? Light on the rum," he added to the waiter.

Fawn pinned Jo with a hostile look. "I'd forgotten how much of a cutup you are, Jo." She gave Jo's dress a thorough once-over. "It seems that hard city life agrees with you. There's no trace of Cedar Bluff breeding left."

"Oh, I don't know." Jo injected every word with wicked humor. "I've been thinking of coming home, maybe setting up a boutique, something for a more youthful crowd."

Fawn's face went pale beneath her blusher, but her voice never lost its sugar-substitute sweetness. "If your attire is an example of what you have in mind, I'm afraid you're doomed to failure. Cedar Bluff women aren't quite so... bold."

"I like Jo's dress," Caleb declared with a little-boy grin. "It's the most interesting piece of clothing I've seen a woman in since you tried on one of them thong bikinis."

Her mouth forming an O of embarrassment, Fawn struck her husband on the arm, but he ignored it, chuckling louder than the others.

Once the production of serving drinks was complete, Steve took charge of the conversation, asking Caleb several questions about his BMW. On the other side, Fawn began a discussion of the merits of the various jewelry stores in town with Adelle.

Freed from the woman's snooping for the moment, Jo sipped her drink. It took only two sips to remind her that she hadn't had any lunch. She set it aside and picked up the menu. She was halfway down the left column when she heard Fawn address her. "Poor Jo, Caleb told me what happened to you."

Reluctantly, Jo lowered the menu.

"Are you certain you're all right?"

"I had a car breakdown, not a seizure," Jo replied, surprised at the belligerence in her tone but unwilling to apologize for it. After the day she'd had, she was in no mood for a grilling. If anyone got burned it would be Mrs. Gordon.

Fawn smiled conspiratorially at Adelle. "We girls know how those things are, don't we? A flat tire can ruin my entire afternoon." Her eyes were two slits of blue when she turned back Jo's way. "I saw you come home and rushed right over to see about you, but you didn't answer the bell."

"I must have been in the shower." Jo helped herself to some of the breadsticks in the basket on the table. The woman was like a dog with a bone. If someone or something didn't muzzle her soon, Jo would simply have to make up an excuse to leave.

"What did you do afterward?"

Jo smiled, aware of the other curious gazes as well as Fawn's avid stare. "Nothing spectacular."

"I don't mind telling you, you gave both Adelle and me a shock when she returned from dance class and there you were, gone, without so much as a note." She turned and laid a blood-red-nailed hand on Adelle's shoulder. "Your cousin was distraught."

"Not really." Adelle offered Jo an apologetic smile. "I know Jo lives alone and guessed it didn't occur to her to leave a note."

"How understanding you are of others' failures, Adelle." Fawn was fairly purring. "By the way, where *did* you go, Jo?"

Jo knew from past experience that the bold question was a favorite tool of Fawn's. She used it like a blunt instrument to knock her victims off guard. "I went fishing."

"Fishing?" Caleb set his long-necked beer bottle back on the table. "You like to fish?"

Jo turned to him, a line thrown to a sinking woman. "Love it. Caught half a dozen crappy this afternoon."

"That's piddling poor game." Caleb hunched forward and planted both elbows squarely on the damask table-cloth, in spite of his wife's frown of disapproval. "Now, you like to fish, you'll want to come with me tomorrow. John and me, neither one lets a week go by in the summer without we go fishing. And tomorrow's the beginning of the BASS Wranglers' Tournament."

"The what?" Jo asked, more than willing to spin out the conversation for as long as possible.

"The tourney leading up to the BASS Masters competition."

"We're talking about bass fishing, right?" Jo asked in bemusement.

"It's BASS with all capitals," Steve supplied. "It stands for the Bass Anglers Sportsman's Society."

Caleb nodded. "Right. By fishing the Wranglers' tourney, John and me aim to gain enough points to become pros."

"Bass pros?" Jo tried to keep a straight face.

"Right, on the Pro BASS Tour. Things work out, we'll do well enough this next week to qualify for the BASS Masters' Classic."

Jo turned to Steve. "He's pulling my leg, right?"

"Not at all. Bass fishing has become quite popular these last years."

"Yeah." Caleb winked at her. "Where you been you ain't heard about it?"

"She's become a Yankee," Fawn supplied, as if the explanation were a condemnation.

"We can take care of that." Caleb reached for his beer bottle and reared back in his chair so far that Jo thought he'd topple over backward. He didn't. As he took a long pull on his beer, Jo stared at his profile and wondered how Fawn kept temptation out of his way, for—mercy—the man was gorgeous, if not her type. "You come with me and John tomorrow," he said when he'd swallowed. "We got plenty of gear. There's a women's division. You'll just need to pay the entrance fee."

"Thanks, but I don't think I want to pay to fish. After all, it's just for fun, right?"

"If you call a twenty-five-thousand-dollar first prize fun."

"Twenty-five thousand?" Jo again sought Steve's confirmation. He nodded.

"Not only that, there's all kinds of boats and motors and other equipment to be won," Caleb continued. "Old McMurtry won himself a deep-sea fishing trip two years back. Brought back a blue marlin. Had it stuffed and mounted over his mantel. Last year I won myself a Ranger bass boat. You ever fish from a Ranger?"

"No," Jo answered.

"Made over in Flippen. Best damn bass boat in the world. You can saw one of them in half and it will still float."

"Amazing," Jo murmured, and reopened her menu. What did one do with half a floating boat?

Surprisingly, the dinner proceeded smoothly for the next hour. Fawn made a few more digs, but once Jo finished her double martini, she didn't feel the need to return incoming fire. Finally, Fawn gave up. Regrouping, no doubt, Jo decided.

The dinner conversation drifted off into talk of local politics. It seemed Fawn wanted Caleb to run for the school board. The fact that he didn't have a high school diploma himself didn't seem to dampen her aspirations. "He's an example of the kind of citizens the Cedar Bluff school system produces, even if the education process is incomplete," she stated passionately at one point. Fawn, at least, was a natural political animal.

Jo ate in silence, content to be excluded. Three years younger than the others, she had never really been a part of their social whirl. Over the years being next-door neighbors had cemented their relationship, while her extended absences had degraded what had once been strong ties to Cedar Bluff and Adelle. She had no connections but to the past. If only she could free herself of those she might be able to get on with her own life.

The jazz quintet hired for the evening came as a pleasant surprise to Jo, who had expected C and W. As they launched into a lively samba, the lights in the room were dramatically lowered.

Steve leaned toward her. "Care to dance?"

"You better ask Adelle first," Jo whispered, and lifted her eyes in Fawn's direction.

Steve followed her meaning and smiled. "Right. Second go-round?"

"Absolutely."

"You know I can't do nothing more than a good two-step," Caleb complained loudly as his wife whispered insistently in his ear. "Hell, Fawn!" He tossed down his napkin and rose to his feet. "Only don't you be calling me clumsy if I step on your foot."

"Trouble in paradise," Adelle murmured as she and Steve passed Jo's chair on the way to the dance floor.

The dining room of the country club was built with huge glass doors leading onto an even larger patio that overlooked the golf course. As the tiny wooden dance floor inside filled up with couples, the waiters slid back a few of the doors so that those who wished could dance under the stars. As the muggy summer night invaded the air-conditioned interior, Jo decided the takers would be few.

She watched her cousin and husband for a few minutes, noting how well they moved together. She suspected they came here often to dance. The Latin rhythms were infectious. Toe tapping became body swaying as she sat in her seat. She loved to dance.

You let the rhythm get the better of you last night, for sure, she mused, suddenly conscious of her body in ways she hadn't been moments before. But that wasn't true. It had been the man himself who had gotten in under her defenses. It took no effort at all to remember how it felt to be in his arms, to remember the brush of his thighs against hers, the insistence of the beat urging their hips together until there was no denying the attraction between them. She'd been surprised the current between them hadn't short-circuited the lights. It had been so natural, so easy to simply go with the mood, and keep going, to go all the way.

Only they didn't. The ride had ended abruptly, leaving her feeling as if she'd been snatched back from the brink, relieved but with a sense of the incomplete.

To break her mood she began tapping out the beat with her fingertips on the tabletop. It did no good to think about last night. It did no good to think about Gus. She'd find some way to subvert this unsatisfied hunger, this low-down ache for him.

"I just couldn't sit by and watch you any longer."

Startled, Jo looked up into an incredibly weathered face, leathered and crisscrossed with creases too numerous to count. A thick shock of hair peppered with gray and droopy mustache made him look as if he'd just stepped out of the pages of a Louis Lamour Western. He even wore a bolo tie with his conventional business suit.

He made a little circling motion with his index finger. "Care to take that powerful urge out on the floor?"

"Certainly." She put out her hand in a forthright manner. "My name's Jo Spencer."

He grinned at her, at least she supposed he did, for his mustache twitched as he clasped her hand. "John Doggett, Miss Spencer."

Once they were on the dance floor, it was apparent that he wasn't as old as she had first thought. He led her through a cha-cha and then a fox-trot without breathing hard. When the band launched into another sexy jazz number, they joined in the free-style formation with the younger crowd. Hips popping, pelvis rocking, Jo circled the floor unencumbered by a partner.

To increase suppleness and flexibility, her college soccer coach had insisted that all players sign up for dance lessons. Just to be different, she had taken up belly dancing. She had thought it would be a hoot. It turned out to be the most demanding physical activity she'd ever undertaken, and the most sensuous. She'd learned to isolate muscles she'd never before given thought to, to express herself in the most tangible sense as a woman, with her body. But best of all, she learned how to stop thinking and only feel, to lose herself in the music.

Closing her eyes, Jo sought that release again, wanting now only to feel and nothing more.

Raising her arms over her head, she let the rhythm of the music glide in slow rolling swells through her body. From fingertips through liquid shoulder rolls, the music moved down through her. Then lower, over the riding swell of her breasts, the swaying arch of her back, sliding through sensual tummy rolls, past liquid hip thrusts into her thighs, legs and feet. Little by little the rhythm absorbed her until she had given up control to its insistent pulse.

The band moved from one song into another without missing a beat. It was a glorious world in the dark behind her closed lids, the chafing annoyances of the day balmed by soothing Latin syncopation.

Gradually, she became aware that she was being watched by one particular onlooker. It was one of those inexplicable sensations where the intensity of the watcher's gaze draws the subject's attention through the sheer power of that interest. Palms pricking, she opened her eyes and turned her head slowly toward the night.

She couldn't make out any details of the man standing at the far side of the patio with his hands in his pockets and feet wide apart. Braced, but for what? A dancer wandered into her line of view, eclipsing him, and then moved on.

He didn't so much as crook a finger to signal her, but Jo started toward him.

Oh, God, she thought with a quickening deep inside. Gus had dared come here, to a place full of people who would instantly recognize his features. Brett Ashwood would have done it for the mere effect. She didn't know Gus Thornton well enough to predict his moods. Yet she sensed he was here for reasons that had nothing to do with anyone else in the room but her.

Chapter 10

The muggy night wrapped moist arms about her as Jo stepped out into the empty patio. To the south, purple clouds thrust their woolly heads above the horizon. Behind them lightning winked like a faulty bulb, changing for an instant the violet wool into pale lavender fleece. In the trees flanking the patio, cicadas cranked up and raked the night with sounds from a Halloween noisemaker. Behind her the band played Joe Sample's "Ashes to Ashes," a melody full of sultry mood and simmering passion.

He didn't make it easy for her. Yet she sensed in his very stillness a tension to match her own caution. He wasn't certain he was welcome. Neither was she.

She paused two yards away, flushed from dancing, her skin slick, heated, tingling.

He removed his hands from his pockets. "I like watching you wear out the inside of that dress."

"Is that a compliment?"

"It's the truth."

"As I recall, you dance."

"I thought you'd never ask."

They moved together, fingers intertwining as they touched. He laid his free hand on her hip just below the indentation of her waist while she draped hers on his shoulder.

She matched her steps to his as he eased into a simple cha-cha. His limp made his steps slightly irregular, but his hips caught the rhythm perfectly. Even in the darkness she couldn't miss the fluid purity of his body line. Sharp and painful longing replaced the serenity she'd just known. She was no longer lost in the music. But she was still feeling, feeling more than before through the motions of her body and his.

She'd once gone to a male strip show, as curious as any woman to know what it was like. But she'd been disappointed by the experience. The dancers were too interested in acrobatics and jackhammer pelvic thrusts to be more than blatantly sexual. Sensuality escaped them. Gus Thornton knew all about subtlety, and sensuality, and that made him a very potent experience.

His hand stirred on her hip, moving in a slow caress that molded the shape of his palm to the tight curve beneath her dress. Then his hand slipped down and back over the full swell of a buttock before circling back to her waist. Her hand tightened on his shoulder, creasing the fabric of his jacket. There was no one to see them, no one to wonder who they were or what they were doing. There was only the music and the night, and him.

She gave up trying to pretend to herself or to him that this was anything less than what she wanted. She stepped in closer, forcing him to a narrower range of movement, and felt the hard line of his thighs along hers. As she leaned in more, her breasts pressed against his chest. The feather-light abrasion of his jacket as they moved brought to life her nipples, which budded up tight behind the spandex. Her hand moved from his shoulder to his neck and delved into the hair above his collar. He bent his head to lean against her forehead as she stroked his nape. He smelled of cologne and the duskier fragrance of warm skin.

"Jo...Jo." His hand went exploring again.

Jo breathed in through parted lips as he cupped her down low and gathered her closer. They were barely moving now, merely swaying as the music swirled in and around town.

She let him tighten his grip, pressing her hips into the hard heat of his.

"I want you, Jo."

She lifted her hands, cradling his head in her fingers as she lifted her mouth to his.

At first he barely made contact, the touch of his lips the merest hint of skin on skin. His hands moved to her back, lifting and pulling her in at the same time. And then his open mouth settled on hers, damp and demanding.

She responded to every kiss, reveling in his touch, his hunger for her. She knew that she could never lie to herself again about wanting him, about needing him as much as he seemed to need her.

His tongue followed the shape of her lips, feeding the heat that was melting her. His fingers found the shape of a breast, rubbing, molding, stroking. He brushed a thumb over the hard center and sighed low in his throat.

When he at last pulled back, her gaze was unfocused, her breath shallow and fast, her mouth deliciously moist from his.

"Let's go, Jo." His voice was no more than an insistent whisper.

Her gaze wandered over his face. "I can't."

"Can't?" His embrace tightened, molding her curves against his harder length until there was no denying the extent of his arousal. "Why are you in such a hurry to be lonely one more night?"

She stared up at him through the darkness, willing him to see in her expression a desire equal to his own need. "You don't understand."

"Don't I?"

A distant flash of lightning illuminated his profile as he shook his head a little wearily. "What you do to me, Jo." He sounded a little sad as his embrace fell away, leaving her bare arms feeling unexpectedly exposed.

"It's not what you think." She whispered as he had done. "I came with people. There'd be questions."

"Just tell them you're going to meet a man. They'll get the idea."

The blunt words knocked the breath out of her. "Is that all . . . all this is about? Sex?"

"Isn't it?"

She bent her head. "I don't know. I don't think so."

"Then don't you think it's time we found out?"

"Having sex with you won't tell me anything I don't already suspect."

"You mean that you'd like it?"

"Yes." The word was wrung from her grudgingly. "That's not enough."

"It's a hell of a start."

It suddenly occurred to her to ask the question that had been circling in her mind for a variety of reasons since yesterday. "How much longer will you be here?"

"Right now that depends on you."

"I don't understand."

"Sure you do."

"So, I'm your American holiday romance."

"If you like."

"Well, I don't like."

She turned abruptly away but he caught her by the arm. Taking her shoulders in his hands, he drew her back against him. His voice sounded ragged, harsh. "Look, Jo, I'm not doing this well. I don't know what you want from me. Tell me and we'll go from there."

"I don't know," she whispered unhappily. "It's just that none of this seems quite right. If you hadn't reminded me of someone else, we'd never have met."

"I'll take my chances with old ghosts."

"I don't know if I can."

"Our Jo's a coward? I don't think so." He turned her in to his arms and bent his head, putting the full force of his considerable persuasion into his kiss.

"Jo?"

She yanked herself away from him, turning so quickly that she stepped on his foot.

"Jo, are you out there?"

"I—" Jo paused to gain control of her vocal cords. "Yes, I'm here."

Backlit by the dining room light, Caleb's body cast a long shadow ahead of him from the doorway. As he came forward Jo spun about to warn Gus, but he had disappeared. As her gaze swung wide across the patio she saw a shadow move in next to a nearby tree.

Caleb was frowning as he came up to her. "Fawn sent me to look for you when she couldn't find you on the floor or in the ladies'." He squinted as he looked left and right. "Didn't I see you dancing with someone?"

Uncertain exactly what he had seen, she decided not to be evasive. "Yes."

"Who was it?"

Caleb's questions might have been in all innocence, but he'd begun to sound like his prying wife. Some perverse desire to tease him made her answer, "He said his name's Thornton."

Caleb jerked back his head as if in surprise. "Thornton?"

Something in his tone alarmed her. "Why? Do you know a Mr. Thornton?"

"Can't say for certain," Caleb murmured, looking decidedly uncomfortable. "You better come on in. Looks to be rain coming up."

At that moment a bolt of lightning arched across half the distance of the sky. The hair on her arms lifted and her scalp felt suddenly alive with a thousand crawling things. As her knees buckled in horror, she felt Caleb shove her down to the ground.

The contact of streaming ions dazzled the night. The resulting thunder broke like the crack of heaven, rattling her teeth and filling her nostrils with the sweet smell of ozone as she lay sprawled on the paving stones. At the edge of the patio the transformer on a pole exploded, spraying, spewing into the night a roman candle of blue flame and white sparks.

"Sweet Jesus! That was a close un," Caleb muttered as he climbed to his feet. He reached down to help Jo as dozens of people poured out to see what had happened. "You all right, Jo?"

"Yes, I'm fine." But her teeth were chattering and she felt a little sick. The double martini she'd drunk seemed bent on revenge.

"Jo! Are you okay?" Adelle rushed up and put her arms around her cousin.

"I'm fine, really." But Jo hugged Adelle tightly.

"Let's get her home," she heard Steve say.

"My Lord, she might have been killed!"

Jo couldn't be certain whether Fawn sounded more appalled or delighted by the prospect of such a grisly outcome. Only then did it occur to her how senselessly reckless she'd been to mention Gus's name to Caleb.

She looked back over her shoulder, hoping to catch Caleb's eye, but his wife had grabbed his full attention, questioning loud enough for all to hear exactly what he had been doing out on the patio with Jo Spencer.

"Poor Caleb," Adelle said as she steered Jo toward the dining room. "One of these days Fawn's going to run him off for good. Now let's get you home before the sky opens."

By the time they reached home, the streetlights were blinking on and off, though the sky was still star spangled and the wind ominously still. "Looks like we're in for one hell of a storm," Steve commented as he turned into his driveway. "Hope we don't lose power tonight."

"I'd forgotten about the town's 'early-warning' system." Jo craned her head to look back at the corner light. For as long as she could remember, when a really bad storm was brewing, the atmospheric disturbance would make the municipal lights fluctuate. "I'd have thought Cedar Bluff would have modernized, put in underground electrical cables, by now."

"Too wet," Steve replied. "Same reason we don't have basements. The water table's at ground level." He stopped by the front porch and shut off the engine. "You ladies go on in. I'll wait here to take the sitter home."

But before Jo or Adelle could get out, the front door opened and Angie, the Lawsons' fifteen-year-old sitter, came racing across the porch and down the steps toward them.

"Mrs. Lawson! Thank God! I've been calling and calling but the line was busy."

Steve was out of the car in a shot. "What's the matter, Angie?"

"It's Sarah, Mr. Lawson. I don't know what's wrong. She just started throwing up a few minutes ago. Then she just kinda of fell out."

"Fainted!" Adelle's words ended on a cry of alarm as she pushed the car door open. "Where is she?"

"I put her on the den sofa. I called the country club but the line—" Adelle rushed past the girl and headed for the house at a run. Distraught, Angie turned to Jo. "The line was out. I was just about to call 911 when I heard your car."

"Go ahead and call 911!" Steve cried over his shoulder as he pursued his wife into the house.

"I don't know what she could have gotten into," Angie wailed, black mascara making sooty trails on her pale cheeks as the family watched the paramedics try to revive Sarah. "I was putting Stevie, Jr., to bed, but she couldn't have been out of my sight for more than ten minutes, tops."

Jo put an arm around the younger girl's narrow shoulders, more in sympathy with her than she knew. "This wasn't your fault, Angie." Her voice sounded as insubstantial as dust to her own ears. "Things happen. We can't be everywhere at once."

"If anything happens to Sarah, I'll just die!"

The anguish in those words tore at the lacerated moorings of Jo's composure. She had once said them herself. But she didn't die. Nor would Angie.

As she watched the men in white aspirate the small body, she bit down hard on her lip and prayed to crowd out of her mind older but similar images. Adelle had been through this once before. The homecoming to disaster. The sirens. The ambulance. *Please God,* she prayed through unshed tears, *it must end differently this time.*

"Pulse thin but steady, but I think she's stabilizing." A medic looked up as Steve entered the room. "Did you find it?"

"I found this in my daughter's room." Steve held out a vial. "Muscle relaxers."

"Oh, God! Oh, God!" Adelle murmured over and over as she turned in to her husband's arms.

The medic read the label and then held out the vial. "Mrs. Lawson? Is this prescription yours?"

Adelle nodded but her eyes were squeezed shut and her face half hidden in her husband's jacket. "I take them occasionally when I overdo it at my dance studio. An old knee injury was bothering me tonight, so I took one. But I'm usually *so* careful with them." She punctuated her words with the soft hammering of her fist against her husband's arm. "They look just like those little breath mints Sarah's so fond of."

"How much of this prescription had you used?"

"It was nearly—" Adelle's chin quivered so much that she could not control it.

"I refilled it yesterday," Steve offered, his voice quavering nearly as much as his wife's.

"Got her!" the second medic said with an edge of triumph in his voice.

"That's all we need." The first medic turned to his companion. "Let's roll."

"I'm going with you," Adelle said as they raised the gurney in order to wheel Sarah out to the waiting ambulance.

"You can ride in the ambulance, but you'll have to ride up front. We need to work in the back," the medic called over his shoulder, as they whisked the young patient out of the room.

Steve paused by Jo, who still held Angie. "I hate to ask, but we need you to stay with Steve, Jr." He gave her shoulder a painful squeeze. "I'll call as soon as we know anything."

The shock of his request delayed Jo's reaction. And then he was past her.

"We're going to drive over to the hospital, to lend support." Until Fawn spoke to her, Jo hadn't noticed that she was present. "Caleb says the storm's going to break loose any minute."

"A real toad strangler," Caleb concurred as he came up beside them. "We best get going."

Their words took time to penetrate Jo's consciousness. Everything seemed confused, out of focus. Other people moved through her range of vision, neighbors drawn by the siren and flashing lights. They offered encouragement and advice, yet the only thing Jo heard clearly was a roaring in her ears. It was happening again. *Again.*

Angie broke away from her embrace with a cry as another woman entered the room. "Mom!"

As the crowd dispersed, Jo followed them to the door. Angie's mother asked Jo a few questions, seeking assurances that her daughter was in no way to blame, and offering to do whatever the Lawsons needed.

In a short space of minutes, the night had turned blustery, the wind grabbing the front door from the man who'd opened it. People streamed out into the night with parting cries.

With every fiber of her being Jo wanted to scream! *No! Please! Please don't leave me alone with the baby!* But she couldn't force the words out. She hung in the doorway, white knuckled from clutching the frame, until a bright blue-white flash backed her inside.

Jo covered her face briefly with her hands. Her fingers felt like ice against her skin. *Get a grip!* she told herself. She was an adult. She could handle this.

Thunder reverberated through the old colonial, rushing down the stairwell to drown out the sound of her slamming the front door. It was just a coincidence. They hadn't thought of what it meant to leave her alone with a baby, with Adelle's infant son.

And then she heard Stevie's wail of fright.

She tried to move swiftly, but her legs seemed weighted with lead shot. *Be calm. He's okay,* she told herself. He was crying. That was good. Noise was good. A sign of life. But memories were gathering, circling buzzards of remembered dread.

By the time she reached the second floor landing, she was breathing hard, her ribs aching from the pressure of rising and falling beneath the stricture of tension. She paused, listening.

The crying had stopped.

Irrational fear drained the blood from her face as she took off down the hall. She struck her hip painfully on the sharp edge of a bureau parked in the hall, but she didn't pause. She flung open the nursery room door and felt frantically for the light switch.

The instant illumination momentarily blinded her, but she didn't pause again until she reached the crib. Blinking back tears of pain, she leaned across the raised railing.

He lay on his stomach, his eyes closed, his soft pink lips parted. Strands of white blond hair radiated from his scalp like a punk rocker's halo. Near one tightly closed pink fist lay his blue pacifier. *Stay calm. Think!*

She touched him fearfully. "Stevie?" He felt warm and solid through his light sleeper. And then she perceived the even fluctuation of his chest. He was sleeping. Just sleeping.

Relief made her grasp the crib rail for support. He was fine. Everything was normal.

Suddenly her hip seemed to catch fire. She put a hand to soft flesh just inside the curve of her hipbone and winced. She was going to have one huge bruise there.

Thunder rolled with seismic force, rattling the windows. Stevie stirred, his little face screwing up as his mouth pursed in pursuit of the comfort of his pacifier. The first splattering of rain raked the house, sounding like a handful of gravel hurled at the windows.

The chimes of the doorbell made Jo jump. Perhaps it was news. Or a neighbor who'd decided she needed company. She needed more than that. She needed rescue.

Her head swung back to Stevie, who had lifted his head and was looking at her with cautious sleepy blue eyes. Should she risk leaving him alone even for a few seconds?

The question was answered in her actions even before it was fully formed in her mind. She scooped him up, summer blanket and all, and headed for the stairs.

She wondered if it was because she was squeezing him too tightly or perhaps it was her pace, or the fact that she was trembling so hard, but Stevie began to cry fretfully.

"It's all right. It's all right," she repeated anxiously, bouncing him harder and harder in her arms as she descended the front stairs. For his sake, she needed to remain calm. But his balky cries turned into a wail of distress as thunder again shook the house.

She paused at the bottom of the stairs as a sound like a loose live wire crackled around them. Eerie white light filled the beveled glass on either side of the front door. The house lights dimmed, flickered on and then faded for good as thunder slammed the walls.

Stevie cringed within her arms and then let loose a keening, unearthly wail.

Hammering at the door was followed by a shout. "Hello? Anybody in there?"

She stumbled the final steps to the door and flung it open. In the gust of wind and rain stood Gus Thornton.

She threw an arm around his neck. "Thank God it's you!" She released him just as quickly and thrust the howling child into his arms. "You've got to do something. Please. Take him! Please!"

Chapter 11

Jo threw her full weight against the door, forcing it closed. A final gust swirled past the crack, whipping her face with rain and grit. And then it was dark, the tinkling chandelier the only sound inside the room.

She turned sharply, searching the darkness. Multiple flares of light snapped sharp silhouettes of Gus Thornton and the child in his arms. Stevie began to whimper again as the rolling rumble crested overhead.

Before she could move or speak, Gus's soothing voice reached her astonished ears. "Hey, big fellow. What's the matter, huh? You're not scared of a bit of boom and bluster, are you?"

How gentle he sounded, how confident and protective. It brought her unlooked-for, nearly painful relief. Rescue, from an unexpected source. Yet the feeling didn't last. The panic came galloping back, no matter how hard she tried to keep it at bay. "Something's happened, Gus. Something awful!"

"Not now, Jo." He lifted a shadowy arm toward her and when she moved into its circle, he drew her against his side. Rain droplets from his jacket dampened her cheek and bare

arm and sank into the fabric of her dress, making her shiver.
"Jo?"

He said her name softly so that she answered in kind.
"Yes?"

"Do you know where they keep candles?"

"I don't—"

"Sure you do." His voice was as calm as hers was agitated. "In the dining room, maybe. Ladies often keep candles with the linen."

He's right, Jo thought. Adelle kept their grandmother's silver candelabra with white tapers on the sideboard. Amazing that he would think of such a thing.

"I'll look."

But he didn't release her. His arm pressed her closer. "Take your time, Jo. We've got lots of time." She felt his lips on her brow. How warm they were against her cold skin.

She found her way into the dining room without incident and picked up a candelabrum. Matches would be in the kitchen. She found them in the drawer next to the gas stove.

She struck the first one as a particularly bright spear of lightning again illuminated the night. Through the kitchen window she saw for a moment the entire backyard, the trees caught in a tortured dance with the wind. Perhaps a branch had broken off, downing the power lines. The next moment her own reflection stared back at her from the surface of the glass, the match in her fingers the only light in the room. She looked like a ghost, a shadow of her real self. It wasn't all illusion. She felt haunted, trapped in a familiar nightmare.

She struck a new match with trembling fingers, dropping more than one match before she was able to light all five tapers.

"Good girl."

Startled, she turned and saw Gus who stood in the kitchen door smiling. Stevie's white blond head had dropped forward onto Gus's chest as he sucked his thumb with deep concentration. "Come on then, Jo. Let's get the tot a fresh nappie."

"Wait." He hadn't moved, but she sensed that he was puzzled by her tone and she didn't blame him. How could she put into words this sense of terror? She couldn't. She held out the candelabrum toward him. "You see to the baby. I—I think I'd better wait here, by the phone. In case Adelle calls from the hospital."

She saw him cock his head, flickering wicks exaggerating the movements of his shadow on the wall behind him. "I'm a stranger to the boy."

There was a long pause. She might have filled it with any number of reasonable statements, but time seemed suspended. Finally she heard him speak again. "What's the boy's name?"

"Steve—Stevie, Steven, Jr."

"So many names? He must be an important person around here."

"He's Adelle's son."

Lightning caught them in its sudden glare, casting the world as a poorly lit black-and-white photo. She couldn't be certain but he seemed startled, staring at the child in his arms. As darkness closed in around them again she asked in alarm, "Is something wrong?"

"No. Nothing." His voice sounded hollow, subdued.

"He should be in bed," she said firmly.

"You'll have to show me the way, Jo."

"Of course."

She moved quickly past him, not wanting to waste a moment. Stevie should be in bed, should be asleep. If Adelle called, she wanted to be able to tell her that, at least. And that someone responsible was keeping guard.

"In here," she said, when they reached the nursery and set the branching candlestick on the chest of drawers. As he brushed past her she nearly reached out to touch his arm but didn't. He needed to concentrate on Stevie. And she needed a moment to collect herself. As ashamed as she was to admit it, she was a little hung over. Perhaps a cup of coffee would help.

She backed into the doorway. "I'll be in the kitchen."

Gus straightened from depositing Stevie in the crib. "You aren't serious about leaving the boy with me?" Candlelight exaggerated his expression of surprise.

"You'll be fine." She picked up the baby monitor. "I can hear everything with this." She nodded toward the changing stand. "Everything you need is in the pockets—wipes and diapers." She took another step backward, out into the hall. "I won't be far."

Her stomach felt like a ball of ice as she descended the front stairs cloaked in darkness. She wondered if someone had turned the air-conditioner thermostat too low. She started to check, then remembered that they were without electricity. She began to shiver.

Coffee was out. The percolator was electric. However, the glow from the pilot light reminded her that the stove was gas. She could make tea to warm herself. But first she had to locate other candles. It didn't take long. After the kettle was on the flame, she reached out and turned up the volume on the baby monitor. Gus was talking softly, making silly sounds. She took a deep breath. The worst was over. No, not until she heard about Sarah.

As she measured tea into the pot, a new thought occurred to her, triggering another surge of anxiety. Turning, she snatched up the receiver of the wall phone. The insistent hum of the dial tone filled her ear. She was not cut off. This was a good sign.

A few minutes later, as she sat down with a cup of tea, she realized just how quiet the house had become. The brunt of the storm had passed, the more volatile elements rushing ahead of it to warn the next community. All that remained was a steady downpour. In the relative quiet she heard footsteps on the stairs.

Gus was annoyed as he descended the stairway in the darkness. It wasn't that he'd had to change a soiled diaper. It wasn't that Stevie had gazed up at him the entire time in injured affront and with a pouting lower lip. What bothered him was the fact that Jo had left the boy with a stranger in the first place. That didn't seem like her.

He'd responded to her tremendous relief at seeing him with good grace because he knew what was going on. He'd driven up just as the ambulance arrived. Not wanting to intrude on the emergency, he had waited until he could stop a neighbor, who told him what had happened. But his mood up to that moment hadn't been good.

He had followed her home because he was tired of this back and forth between them. For the third time she'd left him in a moment of passion so deeply felt that his body still ached from the disappointment. He could think of only one remedy for what ailed them both. It was time they took the cure. Yet before he could confront her, circumstance had again intervened.

Now, all he wanted to know was what the heck was the matter with her. As he entered the kitchen to chide her, her expression stopped him.

She sat at the table, both hands wrapped tightly about a mug. Two candlesticks were burning brightly on the table before her. Flanked by their glow, she looked like one of those pictures of big-eyed waifs that had been so popular a few years ago. Her hair was scattered tangles of burnished red curls, her complexion sallowed by the candle's glow. What affected him, though, were the large eyes staring at him, dry but full of pain and fear.

She came slowly to her feet as he approached. "What are you doing down here?" Her voice faltered. "Is . . . is something wrong with Stevie?"

"He's fine, Jo. Out like the lights." He'd had some experience with trauma, and Jo Spencer was showing definite signs of it. Less than an hour ago she'd been all heat and womanly desire in his arms. Now she looked like a girl who'd been caught playing dress up in her older sister's clothing. The urge to wrap her up in his arms was strong, but he sensed she wasn't ready for that yet.

He glanced deliberately away from her to the cup she had abandoned. "If that's hot, I'll have some."

"It's tea," she said, and turned to snag a second mug from the arrangement hanging on pegs beneath the cupboard. As she did, he swung a leg over the chair opposite hers and sat down.

She glanced back at him, alarm clearly written in her expression. "You *are* going back upstairs? Stevie mustn't be left alone."

He ignored the thready sound of panic in her voice. "Looks like you've got it covered." He pointed to the baby monitor by her cup. The sounds of Stevie's soft snores filled the kitchen. "Relax, Jo. You can count his breaths if you need to."

She brought his mug and set it down beside him. "Sugar? Milk? Lemon?"

"Ta. Sugar." He watched her moving about the kitchen, trying to be patient. "Aren't you going to ask me what I'm doing here?"

She looked back at him, surprised. "Yes."

"I came to get you."

She seemed to let this sink in, but she didn't say anything as she brought the sugar bowl, shaped like a cluster of purple grapes, and teaspoon and put them in front of him.

He lifted his head. She was so close that all he had to do was reach out an arm to pull her against him. He could imagine his face buried in the tender firmness of her stomach, then moving lower to the delta of her thighs. He resisted the urge but it cost him.

She frowned as she stared at him and he wondered, guiltily, if she could read his thoughts in his eyes. She was going through some kind of hell and all he could think about was how horny he was.

She touched his forehead just below the hairline and he held his breath. Her fingers were slick against his damp skin. "You're wet," she said, her fingers sliding into the rain-soaked hair at his temple.

"Right through to the skin." Encouraged by her touch, he reached out to stroke her side, but she recoiled as his fingers grazed her waist.

She looked apologetic immediately, but she didn't touch him again and she stepped back as she said, "Let me get something to dry you."

He shrugged angrily out of his soggy jacket as she pulled a clean terry-cloth dish towel from the linen drawer. She had reacted as if he was some molester slobbering after a six-teen-year-old virgin. But the curves filling out that dress weren't those of an immature girl. He knew the feel and shape of her breasts, had caressed the full swell of her derriere. She'd been like an erotic dream on the dance floor, all incandescent sexiness, and he wanted it back, wanted her. Period. No elaborations necessary. But the moment seemed beyond them.

He took the towel she handed him and roughly rubbed his hair. Something was wrong, something that might or might not have to do with her niece's poisoning. He ached to take her in his lap and just hold her until she felt strong enough to confide in him. But if anything, she seemed to shrink in on herself as she resumed her chair. He knew that wasn't wise. In another few minutes she'd be lost to any reality but her own. He was going to have to dig. And he didn't even know what he was looking for.

"I heard from a neighbor about your niece." He resisted the urge to pry loose the fingers clutched about her cup, but his voice betrayed the strain. "I'm sorry, Jo. I had decided to wait in my car until someone came back. Then I saw the light go on upstairs. I'm glad it was you who answered the door."

Her gaze kept straying to the monitor. "Someone should be up there," she said softly. "Someone should be keeping watch."

"Why, Jo? What could happen that we couldn't hear from here?"

The eyes she raised to his looked haunted. "Things happen."

"Accidents like this one tonight do happen sometimes. But Stevie's asleep. Once I stuck his plug in, he didn't stand a chance. Didn't even squirm before his eyes blinkered shut. Amazing inventions, pacifiers."

The ghost of a smile played over her soft mouth. "You're good with children."

"I've had to be. My secretary brought her infant to work from day one. Sooner or later we all get tapped to sit the nipper. It's a knack you develop, soothing children and frightened things." His gaze gently searched her face. "What's wrong, Jo?"

She stood up abruptly and began pacing, talking more to herself than him. "I'm not good with children. Adelle knows I'm not comfortable around babies." She pressed a hand to her cheek, half covering her mouth. "It was the emergency. She wasn't thinking clearly. But the house was full of neighbors. Any of them would gladly have stayed with Stevie."

"Did you want to go to the hospital with them?"

"No." The slight shake of her head strained aching neck muscles, which she reached up absently to massage. "I just think Adelle should have left her son in more capable hands, that's all."

"I think yours are about the most capable hands around," he said gently as he scrutinized her every gesture for signs of an emotional breakthrough. "You're family."

The sound of the phone sent both their gazes swinging toward the wall. Jo bumped her thigh against the tabletop as she shot past. Tea splashed over the rims of both their mugs, but he saw she didn't notice. She was across the room to snatch up the receiver before the second ring.

"Hello? Oh, Steve, how is she?" He saw her lids fall shut as she whispered, "Thank God!" and felt an echoing "amen" in his own thoughts.

In the candlelight he watched the smoothing out of her brow as she listened intently to the voice on the other end of the line. He wished he could have brought her that relief but was grateful to the man on the line who had. "Yes, he's fine. Asleep."

Suddenly her eyes were wide open again, staring in new panic as worry lines reformed. He half rose from his chair, wishing he could hear what had so frightened her. "The whole night?" she whispered. "But what about Stevie? I don't—"

He could hear that she was being overruled by a stronger tone but couldn't make out the words. He came to his feet. Couldn't Steve hear the panic in her voice, sense the anxiety that had her gripping the phone in two white-knuckled hands?

"Adelle really should..." she began again, only to be cut off a second time. "I know she needs you. It's just that—" He moved up close behind her, reached out to touch her but didn't.

"Right. All right." The resignation of defeat in her words struck him as odd. This wasn't the woman he knew.

She slammed the receiver back into place with a curse and leaned her head against the hand she left resting there.

"There was some good news?"

She turned in his direction, startled by the sound of his voice so close by. "Yes—Sarah's going to be okay." She straightened, visibly trying to pull herself back together. "The doctor said it was a good thing she vomited immediately. It kept most of the medication from reaching her bloodstream. But she's being kept overnight. Steve and Adelle are going to remain with her."

"It's what most parents would do."

"I suppose so." She stuck a thumbnail between her teeth, her gaze turning inward. He had forgotten how little she was. The woman he'd known these past days radiated such energy and confidence that she'd seemed at times six feet tall. But now, out of her heels, she barely reached his shoulder. As she moved toward her chair, he felt as if a whole world of suffering burdened her shoulders. He wanted to shoulder it all, even her, if she'd let him.

"There's something else bothering you, isn't there, Jo?"

She was shaking her head even before he finished, either at his words or some pain he could not guess at. "I don't want to talk about it." Her voice sounded thin, hoarse, immeasurably tired.

"You can talk to me, Jo." He came up beside her and knelt on a knee by her chair. Even more quietly, more gently, he added. "You can tell me anything."

She held up a hand, palm facing him. "I can't talk about it," she said adamantly. "Not to you, not to anyone."

"No one? Not even Brett Ashwood?"

He knew that was a low blow, a gamble he really didn't want to take, but she was pushing him further and further away, and he needed something, anything to shock her back.

The reaction he got shocked him.

Jo rocked forward suddenly, hugging her arms to her body. "It was my fault. My fault!"

The darkness and whispering quietness in the wake of the storm gave the house the air of a confessional.

After a moment she lifted her head toward him, her expression painfully open, unguarded against some truth only she knew. "I'm responsible for the death of Adelle's first son."

Chapter 12

"Hush. Hush, Jo. Baby, you're breaking my heart."

The sobs escaping her shook both their bodies as he held her tightly while he knelt with her on the floor. But she wouldn't be comforted. She was sobbing, openly and the weight of her emotion caused her to choke out her cries. Tears ran freely down her cheeks. Her method of crying wasn't beautiful, but neither was her pain. He doubted she would even have let him touch her if her own distress hadn't been so great that she couldn't hold herself upright. She had slid from her chair into his arms under the weight of her grief.

He was appalled and ashamed of what he'd done, pushing her over the brink. He doubted he would ever completely erase from his mind the stricken look on her face as she said those words.

I'm responsible for the death of Adelle's first son.

So that was it. But he knew this couldn't possibly be right. Yet he couldn't doubt the sincerity of the anguish pouring from her.

Bracing her weight with his left arm just beneath her breasts, he pulled her against him, spreading his legs so that she knelt between his thighs. "Jo. Love, listen." He said the

words slowly, softly, stroking her curls with his right hand.
"Come on, baby. You've got to stop. You'll make yourself
sick."

"I wish I were dead."

The words came out of her haltingly, strangled by tears.
The effort to force them out made her take several deep
breaths and her crying jag diminished.

"You're just in pain, Jo. Old pain that's been festering
deep. It'll be better now that you've released it. You'll see."

How trite the wisdom sounded, even to his own ears. She
seemed to agree. She pushed angrily away from him, moving sideways on her knees. "You don't know. You don't
know what happened."

"I know you didn't harm anyone, Jo."

She turned a tear-streaked face to him, too vulnerable to
even hide it. "It's my fault. No one would even listen to me.
I tried to tell them. But they wouldn't hear me. They
thought it too awful to believe."

He didn't carry a handkerchief, so he reached up to snag
a napkin from the table. When he tried to blot her face, she
grabbed it from him and began her own salvage detail. She
mopped around each eye, still hiccuping in the aftermath of
her stormy weeping. Nature could learn a thing or two about
turbulent storms from Jo Spencer, he thought in grudging
admiration.

Finally she sat on the floor, her legs bent under her, just
staring into space. The seconds ticked past, piled up into a
minute and moved on. The eerie calm in the wake of the
torrent worried him. He laid a hand on her shoulder. "Jo?
Why do you blame yourself?"

He thought she wasn't going to answer. The shoulder under his hand trembled with her breath. But her profile, illuminated by candlelight, gave no clue to her thoughts or
feelings.

When she spoke it was as if she were throwing her voice,
ventriloquist-style. It seemed to come from a place beyond
her, separate and apart.

"Uncle Robert and Aunt Della had taken Adelle on an
overnight trip to Memphis. Adelle had been so sick during
her pregnancy that they wanted to reward her. A national

dance company from New York was touring with a production of *Swan Lake*. Zachary had just passed his six-week checkup. The doctor said he was doing fine, if growing a little slowly. But he was a little colicky."

She paused to brush an imaginary hair from her eyes. "All babies are a little colicky, Aunt Della said. And Adelle deserved a night out."

"So they left you, a sixteen-year-old, with a sick baby?"

She shook her head slowly. "He wasn't sick. He always did best with me. I loved him, you see." She turned her head quickly toward him. "Adelle loved him, too, only she'd been so sick carrying him. And Brett, well, you just about couldn't talk to Brett after his son was born, he was so proud. But he was busy working and going to school, and Adelle didn't like it when he went out drinking. So, I just sort of naturally spent a lot of time with Zachary. It was my responsibility to look after him after school. Adelle had to get up with him during the night, and Aunt Della was teaching school. So, to help out, Zachary became my responsibility from 4:00 p.m. until midnight."

"What happened after they left that night?"

"Nothing. I gave Zachary his bath like always, fed him his last bottle and rocked him to sleep." He saw her chin trembling uncontrollably, but she went on. "I liked to pretend he was mine. Because I wished he was. That night he was to be mine all night. Then Brett came back."

"And?"

"And I—" Jo shook her head slowly. "He was drunk. And angry. Talking crazy. I wanted to comfort him."

"And being the person you are, you did."

She nodded. "We talked, first in the kitchen and then—" her gaze darted away from his "—in bed."

"He took advantage of your kind heart."

"No! It wasn't kindness." Her voice had hardened, sharpened in contrast to a moment before. "I wasn't being kind. I was in love with him."

This time Gus didn't say anything.

"I've shocked you. Sixteen-year-old Jo Spencer was in love with her cousin's husband. It sounds pathetic now, like a subplot in a soap."

"Love is never pathetic."

"This one was. How stupid I must have seemed to him. I hung on every word, believed every one. I thought he meant them."

"Meant what?"

She lifted her head, her chin thrust out, her eyes full of challenge. "He said he loved me that night."

She saw him wince and thought she understood. "Don't feel sorry for me. It was what I wanted to hear, would have given my right arm to hear. Because, then at least, I thought he meant it."

"Perhaps he did."

"Don't defend him!" Jo leapt up from the floor. "He was drunk. Men will say anything when they're drunk."

"And some reveal the sordid secrets of their hearts."

She turned and looked at him. "Is that what you think it was? A sordid secret? This isn't true confessions. We didn't make love. But I wish we had."

She turned abruptly away from him. "He'd drunk too much, needed to lie down. I curled up beside him on his bed to listen. He always said I was the good listener. Even when he and Adelle were dating, he'd always come to me to talk about things, especially after a fight with his father.

"He'd been to see his daddy that evening. Mr. Ashwood had promised to pay Brett's tuition back to Harvard after the child was born. But he'd changed his mind, said Brett wasn't living up to his part of the bargain to make a go of his marriage. But what did his father expect? Adelle had been miserably sick during most of the pregnancy. Even I knew they weren't sleeping together. Brett had started going out with his friends, drinking and raising hell. Blowing off steam was all."

"Young men have pretty hard heads," Gus said quietly.

"Adelle didn't help," Jo said. "She was always crying and complaining about her figure and how she couldn't go out because she was getting too fat. If I'd been pregnant with his child, I'd have bought maternity clothes the day the doctor gave me the news. I'd have gone everywhere, wanted everybody to see my belly and know that it was Brett's child I was carrying."

He had no answer for that, only wondered if she realized how much of herself she was revealing to him.

"He talked a lot that night, about all the things he wanted to do. How he'd never get to do them tied down with a wife who didn't love him. He said he'd have been better off married to me, that at least I knew how to love a child and stand by a friend."

"He said that?"

Jo nodded. "And then he kissed me, really kissed me. And there was nothing ugly in it, only glory. I couldn't believe it. We just kind of rolled around on the bed for a while. I wanted him to love me—really love me. But he wouldn't. He said he wouldn't hurt me that way. He'd made one big mistake and he wasn't going to make another."

"Jo."

She scanned his face, reading his discomfort at her revelation. "You think I should be ashamed to say that?" She shrugged. "Maybe I should. I was offering myself to a married man. But it's how I felt at the time. Only he said he had some scruples."

"You loved him that much?"

She sighed, not really needing to answer.

"But now you hate him. What changed your mind?"

"It was changed for me. Brett changed it."

"Don't you think he meant everything he said to you that night, Jo?"

She hunched her shoulders against his words. He watched as tears appeared and slid silently down her cheeks. "He said he loved me, that someway, someday, he'd find a way to take what I was offering him, but in the meantime he couldn't. He tucked me under the sheet beside him and we slept, me under and him on top of the covers."

"What you did wasn't so great a crime, Jo," he said as she fell silent.

She shook her head. "There's more. Brett was so drunk I don't think an exploding bomb could have awakened him once he fell asleep. But I knew what I was doing. Even after I got up during the night to check on Zachary I got back into bed with him. I just wanted to lie there next to him and pretend that he was mine.

"When I woke up the next morning, Brett was gone. I guess he'd come to his senses and realized what could happen if we were caught. Even so, I thought I'd die of happiness and guilt. Lord, the guilt was excruciating. But the happiness was even sharper. And then I remembered Zachary. It was past eight o'clock and he wasn't fussing for his bottle."

Jo shut her eyes tight, her fingers curling into fists by her sides. "He looked so small in the crib, even smaller than the day before. And quiet. I knew something..." She shuddered. "Blue, he was blue gray, and cold. My fault."

Gus grabbed her and shook her. "Don't think about it!" He hauled her against his chest and crushed her to him. "It happened. Dammit all, Jo! It just happened!"

She just stared at him, her eyes wide pools of liquid light. He released his grip. "Who else knows what you've told me?"

"About what happened that night?" She rubbed her hand up and down over the place where he'd gripped her left wrist. "No one."

"You didn't tell anybody how you felt? Not even Adelle?"

"Adelle collapsed when she heard Zachary was dead. Aunt Della and Uncle Robert had to rush her to the hospital. After that they were too busy looking after things to think much about me."

"They never blamed you, never said anything against you?"

"No, I don't think it really occurred to them to ask what had gone on. They just looked so sad, didn't say much."

"And Brett?"

Her expression flattened out, becoming remote. "I only saw him once after that morning. At the funeral. He was sitting by Adelle looking like hell couldn't hold him. He wouldn't even look me in the face. But I know what he was thinking, that I should have been upstairs watching Zachary instead of trying to seduce him. He bolted the next day."

"No wonder you hate him."

But she didn't seem to be listening to him anymore. "Brett blamed me."

"That's not true." He stood up and crossed over to her. "You must have read about crib death. It's nobody's fault. The babies stop breathing. Even twelve years later there's still not much known about why it happens, Jo. You can't be blamed."

She shook her head. "But if I'd been there—"

"Been where?" he burst out. "Staring down into the crib all night? Nobody expected that of you. You'd even checked on the child, which is more than most mothers do. It could as easily have occurred the next night, with Adelle and her parents all under the roof."

"Then it wouldn't have been my fault."

That pitiful statement wrung his heart. "Oh, Jo." He reached for her, but she turned away from him toward the sink. He was not about to be deterred.

He came up behind her, curled an arm about her waist and buried his face in her hair. "It never was your fault. No one blamed you, not then and not now. Somebody should have said that."

He felt a shuddering breath escape behind the hand he pressed flat against her abdomen. More than anything, he wanted to take her pain away. He pushed the heel of his palm into the soft flesh, rubbing slowly up and down. "Let the pain go, Jo."

She shook her head, whisking his face with her curls. "I've tried."

"Try harder." He lifted the curls at her nape and nuzzled the warm skin there. Her skin tasted salty and sweet at the same time. He thought of her dancing alone at the country club, before she knew he was there, and stepped in closer until the curve of her derriere was pressed fully against his trouser front.

She sighed and gripped the sink, her nails raking the porcelain surface. "Love me, Gus."

He lifted his head. "Jo?"

She turned within his embrace, her breasts brushing first his arm and then his chest. "Have you changed your mind?"

Her tone was the old Jo's—light, teasing, edged with a challenge. Yet her expression was stark, her eyes shadowed by doubt. Even her often smirking mouth was different—softer, more vulnerable, lips parted in anticipation or a sigh of regret ... or a kiss.

"Jo, there's something I ought to tell—"

She covered his mouth with the length of her hand. "Don't tell me I'm a wonderful girl." This time her chin trembled.

"It's about me," he said behind the bar of her fingers.

"Are you married?"

He gave his head a tight shake.

"Then I don't want excuses." She moved her hand. Rising on tiptoe, she pressed her lips lightly against his. "I don't want promises. Reassurances." She punctuated each phrase with a lingering, velvet-lipped kiss. "Or any verbal foreplay. Just take away the pain."

He caught her chin with the hook of his thumb and held her final kiss until her lips parted under his and the warmth of her breath flooded his mouth. He brought her against him, taking her in a deep steady kiss that at its center held the heated stroke of his tongue.

He tasted all of her, the contours of her lips, the deep plush outer fullness and then the damp sensitive inside. He was thorough and gentle. They had time. They had the rest of the night. He wanted to give her pleasure, more than enough to heal the pain she'd just revealed. He shared it, understood it better than she knew. And like her, he wanted respite from it.

His kisses moved to her cheek, to her cheekbone, and then over the damp fringe of her lashes. He licked under the edges, wanting to erase with his tongue the salt and sorrow of her tears. Her hands moved to his waist as she adjusted her body to fit more closely to his. He found her ear with his lips, nuzzled the whorl with his nose and then pressed the tip of his tongue into the center. She leaned into him with a sigh, her hands flexing on his waist. He moved her back until her hips were buttressed by the sink and then he pressed the full length of his body against hers. Luxuriating in the feel of her breasts, the hard nipples prodding him through the dampness of his shirt, he rubbed his body in a slow tantalizing full-length body massage over hers.

"You feel so good," he said into her ear, then brought his mouth back to capture hers before he could say more.

She'd asked him not to talk. It was usually the other way around, in his experience. But he wanted her to have what she wanted. He would have liked to tell her how good she tasted, how delightedly surprised he was each time by their first kiss. How watching her on the dance floor had given him the longest, hardest erection of his life. But, he supposed, he didn't need to say that. Her hands were moving shyly over his stomach. He eased off her and the fluttery sensation of her touch moved to his belt buckle and then his zipper.

Strange, he'd never felt so strong an urge to talk, to tell her how good it felt, how glad he was that she wasn't afraid of him. But he felt muzzled. And the struggle to control himself in one way was increasing the pressure for release in another area.

He reached down for the hem of her dress and began inching it up. The silky skin of her thighs grazed the back of his fingers as the form-fitting material peeled away. His temperature soared three degrees. He hadn't thought it possible that she could be wearing anything other than panty hose under a dress like this. When he found her legs bare, his imagination went wild. Moments later he encountered the lower edge of panties. There was something comforting about the discovery, confirming his original opinion that Jo Spencer was a lady.

Her fingers were unbuttoning his shirt, peeling it back away from his shoulders and then pushing it down the ends of his hands. As she delved tongue-first into his chest hair, he smiled. She wasn't too much of a lady, thank the gods. He let her play, amazed by the absorption with which she went about discovering the textures and shape of his body. Her eyes had taken on a smoky hue in the meager candlelight that reflected deep copper and wine plum shades from her curls. Her deep concentration was part of her need to block out the world that had, tonight, come in too painfully close. It didn't matter. As she rimmed first one flat male nipple and then the other, he stopped thinking about her needs for the moment, zeroing in on his own urgent cravings.

Removing her dress was as easy as stripping off a leather glove. And then she was standing before him in her brief panties and lace-cupped bra. He touched her just above one lacy edge, slipping the tips of his fingers inside. Her eyes were as big as saucers as she watched him, his face, not his hand. He wondered what she was thinking. Or if she was only feeling.

He was feeling—the textures of unbelievably soft skin, and warm fullness and finally the taut bud of a nipple. He flicked his thumb lightly over it and saw her lips part in response. She had braced her hands behind her on the edge of the counter, but now her hands came up behind his neck to draw him closer. He unhooked her bra, accepting the naked fullness in his hands.

"Jo," he said against her mouth. "We need privacy."

She led him upstairs without any light to guide them. They didn't need it. He could have found her by his own personal radar, so in tune was he to her every move. He reached out to stroke her hip as she climbed the steps ahead of him. The feel of her bottom moving beneath the sheer layer of her panties drew vivid pictures in his mind. When she turned into the room at the top of the stairs, he waited in the hall. It was Stevie's room and he knew she had gone to check on him. Half a minute later she returned and took his hand. "This way."

He brought her hand up to his lips. "Are you certain, Jo?"

Instead of answering, she leaned forward and kissed him. Afterward, he followed her eagerly.

"It's only a twin bed," she said, leading him across the carpet to their unseen destination.

"One body width is all we need," he assured her and tugged on her arm to stop her progress.

As she turned to him, he enfolded her in a long, heart-shattering kiss that left them clinging to one another, their rapid breathing the only sound in the house.

He followed her down onto the mattress, his trousers and her panties left by the side of the bed. Her breasts seemed to grow even firmer and fuller under the attention of his hands and mouth. Her hands held him, caressed him, stroked him until he moaned. He reached low, finding more curls and inviting wetness. Her soft moans stoked his. This time he didn't have to wrestle with his conscience. He reached over the side of the bed and fished a foil-wrapped package from his trouser pocket. Then he was there, hard and hot, and pressing into her womanly body.

"Jo. Jo," he whispered, ready to burst with praise for the pleasure she was giving him. But she was meeting him thrust for thrust, reaching down to hold him close. Then she stopped. Her back arched, her head moving from side to side on the pillow as little inarticulate sounds came from her throat.

He covered her lips with his, exulting in her cries of pleasure as her body gently contracted around his erection. He had waited what seemed like a lifetime to experience this—her moisture, her heat, her need fulfilled by his thrusting body.

When she lay softly panting beneath him, he nuzzled her neck, then bent lower to take a nipple in his mouth. He reached between their bodies, wanting to pleasure her further. As he caressed her, her fingers curled into his shoulders, her nails dimpling the skin of his back. When she came a second time he knew the moment—the taste and textures and sound of her—was forever imprinted on his soul.

He was helpless to control the climax that shook him, drained him.

Afterward, his pleasure was so immense, so complete, that he couldn't think of anything to say. Her tears came quickly, a torrent so heartfelt that he could only hold her as she clung to him and wait it out.

When she was quiet again, he turned her toward him, wrapping a leg over hers and then kissing her deeply. There was something he should have told her, something she should have heard. But now it was too late.

"Forgive me, Jo, for hurting you."

She didn't answer, only snuggled closer to him. Deep in thought, he wondered if he could live the rest of his life without her. No, he couldn't. Even now his body was stirring with a renewed need of her.

He took them more slowly this time, stopping to learn what made her sigh or gasp or just purr. He found ways of making her sing soft choruses of ecstasy, then echoed them in a deeper timbre as she shyly explored his body with her hands and mouth. When, deep into the silence of the night, they lay spent and heavy with satisfaction in one another's arms, she curled her hand against his cheek and kissed him so softly that it brought tears to his eyes.

Jo awoke to darkness, uncertain where she was. And then she remembered. She reached out for him but found only a cool impression where he had been tucked tightly against her.

She sat up and discovered the glow of a light beneath her closed bedroom door. The electricity was on. Had someone come home? Guilt pricked her and she reached for her bedside lamp. Light filtered through the pink lace shade revealed a trail of discarded clothing, male and female. She didn't pause to scoop up the evidence. She snatched her robe from the upholstered bench at the foot of the bed and stuck her arms through the sleeves. If Adelle and Steve were home, she was going to have to do a lot of fast talking. Then she remembered that she was supposed to be caring for Stevie.

Heart knocking in her chest, she flung open her door, running down the hall even before her robe was completely closed.

If anything had happened, anything at all—

Dry mouthed, she swung into the nursery doorway, every sense alert for disaster, and paused.

Gus sat in the rocking chair with Stevie curled protectively in the crook of his right arm. He wore only trousers, and the child's fair head looked angelic nestled in the dark mat of his chest hair. A Ninja Turtle blanket trailed from Stevie's torso across his legs, which were splayed out before him on the braided rug. On the floor beside one bare foot stood a half-finished bottle of milk. They were both asleep with heads thrown back, mouths ajar. Two ages of man in perfect harmony.

Tears stung her eyes. He must have heard the child, had not wanted to disturb her. The rush of strong emotion filled her with sudden warmth. She felt protected. It was a new, odd, but desperately sought feeling.

As she slipped back into the dark hallway, she couldn't stop her mouth from forming a big silly grin. She'd known him only two days. She had tossed every bit of common sense and natural female caution to the winds for a stranger. Despite that, there was no avoiding the feeling. Something else tugged at her heart. She'd felt it only once before in her life.

She was almost asleep again when she heard him whisper, "Jo?" She turned toward the doorway. He was slipping his trousers past his hips. "Jo, Jo, I need you." He came and knelt on the bed. "Can I— You're not too tired?"

Smiling, she reached up and touched his face. "We can sleep tomorrow."

Chapter 13

Gus left the Spencer residence just before dawn. Jo had wakened him with a cup of coffee and a kiss. She looked especially pretty in her short terry robe, her hair still damp from her shower, clinging in damp tendrils to her cheeks and brow. Her eyes had regained their gentle candor. But more than that she seemed refreshed, serene in the aftermath of the internal storm that had shaken them both.

He didn't touch her again; he didn't dare. He had left quickly, though she had offered to make him breakfast. She hadn't asked when or if she'd see him again. In fact, she'd said very little. She just looked radiant with some new knowledge of herself. It wasn't sexual but something deeper, quiet, going to the core of her self-awareness. She had asked him to take away the pain. Could it be he had succeeded? That thought had haunted him as he had taken that final glimpse of her with him down the steps and out into the street.

It remained with him now as he walked up the block and turned right. The streets were still wet from the rain, shimmering like oil slicks in the gunmetal gray of first light. The street lamps, gleaming yellow eyes beneath their old-fashioned hooded shades, maintained their nightly vigil.

Hands in pockets, he did not hurry his pace. It was too early for joggers and too late for prowlers. But the blocks melted away under his stride. The raucous twitter of birds filled the air. The smell of honeysuckle greeted his nostrils as he turned a corner.

The block was a broad avenue bisected by a wide green median where shade trees grew and a brick fountain, now inoperative, sat silent in the morning air. A mockingbird, the early riser of the South, perched on the edge and sang his homage to the approaching day.

He passed the brick Federal house on the corner, walked past the Victorian with the wrought-iron fence and copper gable. The next two houses never came fully into his range of view. He was approaching an imposing white colonial on the opposite side of the avenue. It sat back from the street, a plantation colonial with long columns rising two stories to support the full balcony that ran the length of the second floor.

He stood looking at it a long time. It was familiar to him. It was the seldom-occupied residence of a former mayor of Cedar Bluff. It was once his home.

Memories of that final morning rose phoenixlike from the remains of a life he had buried long ago and left untouched until three days ago.

"You aren't fit to be my son!" The veins standing out on his father's brow looked like roadways to hell. "After all I've done— And your mother! You're killing your mother. How do you expect her to hold up her head in public after this?"

"I suspect she'll manage."

The crack of his father's palm across his face came as no surprise. He'd felt it often enough before. But never again.

"Don't ever touch me again," he said past lips already thickening from the impact of being driven against his teeth.

Something in his face made his father blanch. "You wouldn't dare."

Brett backed up a step as his father glared at him, but his hands were knotted into damaging fists as he raised them from his sides. He wasn't as heavy or broad as the man before him, but he was taller and younger, and just as angry. And he had new armor, the grief and guilt of the loss of his own son. Nothing his father could say could hurt him now. His father was right. He was a loser, a failure. Yet there was an odd kind of strength in his self-loathing. He felt immune from further injury, wrapped in a soul-searing misery that protected him this time from his father's abuse. It was over. He was leaving. The bag he'd packed stood in the front hall a few feet away, crammed with the last things he'd ever accept from this man. "Suppose you just get out of my way."

"That's what you'd like, isn't it? Then when you fall on your ass you can tell the world your father threw you out. Well, it won't wash, mister. I've given you everything. All your life you've only had to ask and it was yours. Cars. Money. Bailed you out of trouble more times than I care to think about. How do you think you got to Harvard?"

He smirked, feeling on safe ground at last. "I earned it."

"You earned squat! You don't think you got in on your good looks and personality?" His father bared his teeth as though he was enjoying the battle. "Valedictorian of Cedar Bluff meant nothing to that review board. Hell! You have no idea the strings I pulled to get you in." He jabbed a finger toward Brett's chest. "*My* political clout. *My* IOUs. *My* money got you in."

Brett stared at him with sullen eyes. "Looks like you didn't get your money's worth." But it hurt, found the chink in what he thought was an impenetrable guard. The words cut into his gut like slashes of a razor blade. He hadn't known of his father's machinations. He wished he still didn't.

"I made you. I bullied and cajoled and pushed and—"

"And hit," Brett added, wiping a trickle of blood from the corner of his mouth. "I learned my fighting skills from you, Dad."

His father threw up his hands. "That's right. It's fashionable these days to blame the sins of the son on the father. But I won't be made the goat. You never learned to drink and whore from me."

"Adelle isn't a whore."

"Then why did you treat her like one?"

His father swung away from him and began to massage his brow, an indication that his migraine was flaring up under the blast of his temper. "I didn't mean that about Adelle. She's a good girl from a good family."

He turned back. "That's why you can't just walk out on her. After all that's happened, now that little Zach's…" He paused to swallow a threatening emotion, then, like tracking radar, he was back on course. "You've got to begin taking responsibility. Be a man."

Brett maintained a stony-faced silence. *"Be a man."* Those three words had defined the parameters of his existence since he'd been born. He'd never stood a chance. No son of his— He backtracked hurriedly from that abyss of grief. He no longer had a son, but he wasn't about to give his father the satisfaction of any show of misery.

His father faced him fully again, his expression a blend of exasperation and fury. "Well? Say something, dammit!"

"Sorry I've disappointed you." He added without blinking, "Goodbye."

He was shocked when his father backed away from him, making a clear path to his bag and the front door. Stiff legged from tension and an indefinable sense of defeat, he went and picked up his luggage. Nineteen years packed into a space not much bigger than the pillow on which he laid his head, it was a mocking reminder of just how little of his past he was taking away with him.

"You won't get far." His father followed him to the door, talking low but fast. "You haven't got what it takes to make it on your own. You'll be nowhere, nothing without me!"

He lowered his head and kept moving, refusing to speak the words that came to his defense. *I'm nothing because of you.*

"What about Adelle?"

He turned back at the door. "Tell her to divorce me. Her father's a lawyer. It should be easy."

"You little bastard."

"Right, Dad."

He thought his father would blow an artery. Instead he whispered as Brett opened the door, "You're no son of mine."

Gus had made his way around the side of the house, making certain no cars were parked on the drive or in the garage, before approaching the front door.

It's funny, he thought, how some things stay with a person when other, maybe more hurtful, things get lost in the clutter of a bruised mind. No son of his. It was the final statement his father had made and he'd taken it to heart.

Changing his name had been unbelievably easy. One sleight of hand led to another. Within a month, he was aboard a freighter bound for South America, carrying a passport with the name Gus Thornton. He had chosen Gus from his mother's grandfather, Andrew Augustus Adams, the only man he'd ever admired. Thornton was culled from the front page of the local paper the day he left town. A local businessman named Chester Thornton was suing the mayor and city council for alleged dishonest practices in dealing with bids for a city work project. Someone was taking on his father. He had hoped the guy would win, but he'd never found out.

He sat down on the top step of the veranda and braced his back against one white column. The words of a country-and-Western song drifted through his mind.

"All the things you do two by two,
you pay for one by one."

He thought he had paid, in full, until last night.

In spite of his bravado with his father, he had gone by the Spencer house, but not to see Adelle. He wished they could have grieved together over the loss of their son, but they couldn't even do that. There was nothing between them, never really had been. There was only one person who understood his pain. That was Jo. He'd seen her only once, at the funeral, but he couldn't talk to her there.

The stark simplicity of her declaration of love had
shocked him. His fondness for her had been steadily building over the months. She was good with the baby, better
than Adelle. She never turned him away when he needed to
talk. But until the night of Zachary's death, he hadn't allowed himself to think the impossible, that he and Jo be-
longed together. Now even that hope seemed beyond his
grasp. He hadn't even spoken to her since the morning
they'd discovered Zachary.

He'd never felt more stone-cold sober than he had that
morning. Shock neutralized his hangover. He couldn't believe it, couldn't fathom that his son—Jesus! How had he
come to have a son?—was dead. He had not wanted the
child before it was born. But once his Zachary was a fact,
he'd not been able to quite believe how proud he was of the
accomplishment. Something good out of something rotten.
Perhaps the months of pain and frustration were going to be
worth it. But now his son of six weeks was gone, snatched
away before he would fully appreciate his good fortune.

He remembered Jo's standing with her back to the wall,
her ginger freckles standing in stark relief to the ghostly
coloring of her skin, her gaze fixed upon the unmoving body
in the crib. She looked as if she was about to simply fade out
of sight. And then she started to cry.

He'd never felt more helpless, and his father had given
him plenty of occasions to know what gut-wrenching help-
lessness felt like. He had covered the small body with a receiving blanket, tears he'd never show to anyone else sliding
in hot streaks down his face. Somehow he had found the
presence of mind to call for help.

An ambulance and police car had come, followed almost
immediately by Adelle and her parents. Somewhere in the
confusion, Jo had slipped away.

He skirted the front of the house, not wanting to deal with
Adelle's parents, or Adelle herself. What they had to say to
one another had been said months before Zach was born.
They had agreed to marry to save their folks, specifically
their mothers, embarrassment. And to legitimize the baby.

Unfortunately, the girl he had taken out to the levee in
August had disappeared by the time they exchanged wed-

ding vows in November. Adelle not only didn't want to make love with him anymore, she positively loathed the idea. He had tried to make light of their situation; at least she didn't have to worry about getting pregnant. She had lost even her sense of humor. She blamed him for everything from her queasy stomach to her lost waistline to her hangnails. If he so much as kissed her openmouthed, she shrank away. To keep down the number of fights, the Spencers gave him his own room. He was young, he was randy and he was accustomed to having his physical needs met. Drinking seemed a lesser evil than picking up women. And so he drank. A lot. And often.

He knew Jo's window. Picking up a pebble, he flung it at the glass. Jo was his pal, his confidante. He couldn't get out of his mind the picture of her lying on his bed so warm and willing. And she had said she was in love with him, wanted him to make love to her.

Poor kid, if only she knew how much he had wanted to do just that. It wasn't just the sex, which he'd been denied for months. After living for seven months under the same roof with Jo, he had come to the conclusion that he had unconsciously substituted Adelle for Jo, who had been too young for his kind of fun the summer he and Adelle had been making it out on the levee. Yet Jo was a funny sort of girl, full of secrets and shyness... until that night.

She had tasted so sweet. The kisses he stole from her that night should have damned him to hell, but all he could think about was what he had missed, what, maybe, he could have had in substitution for sex with Adelle. But he had been looking to get lucky, and Adelle was beautiful and adventurous. Only they weren't supposed to get caught. Nobody was supposed to get hurt.

He tossed a few more pebbles at the glass, each striking with increasing force. There were things he wanted to say to her, things he had no right to say, yet things he thought she ought to hear. He would come back for her, when he'd established himself. If she'd wait, he'd come back for her.

The longer he stood under that window, the less certain he was what she wanted to hear. Maybe she was ashamed of what she had done. Maybe, since he'd screwed up every-

thing else in his life so far, she wouldn't believe or trust him.
Maybe he should wait until he'd proved himself before he
told her what he wanted from her. Yes, that was what he
would do. Then no matter what anyone thought or said,
he'd have earned the right to be with her.

He left Cedar Bluff feeling lighter in spirit than he had
any right to be. He owed that renewal of heart to Jo. He'd
come back for her. But first he'd make her proud. She knew
how to love with her whole heart and will and body. He
wanted to be able to offer equally from his own self-worth.
He'd start over, reinvent himself for her. He had time. She
was only a junior in high school. And he'd write. Soon.

Gus plucked a cornet of jasmine from the vine twining
over the railing of the house, pulled the stamen from it and
sucked the bead of honey from its tip. Jo's kisses the night
before had been sweeter. As was her body. After twelve
years he now knew he had been right about her, and her
ability to love. Just as he now knew his feelings for her
hadn't died.

He never did write her. There were dozens of excuses he
could have invented but the reason boiled down to one very
simple one—he lost his nerve.

Life on the road was harder than anything he could have
imagined. His father's prediction that he would fail
hounded him constantly. Hopping that New Orleans
freighter at the end of a weary, hungry, lonely month had
been an act of desperation.

After that his life became long stretches of idle time at sea
broken by short stays in a series of foreign ports. Weeks became months and then years. Three years, to be exact. He
might have stayed with the merchant marines for years if he
hadn't gotten sick while in port at Sydney and been left behind. Once again, life had thrown him a curve. This one he
caught.

He'd made a friend in hospital, Shep Hollins, a Queensland lad who talked nonstop about his home. It was in
mimicking Shep's accent for the amusement of the staff that
he began to adopt it as his own. He'd already taken on a new
name. Why not a new accent to go with it? Recently re-

leased from the navy, Shep invited him to go north with him. That began a new era in his life. Together they worked any job to be had, from clearing jungle for roadways to running rickshaws on the beach at Cairns. Shep was game for anything, even dreamed up a hustle for the locals: was his pal or was he not a native Aussie. Nine times out of ten he won the bet, perfecting his accent as he went.

He ended up learning to fly a plane on a dare. That's when life came together for him. For weeks he traded flying lessons for free labor; bartering seemed to be a way of life in the Outback. There were women, a few, but less and less of his self-esteem came from scoring and drinking in pubs. For one, he couldn't afford the time or money. For another, he had found something real to hold on to for the first time in his life. The playboy of the Western world had become the entrepreneur of make do, patch together.

He fast-talked an airport hangar operator out of a grounded biplane. While enduring the daily humor of his friends, which, being Aussie, was broad, barbed and rough, he'd patched it back together. One of the best days of his life was the morning he took it up and brought it back for a safe landing. Thornton Enterprises had begun.

Gradually, he even put away his hope of returning for Jo.

The one time he'd called the States, Adelle had answered the phone. After he got over his shock at hearing her voice, he'd asked for Jo and learned she was away in college, a sophomore. Had it been four years? It didn't seem possible. He couldn't ask more without revealing his identity. All he knew was that Jo Spencer was a woman now, and probably in love with some other man. It had taken him two days to get up the courage to use the number at the University of Virginia that Adelle had given him.

He rubbed his palms on his trouser legs, feeling a twinge of the anxiety that had plagued him as he made that call. He'd had to wait for her roommate to locate her. Then when he heard her voice, he couldn't speak. She sounded so different, so assured, so grown. He couldn't do anything to spoil that. He wouldn't. She'd gotten on with her life. He had to get on with his. He had hung up without a word to her.

Until a crash almost ended his life nearly a year ago, he thought he had come fully to terms with his past. He thought he knew the full toll of his mistakes on the people about him. But a brush with death made him rethink the years, and the months in the hospital made him regret the waste. What did he have to show for his life? He had built a business, learned how to control, limit and make the most of his volatile nature. Yet there was an emptiness no amount of success could fill. If he had died, he'd have left this life without ever having known true love.

When his doctor prescribed a vacation to rid him of the last vestiges of his prolonged hospital stay, he had decided to come to the States, to return to Cedar Bluff just to view— from a distance—the results of his past. Only then did he feel he could return to his new life. But the unexpected happened. He'd found Jo Spencer.

"Jo. Jo," he murmured softly. He still loved her. Probably always would. But that realization didn't make their present situation any easier than the one twelve years earlier.

The agony of her confession the night before had cut into him, twisting like a knife blade in his gut. He couldn't quite believe how open and vulnerable she had been. He would have spared her that. Yet, because of it, he now knew things he would never have otherwise learned.

All these years she'd thought Zachary's death was some cosmic judgment against her, against her behavior with her cousin's husband. He'd never thought of blaming her in any way for Zach's death. If anything, he was to blame. He'd been there, too. Zach was his son. He should have been caring for him instead of seducing his wife's cousin. His one noble gesture had been to leave Jo alone. Was his life always to be plagued by wrong decisions in his past?

He was torn. He'd wooed her as Gus Thornton. She'd made love with Gus Thornton. That wasn't deceit. Brett Ashwood was someone from another lifetime. He wanted Jo to love the man he had become, not the boy he had once been. After her confession, he'd tried to tell her who he was. She wouldn't listen. Later, after they'd made love, he couldn't. He'd just as soon go on being Gus if it meant he could have her. But for how long? And what would happen when she learned the truth?

As the first rays of morning sunlight topped the fence line between the houses opposite, they caught him in their full glare. As he squinted, blinded, something struck the step just below his feet with a loud *thwack*. From the corner of one eye he saw a paperboy on a bicycle fling up a hand of greeting as he pedaled on.

He bent forward to pick up the paper. If there was delivery, there must be a resident inside. He laid the paper very carefully on the veranda and stood up. Swift steps carried him away from the house. He had to talk to Jo. Tell her the truth. The sooner the better. After that, he would know if they had a future.

He had reached the median before something made him turn back. Perhaps it was a mistake, but it was also inevitable.

The man who had stepped out onto the veranda wore a long navy robe, his gray hair gleaming softly in the morning light.

Gus retraced his steps slowly as the man bent over to pick up the paper. He knew the exact moment the older man saw him. He straightened and clutched the paper he had retrieved to his chest.

Gus came back up the sidewalk, his eyes on the face of the man watching him. Twelve years was a long time. He had changed in many ways. Perhaps things had changed, as well. If not, he was prepared.

He climbed the steps slowly, giving the man time to turn away. But he didn't. The man in the robe just stood watching him. When Gus paused one step from him, he smiled. "Hello, Brett."

Gus did not smile in return. "Hello, Dad."

Chapter 14

From the back steps Jo watched the sun top the roofline of the house across the backyard. With coffee mug balanced on the top of her knees by her framing hands, she listened to the soft sounds of Stevie's even breathing through the monitor at her elbow. A few short hours ago she couldn't have imagined that she could feel so calm, so secure in the knowledge that the baby in her care was safe.

She had panicked. The old terror of remembered tragedy had nearly driven her to completely lose control. If Gus hadn't appeared when he did, she didn't know what she would have done. She wanted to believe that she would have pulled herself together, that no matter how poorly she had done the job, she would have gotten through the night with Stevie. But Gus had been there. And his presence had made all the difference in the world.

If only the rest of her life were as simple.

For the first time in twelve years, she had let someone under her guard, into her heart. There had been a few men in her life, but the choices had never been right, and she had finally just stopped hoping. Now it seemed as if life were giving her a second chance, and his name was Gus Thornton. It had happened so quickly, without any regard for

practicality, distance, even time. But it was real. She felt that
all the way to her bones. She was in love.

Jo ducked her head into her arm. She couldn't stop smiling, couldn't stop thinking about him. Where was he? What
was he thinking? Was he as amazed by the passion between
them as she had been?

He hadn't said much when he left. She understood. If he
felt even half of what she did, he must be walking about in
a daze. But she knew he would call. They would go on from
there. All the loss and hurt and pain of the past was behind
her at last.

"Such an exciting evening! What with the storm and then
the near tragedy with dear little Sarah. But it's turned out so
well, hasn't it?"

"That's one way of phrasing it." Jo set a china cup and
saucer before her unwelcome guest. Only Fawn would call
every parents' worst nightmare a well turned out event. But
then Fawn had her own way of looking at the world. She
even had a prejudice against drinking from a mug. "So unladylike, don't you think?" she'd said a moment before.

Jo picked up her own mug and refilled it. She had wanted
to be alone this morning with her thoughts. No such luck.

"What time do you expect Adelle and Steve to return with
Sarah?" Fawn asked.

"Not before about noon. The doctor wanted to see how
Sarah got through the morning." She glanced at the clock
on the wall. It was a ceramic daisy with bright yellow petals
and hands painted to resemble green stems with a leaf on
each end. The long one pointed to the petal with an eleven
on it and short one to the petal with a nine. If Gus hadn't
called by noon, she would call him. She opened the refrigerator. "Milk or cream, Fawn?"

"Milk—skim, if Adelle has it. Those of us who've crossed
the dreaded barrier of thirty have to be especially careful.
You just wait."

Jo poured skim milk into the creamer, wishing she could
add some sort of repellent to it that would shoo Fawn away
from this house. For reasons she couldn't decipher, she had
the distinct feeling that Fawn had not come over here for

just a friendly chat. The woman looked like a cat watching a bird, and she was the bird.

Fawn toyed with her teaspoon, her gaze slanted toward Jo. "How did you like dancing with my husband?"

The possessive emphasis on the last two words created a blip on Jo's personal radar screen. She picked up the pitcher and came toward the table. "I didn't dance with Caleb. Why would you think that?"

"Well, you two were out on the patio when lightning struck, and I distinctly remember noticing a couple out there a few minutes before." Her eyes narrowed. "Dancing *very* closely."

Another time Jo would have enjoyed stringing Fawn along, but today she had other things on her mind. She placed the pitcher next to Fawn's cup. "That was me, all right, but I was dancing with Mr. Thornton."

"Thornton?" Skepticism arched her brows. "Who is he?"

Jo smiled. "You mean somebody sneaked inside the city limits without you hearing about it?"

Fawn poured milk and stirred her coffee quickly, holding the spoon by the very tip. "There's no need to be rude."

"Didn't you ask Caleb if he danced with me?"

A little smile curved up just the corners of her thin mouth. "What wife expects to get a straight answer from her husband about a thing like that?"

I would, thought Jo. She remembered Adelle's whispered comment about trouble between Fawn and Caleb. She could well understand it. Fawn's suspicious nature was enough to drive any man around the bend. "Has he given you reason to doubt him?"

"Why, Jo! What an indelicate question!" She sounded flustered, but her eyes remained focused with enmity on Jo.

Jo smiled. "I don't have any designs on your husband, Fawn. I like Caleb, but he's not my type."

"Oh?" Fawn lowered her gaze for the first time as she picked up her cup. "Do you have a type?"

Yes, and his name is Gus Thornton. The thought made her smile turn dreamy. "I like men who can dance."

"Then you never could abide Caleb." Fawn's laughter was thin and forced. "I swan, that man has two left feet and both of them are tied on backward."

"'I swan'? Gosh and gee, Fawn. I haven't heard that phrase since I graduated sixth grade." Jo glanced again at the clock, wondering why the morning seemed to be passing so slowly. "Is there anything else you wanted, Fawn? I'm really rather busy."

Fawn set her cup back in its saucer. "Actually, there was." She turned a guileless look on Jo. "I saw someone, specifically a *man*, leaving this house about five-forty-five this morning."

"You're certain it wasn't five-forty-six?" Jo was glad her voice retained its mocking edge. If Fawn had seen Gus, then she must also suspect that he'd spent the night. "What were you doing up at that hour?"

"I couldn't sleep. *You* know how that is, don't you?"

The barbs were coming thick and fast. Jo had no idea of the reason behind them, but she wasn't going to be backed into a corner by the likes of Fawn Gordon. "If you have anything to say, Fawn, why don't you just spit it out?"

Fawn clasped her hands before her as if she were about to say grace, but the malice in her gaze was strictly unholy. "Did my husband spend the night here?"

"What?" Astonishment made Jo's jaw drop. She couldn't, mustn't, laugh in Fawn's face or all hell would break loose. A moment later she heard Caleb's voice just outside the kitchen door.

"Jo, you in there?"

He appeared before the screen in a greasy overall and a big lopsided grin that could make any woman limp with joy. "Can I come in? Fawn's set the dead bolt against me."

"Hi, Caleb." Jo went to unlatch the screen, grinning in amusement. She knew she should be concerned that Caleb had appeared at this particular moment, but all she could see was the humor in it.

He pulled the screen open and reached in to snag Jo by the chin, drawing her face up to his. His sky blue eyes skimmed her face with concern. "You okay, after last night?"

Boy, was that a question that could be misunderstood by an irate wife. Jo nodded her head, not trusting herself to speak.

"Smells like coffee," he said hopefully as he slid a friendly arm about her shoulders and stepped inside. "You got some for me?"

"Anytime," Jo replied, trying to wriggle unsuccessfully out of his embrace. "Want a cup?"

"Yes, ma'am!" He squeezed her a little tighter as he planted a kiss on her cheek. "Brett was right. One of us should've waited for you. You know how to treat a man."

"I guess that answers my question." Fawn had withdrawn from the table and stood in the shadow of the refrigerator, her arms folded like a wooden Indian's.

Jo backed out of the line of fire, feeling as if she'd stepped into a farce—or the climactic standoff in a Western. With his winsome blond looks, Caleb seemed to belong in a production of *A Midsummer Night's Dream*. Yet Fawn definitely looked primed for a reenactment of *High Noon*.

"Fawn." Caleb snatched his cap from his head just like a little boy encountering the reproving glance of his mother.

Fawn's expression changed by palpable degrees from shock and outrage to cold fury, taking the temperature of the room with it into the plunge. "Where have you been?"

He glowered at her. "Working on Mr. Fordyce's twin cam engine."

"All night?"

His gorgeous blue eyes turned smoky, his handsome face even more sexy when set in a sulky pout. "Looks like it."

"What does that mean?"

"Hell! I ain't been home all night, have I?"

Jo saw Fawn blanch, but it wasn't embarrassment, it was fury. "Don't you curse at me! You come home with me right now, Mr. Gordon. I have a few things I'd like to say to you." She cut her eyes at Jo. "In private."

Caleb shrugged. "You'll get your say. You always do," he added under his breath. "Only I think I'll take Jo up on that cup of coffee first."

Jo thought Fawn would come across the room at him, red talons poised to shred his fascinating face into chili meat.

She didn't. She collected her purse from the table, woven shades of pastel straw to match her pastel sundress and sandals, and smoothed her unmussed hair with a hand. Injured affront had never had a better interpreter as she walked head held high across the Spanish tile of the kitchen floor.

She turned when she reached the door, her chin cutting an acute angle, which made it possible for her to look down her nose at her husband. "Come home now, Caleb, or don't bother. Ever."

"Hell." He said it low, he said it softly, but he said it.

Fawn's head snapped toward the doorway, which she walked through without another word.

"Sometimes that woman," Caleb said with finality, as though the words summed up his entire philosophy of relationships. He subsided into one of the kitchen chairs.

Jo set a mug of coffee before him. "Don't you think maybe you should go after her?"

He wagged his head. "Been doing that nearly six years. Tired. Dog tired of it."

Jo sat down opposite him. "I think you should know Fawn thinks you spent the night here ... with me."

He lifted his head from a contemplation of his cup. "You serious? Why'd she think that?"

His kind but candid gaze made Jo uncomfortable. "She thought she saw you and me on the patio dancing last night."

"Kissing, you mean. Yeah, I saw you," he added with a grin, as Jo's skin flushed. "Figured it was none of my business. So I'm not asking."

"Thanks." His response was so unlike his wife's that she had to ask, "Why did you marry her?"

His grin turned sheepish. "Got tired of running."

"She pursued you?" The idea of a former runner-up to Miss Arkansas having to chase any man seemed incongruous.

He nodded as he sipped his coffee. "Her car was in my shop every other day that summer. I swear the woman pulled out the wires herself just to have an excuse to come in. Then the rumor got around about why she was back after living in Dallas for four years. She'd just been dumped by this feller from Waco. He was some Texas bigshot. Owned a string of small radio stations, was going into politics in a big way. Seems Fawn was sorta indiscreet in her public remarks a couple of times. It made the papers. He dropped her faster than a truckload of manure. After I heard that, I sorta felt sorry for her, reduced to chasing a grease monkey like me. Seemed the decent thing to do was to give in."

He took a long slurp of his coffee before going on. "I know she's got her faults. Folks call her a snoop behind her back. But who do they call whenever they want to know what's going on in town? My wife."

Jo smiled, liking Caleb better and better with every moment. Many men would have disavowed Fawn's gossiping nature. He saw it as just another human foible. "Fawn's very lucky to have you."

He wagged his head. "I know I'm an embarrassment to her. I don't talk good and I'd as soon be dragged backward through brambles as set foot in that country club she's so blamed fond of. But she ain't always a helpmeet to me, either. Once I wanted to have some French fellers over for dinner, on account of they was here to talk about their Grand Prix. All she was interested in was whether or not she could fly in real caviar and frogs' legs in from New Orleans. I told her, Fawn, them fellers have frogs' legs all the time. Give 'em catfish and barbecue—that's what we eat. It upset her, so she called it off." He looked pained.

"Did it cost you a job at the Grand Prix?" Jo asked in sympathy.

"Heck, no! But I had to get dressed up in a suit *and* tie and drive them all the way to Little Rock for a decent meal."

Jo smiled. She might have known the tie was the kicker. "Sounds like you'll work this out. You have before."

He looked across at her, his smile gone. "No, me and Fawn ain't meant to be together. Gonna get around to saying so any day now."

The simple statement took Jo aback. She hardly knew Fawn and Caleb. It seemed almost indecent that he should

tell her that he was thinking of divorcing his wife before
Fawn knew of it.

"You might want to think about it."

"I have been this last year." He held the mug in both
hands, staring into its depths. "Don't you wonder why we
ain't got any kids?" Before Jo could deny her interest in his
procreation possibilities, he added, "I do. Fawn says we
should wait until we're settled. We got plenty of time. I say
the woman is thirty-one. Past time she got on with it. Plain
truth is, she doesn't want kids. I do. Seems like grounds for
divorce to me."

"Divorces can be..." Jo sought for diplomatic words.
"Sometimes the parties in a divorce get caught up in trying
to outdo one another. I wouldn't be surprised if Fawn hired
one of those fancy divorce lawyers from Dallas or Hous-
ton."

"Won't do her any good." He grinned. "No, ma'am, it
won't. 'Cause her daddy insisted we sign a *prenuptial*
agreement."

"Why would he do that?"

"He thought I was after Fawn's property over near El
Dorado. Some years back, speculators told him there might
be oil under the ground. I said that was okay by me. Her
property was hers." He winked. "Providing my assets remained mine."

Jo looked at him with new respect. He might not be a
brain trust, but he was no fool, either. "So then in a divorce..."

"I get to keep a considerable portion of my million and a
half."

Jo's jaw dropped for a second time this morning. "Caleb,
that's amazing."

"Ain't it? I never knew them purses were that big till we
won a few races. Not that I need that kind of money. My
shop keeps me in overalls and spending change. It goes in
the bank, gets invested, breeds a damn sight better than
Fawn."

Jo considered what he'd said. It was easy enough to
imagine women the world over throwing themselves at him.
The man could draw crowds by just walking down the street.

Add in his worth at a million and a half, and it was nearly impossible not to feel sympathy for the woman who was his wife. Imagined or real, Fawn's feelings of insecurity were understandable. "Caleb, maybe Fawn's afraid of losing her looks. Maybe that's why she doesn't want to have children."

"What are you talking about? A woman's never more beautiful to a man than when she's carrying his child."

"Have you told Fawn that?"

He hunched his shoulders. "She won't even listen to me when I start talking about having a kid."

Jo reached across the table and touched his arm to draw his eyes to her. "Listen to me, Caleb. You're a handsome, wealthy man. Fawn must go nuts when you leave the country, worrying about who you're with and what you're doing."

"I ain't ever give her cause—"

"Some women don't need cause. Fawn was a beauty queen. She made her name on her looks. Perhaps she thinks her looks are all she has to offer you. She may think if she lost them, you might leave her. Jealousy comes from insecurity. That may be her way of showing she loves you. Perhaps she needs reassurance that you still love her."

He stared at her with a blank expression that gradually warmed until Jo felt the breathtaking radiance of it on her skin. No wonder Fawn was kelly green with jealousy. "You might just have hit on something, Jo. You just might." He suddenly blushed, the deepening color spreading over his skin enough to trigger a woman's erotic daydream. "'Cause, truth is, I do love her."

"Tell her, Caleb." Jo rose from her chair, eager to have both Gordons out of her life. "Now."

He drained his cup and rose, snatching his cap off the table. "You're a wonder, Jo Spencer. Anything I can ever do for you, you just ask."

"I may need a job," she returned casually.

His brows arched over his sea blue eyes. "Aren't you going back East?"

"I don't think so." To her surprise, she meant it. There was no compelling reason to return to Baltimore. Seven years and three jobs later, she had nothing substantial to show for the time spent there. Yet returning to Cedar Bluff didn't seem like the right answer, either. And there was Gus.

Caleb adjusted his cap on his head. "You wouldn't happened to know French, would you?"

"As a matter of fact, I do. It got me my job in international flight service for East Coast Air."

He pulled a grease-stained blue airmail envelope from his pocket and held it out to her. "Been carrying this around till I could get the monsignor over at St. Michael's to read it."

Jo opened the letter and scanned the first few lines. "It's from a Monsieur Bellegarde. About a race in Monte Carlo next week."

Caleb frowned. "Don't know I can make it. Got to pull out Mrs. Dunlap's engine and replace the universal joint. Promised Ned Sharp I'd help him rebuild his Mustang after that. It's a '62. Not many chances to work on a car like that."

Jo smiled. Only Caleb would resist a chance to go to Monte Carlo because he could tune a Mustang instead. She lowered her gaze to the letter and finished reading it. "Monsieur Bellegarde assures you that he only needs you for three days. I'm not certain about the details, something about a motor piece you helped design last year. But I think he's offering to cover all travel expenses plus your fee."

"You're hired."

"To do what?"

"Read the mail. Write my letters. Talk to foreigners for me."

"I don't know anything about the auto business, Caleb."

"And I don't know a thing about them foreign languages. I need you."

"What about Fawn?"

"I'll handle Fawn." He smiled at her. "Seems we've solved each other's troubles, don't it?"

After he left, Jo wondered just what she was getting herself into. She suspected Fawn would tolerate her presence at Caleb's place of business the way she would a run in her panty hose. Playing front man for a body shop wasn't exactly what she had in mind, either.

She wandered back through the house to the front door, one ear cocked toward the monitor in her pocket. From the sounds coming forth, Stevie was sleeping in. It seemed she had a few more minutes to herself. She opened the door and sprinted down the front steps to retrieve the paper lying on the lawn.

She slipped off the plastic and unfurled it slowly, looking at the headlines. The night's storm had the lead. No deaths but flash flooding and power outages had been common. Skimming across the national news, she flipped the paper over to read the bottom half.

She recognized the picture before her focus brought the name into clear view. "Senator Ashwood arrives in town to speak to the Women's Political Coalition on Saturday."

She folded the paper slowly, tingling inside. She had come a long way since last night. For the first time since it happened, she no longer felt responsible for Zachary's death. Here was her chance to lay another ghost to rest, to learn what had become of Brett Ashwood.

Chapter 15

Jo approached the Ashwood residence nervously. She had dressed in the suit she'd worn on her flight from Baltimore. It was conservative in tailoring, a pale yellow linen with a surplice silk blouse of ice blue. She had even put on hose for the meeting. She wasn't certain why she felt the formality was necessary, but she couldn't shake the sense that she was about to take an important step in her life.

She had waited until Steve and Adelle had settled Sarah in her own bed and then gone to bed to catch up on the sleep they had missed the night before. Feeling that she wouldn't be missed for a while, she'd called the Ashwood residence.

Perhaps it was the way Congressman Ashwood had responded to her call. He seemed surprised, pleased even, to hear from a member of the Spencer family, yet reluctant to have her visit today. She knew she must have sounded forceful, almost rude, but she wanted to get it over before her nerve failed. When she mentioned that it concerned his son, Brett, he had relented almost at once, asking her to drop by at noon.

The sound of the doorbell brought a maid in black uniform and white apron. "I'm here to see Congressman Ashwood," Jo said with a smile.

"Your name?" the woman asked politely, her gray gaze resting speculatively on Jo's suit.

"Jo Spencer."

The young woman smiled. "Jo! You don't remember me, do you? Marilyn Fuchs? A-Squad all-conference cheerleader? Class of '81." She blushed. "Guess you never thought to see me in a maid's uniform."

Jo smiled, wondering how to answer a question like that. "It's good to see you, Marilyn. You look great."

"Not as good as you." Marilyn gave her the fish-eye. "You must be an executive or something by now."

"Not quite. I'm unemployed, actually. Got my pink slip last Friday." It felt good to admit it.

Marilyn shook her head in sympathy. "Happens to the best of us. Lost my job at the paper mill six months ago. Couldn't find a thing until Mrs. Ashwood upped and offered me a position as her maid. Some folks might not do it, but I'm not too proud to put food in my kids' mouths. Their daddy's long gone. You remember Russ Taylor?"

"I, uh . . ."

"My ex. You wouldn't believe—"

"Ms. Spencer?"

Jo turned to the speaker and saw her host coming toward her. Even though it had to be ninety degrees outside, he was dressed in suit and tie. Her instincts had been correct. "Mr. Ashwood," she greeted him, extending her hand.

He clasped it firmly. "Little Jo Spencer. It must be fully ten years since I clamped eyes on you. You've grown up." He turned to Marilyn. "Please serve lemonade on the terrace." He looked back at Jo. "What would you like? We keep nearly every sort of beverage on hand, but for an old fogy like me, summertime means only one thing—fresh-squeezed lemonade."

"Sounds wonderful," Jo replied.

He nodded. "That will be all, Marilyn."

Marilyn winked at Jo. "Ask Mr. Ashwood about that secretarial job he's going to be interviewing for tomorrow."

Irony edged Jo's smile. Her unemployed status would be common knowledge within the hour. "Thanks, Marilyn."

When she was gone Mr. Ashwood winked at Jo. "Marilyn's a dear young woman but a bit talkative for a man who spends his life speechifying. This way." He indicated that Jo was to go ahead of him toward the rear of the house.

Jo had only been in this house once before, and she had forgotten the majestic sweep of its rooms. As she walked through it, she recalled how Brett detested the fact that he lived in what had once been a plantation home. Built before the Civil War, the fireplaces were the size of closets and the doorways were wide enough to accommodate hooped skirts. Through the open doorways she passed she spied the gleaming surfaces of ornately carved wood surfaces, expensive rugs and the sparkle of crystal chandeliers.

The central hallway led out onto a brick terrace complete with white balustrade. The two-story house still shaded the terrace from the sun, and he offered her a chair before a table set with linen and flatware. "I hope you'll join me for lunch. My wife stayed behind in Washington this trip, and I despise eating alone."

"I'd be delighted," Jo answered, though she suspected that he was simply being polite.

As her host directed the service of the meal, Jo had a chance to study him. Seen through Brett's eyes, he had always seemed something of an ogre, a distant, harsh man who could not be pleased. Yet she knew from Adelle's letters that he was well respected by his constituency, had been recently reelected for his fourth term. His gaze was clear and the same whiskey-neat amber as Brett's, yet there was a downward slant to those eyes and permanent scores in his cheeks that dragged at the corners of his mouth. His dark hair had silvered. He seemed less arrogant than she remembered, less military in his bearing. Had time beaten him down or his son's desertion?

When a mixed green salad and glass of lemonade had been set before each of them, Mr. Ashwood picked up his glass and saluted her, saying, "What's this about you needing a job?"

Jo jumped as though stung. "That's not why I'm here, Mr. Ashwood. I didn't come about a job."

He looked at her over the rim of his glass. "But you need one."

"I assure you I didn't finagle my way into your home to—" Jo began, only to be stopped by his chuckle.

"You haven't changed, Jo. That earnestness was evident the first time I ever saw you. You'd come to my door selling Girl Scout cookies. You couldn't have been more than ten, but you wore your uniform like a five-star general. When I offered to buy only two boxes, you grew quite indignant. I remember your exact words. 'You're a prominent person, Mr. Ashwood. People look to you to set an example. If you only buy two boxes, then everyone who signs up after you will do the same. Don't you want me to win my troop's award?'"

As he chuckled a second time Jo felt a blush creeping up her cheeks. "Did you buy more?"

"Eight boxes," he replied. "Did you win?"

"I don't remember." But she did. The ribbon had had a place of honor on her bulletin board until she had left for college.

"If it's not a job, what exactly brings you to my door?"

Jo picked up her lemonade and took a sip. This was it, the last door opening onto the past. "I want to ask you about Brett."

They heard the crunch of tires on the driveway at the same moment and looked around. The black Mercedes with government license plates pulled up at the foot of the terrace. A man got out. The glass Jo held thudded heavily as it slipped from her hand back onto the tabletop.

Coming into the shade after the glare of the sun, he must not have seen her clearly. He took several long quick strides that brought him up from the driveway onto the brick terrace, stopping just feet from the table. He removed his sunglasses, blinking to adjust his eyes. Finally their gaze met and locked, and she saw him blanch.

Mr. Ashwood had risen to his feet. "Speak of the devil, huh, Ms. Spencer? You remember my son, Brett."

"I...yes." Jo felt as if hands had wrapped around her throat and were squeezing slowly. Brett Ashwood and Gus

Thornton were one and the same. No! It couldn't be! Please, dear God, not this!

He looked as shocked as she, his eyes wide, his mouth slightly open. Yet he couldn't feel as sick as she. The blood roared through her ears. Her vision narrowed to a pinprick of light and then flared, hurting her eyes.

She hadn't realized she had come to her feet until she heard her own voice speaking again. "... really must go. I just remembered Adelle was expecting me to come right back."

"If you must," Mr. Ashwood said uncertainly, "but you were just about to ask me about Brett, and here he is. Ask him yourself."

"Leave it, Dad."

His voice sounded strangely unfamiliar without its Australian accent. Jo felt cold, as if she'd swallowed a huge chunk of ice. All the way down it burned a slick frigid track that left her numb. It was all too numb. She reached for her purse, but it had disappeared. Like someone blind, she began feeling for it without looking down.

Brett reached down and scooped it up from the terrace. He didn't offer it to her but tucked it under his arm, his expression unreadable. "I'll walk you to the door."

"No!" She caught herself in midgesture, fending off the hand he'd extended toward her. She turned from him, couldn't bear the sight of him any longer. Smiling was an effort that made her jaws ache as she turned to the father. "Goodbye, Mr. Ashwood. Thank you for your hospitality."

She didn't glance again at the man who fell into step beside her as she crossed the terrace toward the house. The sight of his achingly familiar face would have driven her to violence. Lies! He'd told her nothing but lies. And she'd believed him. Because she so desperately wanted to.

He didn't say anything until she had stepped into the back hall, then he reached out and took her by the arm, halting her in midstride. "I ... we need to talk."

"Go to hell!" She jerked away so quickly that he couldn't release her fast enough, and she winced in pain as her arm strained free. Head tucked down, she continued down the hall.

"Jo? Jo!" He came after her, his footfalls echoing hers on the parquet floor.

Her temper came roaring back, overriding shock as she turned on him. "Leave me alone. Get it? Entirely alone."

He shook his head, his mouth compressed into a stubborn line. "Not like this. I've something to say."

"Too late. I know your dirty little secret."

He looked as if she had slapped him. "Dammit, Jo!" His voice was low, not more than a guttural whisper. "Do you think I wanted it to happen like this?"

She looked away from him. She could no longer look at the man who had haunted her life these past years, watch the mouth that had kissed and loved her so well only a few short hours ago, or she would go mad.

He reached out for her again. "Let me—"

She hit him, struck down his arm with the flat of her hand. And then she was running down the hall, uncaring what anyone might think who saw her.

She didn't get far before he caught her. Even as she struggled against the arm he wrapped about her waist from behind, he lifted her off the floor. She dug her elbows backward into his ribs. Though he grunted in pain, he didn't release her. Instead he half-carried, half-dragged her into the nearest room and kicked the door shut before releasing her.

Jo flung herself away from him, moving several feet into the salon before turning back, poised for anything. "Stay away from me or I won't be responsible for my actions."

"All right. You want to fight. Let's fight." He swept back the hair that had fallen onto his brow with an impatient hand. "But now, Jo. Now."

She bared her teeth. "You bastard!"

He nodded, hands on hips. "That's right. Say whatever you need to."

His self-possessed tone only further infuriated her. How dared he stay calm when her world was in flames. The back of her throat burned with unshed tears of rage. She was breathing hard. Each sentence became a gulp of air. "You filthy rotten liar! I hope you're happy. You got me good.

That was the plan, wasn't it? String stupid gullible Jo Spencer along. Teach her a lesson for boasting that she could unmask you."

"Jesus, Jo! Give me a little credit."

"Oh, I'll give you that. You played it perfectly. The accent never slipped. Four hours in your company and I was ready to...to—"

"Don't!"

"Don't what? Embarrass myself? You?"

"Don't make it sound sordid. It wasn't like that, and you know it."

He took a step toward her, but she scooped up a silver candlestick from the nearby table and raised it like a club. In her hand it looked like a formidable weapon. He didn't move again. "If you will just sit down a minute and listen to me."

"If you think I'm going to swallow any more of your tripe—"

He threw up his hands. "Is that it? Your pride's hurt?"

"Pride? What pride?" She paused, eyes closing against the assault of recent memory. "I told you everything! Things nobody else ever knew! And you listened! You let me strip myself bare! And you didn't say *anything!*"

As she covered her eyes with her free hand and choked back a sob, Brett swore viciously. He had thought that listening to her confession the night before had been the most painful thing he had ever done. But watching her now was worse. She was like a wounded animal, and he didn't know how to save her a moment of tortured feeling.

"I tried to tell you last night, but you stopped me."

She lifted her head from her hand, her eyes daring him to repeat so weak an excuse.

"All right, so I didn't try very hard. But that was as much your fault as it was mine. You asked me to love you, Jo. It's what I...what we both wanted. And we were right. It was so good between us."

"Don't talk to me about last night."

"Then tell me what you want me to say."

Jo turned her back on him. "Just tell me why. Why would you want to hurt me like this?"

"I didn't. I swear I never meant to hurt you."

"Then why do I feel like I'm dying inside?"

He didn't quite know how to answer that. Nothing had gone as he had planned since the moment he had turned back and seen his father on the front steps of his home this morning. Suddenly nothing was simple. He felt besieged on all sides. There was another confrontation waiting for him, on the terrace with his father. But he couldn't let her go like this.

He came up behind her, wanting to hold her, stroke her bright hair, have her lean into him for comfort, but he knew that was impossible. "It's going to be okay. Your feelings are safe with me, Jo."

She spun around, her face wet with tears. "Liar! I hate you! I hated you twelve years ago but I hate you even more now. Why did you do it? Why make me care again?"

"I can't defend it, Jo." He sounded defeated. Misery dimmed his gaze. "I'm sorry."

She threw up her hands as though his words were brickbats. "Not good enough! Not nearly. You didn't have to do this." She pressed the heel of her palm into her chest to ease the ache there, but it didn't help. "You didn't have to come back."

"Maybe you're right." He angled his head into the crescent of his hand and massaged his brow. "I don't know anymore. But it was unfinished business for me, too."

"What? Haven't you wrecked enough lives? What does it take to get rid of you?"

The color drained out of his face, leaving him looking gaunt and older. All the tiny lines that months of pain had etched into his face were sharply defined. He didn't say anything, just stood staring at her until she turned away from him.

"I never forgot you, Jo."

"No." She shook her head. "You can't say that to me."

"But it's true. And I know you once cared—"

"The boy I fell in love with wasn't a coward," she shot back.

"The boy you fell in love with doesn't exist."

She turned back to him, her expression defiant. "He did. He loved me."

"I love you."

"I don't know who you are."

"Learn me, Jo."

"I can't." She stiffened, her trembling lip sucked in to protect its vulnerability. "I won't."

"Why? Because you're afraid of getting hurt? What more could happen, Jo? You know my secret as I know yours. That gives us a beginning."

"It's all lies—my secret, your secret. None of it is real or true, not even your name."

His face stiffened. "You're wrong about that. I am Gus Thornton. I've earned the right to that name."

Jo brushed his declaration away with a hand. Without glancing in his direction, she replaced the candlestick on its table and started for the door. She half expected that he would try to stop her again, but he didn't.

When the knob turned in her hand, she sighed in relief, leaning her head for a moment against the smooth walnut surface of the door. "Just get out of my life, Brett Ashwood or Gus Thornton, or whoever you think you are. Get out and stay out."

She walked back to her cousin's house. Nothing on earth could have induced her to return for the car keys in the purse she'd left behind. She didn't know what she'd say to Adelle when she asked about her car. At the moment, that didn't seem important.

She felt as though she had contracted some awful disease, that at any moment she might begin to exhibit symptoms of the thing that separated her from every other "normal" person.

Don't let it get to you, she told herself. Yet the pain was beating in her temples and knocking against her ribs. She had become good at holding herself a little apart, away from any pain until it became a way of life. The old habits would return once this fresh wounding subsided. If it subsided. At the moment she felt that this time the internal bleeding might just kill her.

Without consciously choosing it, she had learned to survive disaster early in her life. After the deaths of her parents she had come to live in the Spencer house because she understood that it would be the closest thing to a home she would have after that. Her uncle and aunt had been generous in their love, but it had not been the same. Even as a nine-year-old, she had understood that nothing would ever again be the same. She was the stranger in their midst, the child everyone looked on with sympathetic pity.

She knew neighbors whispered about her when they thought she was out of earshot. "Poor Little Jo. So kind of her relatives to take her in, treat her as their own child. Isn't she bearing up well?"

She had borne up, out of the human instinct to survive. But it had been at a cost. Nothing and no one was allowed to get too close. She adored Adelle, but as a fan does a rock star, from a distance without any real expectation of having the ardor returned. It had taken a teenage infatuation with Brett Ashwood to stir her deep-buried feelings. All the need and love and hope she had squirreled away she had offered to him. Now, twelve years later, she had made the same mistake again.

"Something must be wrong with me," she whispered hoarsely. What Brett had done was despicable, but as much as it galled her to admit it, it wasn't entirely his fault. She had encouraged him. A groan of shame escaped her as she increased the pace of her steps. She had told him of her own volition of her secret torments and of her unfulfilled love for the young man he once was. Worse than that, *she* had asked *him* to make love to her. Was last night his way of offering her a consolation prize for his earlier rejection? How pathetic she must have seemed, and how humiliated she felt.

She paused in the shade of a tree to catch her breath and wiped the perspiration slicking her face with a trembling hand. She had to stop thinking. Every thought was piling up more pain on top of the main injury. There was only one thing she had to keep in mind. No involvement with Brett Ashwood had ever brought her happiness, only the prelude to another disaster. It must never happen again. Not ever.

Chapter 16

Mr. Ashwood found his son staring out the windows of the front parlor. His hands were shoved deeply into his pockets, and he stood with feet far apart, as though braced against some unseen force. The congressman entered silently, uncertain what to say to this tall handsome stranger who was his son.

He had felt amazed, stunned, dropped down the rabbit hole of impossibility when he had first recognized the figure coming toward him in the early-morning light. He couldn't recall their conversation, not even the sequence of the pleasantries that led Brett to offer to run an errand for him. They had clutched at anything that came to hand like thieves on a spree in Tiffany's. Neither had wanted to bridge the main gap between them—Brett's twelve years of absence.

The rage over his son's departure twelve years earlier had lasted exactly seven days. After that, he had joined in his wife's immediate panic that something dreadful might happen to a handsome young man on the road without money or purpose. The detective he had hired had picked up Brett's trail in Louisiana but lost him in New Orleans. Colder than a snail's trail was the detective's final report. That's when the sightings began.

During the first year, he thought he glimpsed his son a dozen times a week. Each time the mistake left him trembling in the aftermath of cattle-prod shock. Later on, at night after his wife was sleeping, he began scouring family albums and yearbooks, trying to keep fresh the exact likeness of his son's face. Gradual despair led him to rummage through Brett's belongings, reading history papers and studying his English essays, cataloging his collection of memorabilia, looking for clues that would explain their turbulent father-son history. By the end of Brett's first year of absence, he knew his son better than he had at any time since he was born. That realization answered a lot of questions.

He hired other detectives, investigated runaway shelters and lived with the sightings that came a dozen times a month. Finally, the watery-gut feeling of recognition diminished to the rare unpleasant jolt outside a restaurant or when entering a hotel. Some young man would hold his head familiarly. A profile would look similar. It was strange, though. When he actually saw his son this morning he knew instantly that all the other sightings had been mistakes. This was the real Brett, as brilliantly different from his look-alikes as a diamond is from zirconium.

The man facing the window was surprisingly tall, having grown a bit since nineteen, and was much broader of physique. Gone, too, was the sulky slouch and perpetually jutted hip. The silver winging into his temples gave him an air of maturity, a dignity that the rebellious boy had once seemed incapable of achieving. Time had carved away the boyishness, leaving behind the refined contours of a self-sufficient man.

Pride naturally flowed through his veins at the sight of the results of his and Louise's genes. From the little he'd seen so far, Brett had become as fine an example of a son as any man could have hoped for. Until a few hours ago, he had felt childless. But—by damn!—he had his son back. Now all he had to do was figure out how to keep him.

He cleared his throat a bit theatrically. The slight sound snapped his son's head around. "That was quite some fireworks display." He smiled broadly. "You always had an effect on women."

His son turned from the window, scowling. "How much did you hear?"

Mr. Ashwood lifted his hands in protest. "Just enough to realize you've been back sufficiently long to have woman trouble."

His son's eyes narrowed. "Naturally you're not surprised."

The older man's smile faltered. "That's not what I meant."

"It doesn't matter."

Bad beginning. Try again. "Are you hungry? Cook just—"

"No." The syllable was like a pistol's report, sharp and startling.

"Fine. We'll eat later." He indicated the pair of Queen Anne wing chairs flanking the fireplace. "Why don't you sit down and we'll talk, son."

The younger man's lips curved ever so slightly. "When did I regain that title? *Son,*" he added pointedly, in response to his father's perplexed expression.

Mr. Ashwood smiled mildly. He didn't expect his son would make it easy for him. The question was, would he allow a reconciliation of any kind? He took one of the chairs. "Where shall we begin?"

"With some ground rules. I didn't come back for this." Gus swept a hand across the room. "Or this." He tossed his father the keys to his Mercedes, which he had picked up for him at a local garage. "No need to change your will again. Understood?"

Mr. Ashwood nodded but reddened. He'd faced adversaries across the House of Representatives with less trepidation than he did now his own flesh and blood. "This isn't easy for either of us."

His son shrugged. "It never was. Dealing with your son had always been a reminder that you weren't perfect, had a flaw. Me."

His father sounded resigned. "You're still bitter."

"Was. Past tense." His expression was blank as he crossed the room and dropped into a wing chair opposite his father's and crossed one ankle over his knee. "Why don't we move on to the next topic."

Mr. Ashwood wanted to ask about the reason for his son's limp, but he decided not to begin so personally. "Your mother would like to know you're here."

"I'll call her later."

"How many other people, besides Jo, know of your return?"

"No one. I'd rather it remain that way but . . ."

"It's bound to leak out," his father finished for him. "In a town this size, it will be big news. Perhaps we should issue a statement."

Gus's gaze snapped up from a contemplation of his shoe tip. "Absolutely not! This isn't the return of the prodigal. My reasons for returning are personal, and I don't want a barbecue and brass band. If you force this into some kind of media event I won't do your political career any good."

The enmity in the threat caught Ashwood with unexpected force. He stared at the man whose gaze was a duplicate of his. "I was wrong before. You're not bitter. You still hate me."

Gus smiled, but there was no warmth in it. "Hate left my range of emotions a long time ago. I simply don't care one way or the other."

"Then why are you back, Brett?"

Gus flinched. That question had been thrown at him from every source possible, and he still couldn't answer it satisfactorily. "I guess you might say I was looking at the future and figured maybe the past needed to be put in perspective."

Mr. Ashwood pounced on those words. They were the first indication that his son shared his hopes for some kind of resolution to their estrangement. He sought a neutral topic. "The last news we had from you was six years ago. Are you still in the merchant marines?"

"No. I'm living in North Queensland, Australia."

"The other side of the world," his father said mildly. Why wasn't he surprised. "What…how did you happen to settle there?"

"Washed up on shore like flotsam, Dad. You always said scum as well as cream rises to the top."

Touché. "I hired various detectives over the years to look for you."

"They could never have found Brett Ashwood," his son returned, "because he no longer exists. First thing I did was change my name. I'm called Gus Thornton."

This thrust hurt more than all the others. His son had changed his name.

Gus watched his father's struggle reflected in his expression, gauging just how much pain he had inflicted. Once he would have savored the moment, satisfied to have wounded in the same degree that he once had been wounded by the words "you're no son of mine." Now it seemed like a childish gesture, a waste, beneath him.

"You think our disagreements were all about image?"

"Weren't they? You told me often enough that people expected things of me because I was your son. I was supposed to reflect your glory, right? Brett Ashwood, mayor's son, the athlete whose father never had time to make the games, unless—" he smiled slowly "—it was in an election year. 'Keep your nose clean son, you never know who's listening, watching, waiting to trip you up.' Only thing was, Dad, no one gave a damn about tripping me. It was you they were interested in. I just gave them something to use against you."

"Is that why you drank—to hurt me?"

"You don't get it. It wasn't about you. Never was. I happened to like the way it made me feel, like I was somebody."

Mr. Ashwood frowned. "You always were somebody."

"No. You were somebody. I was Mayor Ashwood's son. There's a difference."

"I don't understand the distinction."

Gus smiled. "That was the problem. That's why I had to get out."

"I may have made some mistakes..." Mr. Ashwood looked away from the sardonic amusement in his son's eyes. "Right. I did make mistakes. But I never gave up trying to do what I thought was best."

"Is this going to be one of those 'bloody but unbowed' speeches? Or is it the one about how only great men can make great mistakes?"

Mr. Ashwood's face flushed with indignation. "You came to me."

"Bad habits are the hardest to break."

For the space of several seconds the two men glared at one another. The initial flare-up was the age-old battle between father and son: youth versus experience. Each side had its advantages but the outcome remained in doubt. Gradually as whiskey brown eyes held tiger's eye ones, it dawned on each of them that those differences had been mellowed, the distinctions blurred by time. The youthful son had gained by his experience and experience had made the father wiser.

"Tell me about Jo Spencer," his father said after a moment.

Gus's gaze didn't waver. "Why?"

"I understand she's looking for a job." He was gratified to see surprise register in his son's face.

"Is that why she was here?"

"I'm looking for a personal secretary," Mr. Ashwood continued, avoiding a direct answer, "someone to help me organize my papers. The university press has expressed interest in publishing a book on my work revitalizing the state's economic structure. Do you think a Spencer will work for an Ashwood?"

"You'll have to ask her," he replied noncommittally.

"Would you like me to?"

"Don't try to buy her for me. I won't be in town long enough."

The mention of his leaving gave Mr. Ashwood his first serious moment of doubt about a reconciliation. "When are you leaving?"

Gus stood up. "It depends."

"On Jo?"

"On things that have nothing to do with you," he said dismissively. He ran a hand through his hair, leaving furrows where his fingers passed. "I've got some things to sort out."

"You're welcome to stay here."

Gus's head moved in a quick negative. "I'll take a room at a hotel here in town." He glanced at his father. "It's better this way."

"Your mother?"

"I'll call her."

As his son left the room, Mr. Ashwood couldn't keep back a smile. He'd bet the farm that his son's "sorting out" had to do with Jo Spencer. Once they had been father and son, but early in Brett's life they had degenerated into adversaries until finally there had been nothing left but bitterness and recriminations. Now, after a dozen years, fate was giving them another chance. He had made mistakes. But he wasn't a quitter. He might yet prove useful to his proud son.

"Brett Ashwood? You're certain?" Adelle exclaimed as she gently rocked her children in the porch swing. Her daughter and son were curled one on each side, their heads on her lap.

"Knock on the Ashwood front door, if you don't believe me," Jo answered shortly. "I told you it was him at the cemetery. If only you'd listened to me."

"Then what?" Adelle shook her head. "Honestly, Jo, I don't know what I was supposed to do even if he had admitted who he was right from the start. Seems to me he didn't want to acknowledge us. As far as I'm concerned, it's his privilege."

"But he lied!" Jo began pacing before the swing, ticking off her grievances on her fingers. "The phony accent. The lies about Australia. The name Gus Thornton. God only knows what else he would have said, given the chance."

"I just don't understand why you're so upset, Jo. One would think he'd personally injured you."

"He did!" Jo said vehemently. Then she added belatedly, "He wounded the entire family."

"Oh, please! This is not a blood feud. The past is forgiven and forgotten."

"How can you say that? He seduced you, Adelle. Told you what you wanted to hear. Kissed and touched you! Made you think you loved him when he was only looking to get laid."

Adelle looked at her cousin a little strangely as her voice rose in volume and agitation. "Thank you for the defense, Jo, but it's misdirected. Brett Ashwood never did a thing to me I didn't want done. Okay, I didn't want to get pregnant. But it takes two. We both made mistakes. There's no need for you to bear a grudge against him for my sake."

If only it was Adelle's sake, Jo thought, reduced to chagrin by her cousin's reasonable tone. She had been speaking of herself, not Adelle. He had seduced her, told her things she wanted to hear, made love to her when all the time he knew it was a lie. She couldn't shake the shock and outrage of learning the truth by accident. And just when she had given him her complete trust.

"I understand that in your surprise you walked out. But you are going back and get my car, Jo?"

Jo blinked at her cousin. "Yes. Sure. Later." After she had made certain he wasn't around.

"He won't bite, Jo. He's a man."

Don't I know that, Jo mused. Much to her rage and regret. "I just don't want to see him again ever."

The phone just inside the front door rang. "Would you mind," Adelle asked, spreading her hand to include the two blond heads in her lap.

Jo picked up the phone on the third ring. "Hello, Lawson residence."

"Is that you, Jo?"

Jo took a breath. "Mr. Ashwood?"

"Right the first time. I was sorry we couldn't finish our discussion earlier. I'm especially eager to see you again."

"If your son asked . . ." Jo began.

"This has nothing to do with Brett. I have my very own selfish reasons for needing to see you. Say, 10:00 a.m. tomorrow?"

"I don't know, Mr. Ashwood. I'm sure that after this morning's altercation, you're aware that your son and I don't get along."

"Brett's not staying here, if that's what's on your mind. I certainly hope that past differences between our families won't prevent you from doing me the courtesy of another visit."

Jo thought about it. She had to go back and get Adelle's car, anyway. She might as well get this over with. "Could we possibly have this meeting in, say, half an hour?"

"Whatever is most convenient. I'm looking forward to our chat."

Jo hung up, wondering just what she was about to get herself into.

She had put her hand up to push the front screen open when she heard Fawn Gordon's voice saying, "Imagine that, Adelle! Marilyn said they had a great set-to right in the Ashwood front salon! Now why do you suppose Jo kept it from us?"

She stepped back from the screen, hoping she hadn't been spotted. In the mood she was in at the moment, she would likely pin back Fawn Gordon's delicate ears with a litany of four-letter words, and she had a feeling Caleb wouldn't like that.

She was through the house and out the back door before either woman noticed her absence.

"I'm not even certain how long I'll be in Cedar Bluff," Jo answered, sipping some of the delicious lemonade she had been promised two hours earlier.

"Then simply agree to work for me for the time you're here," Mr. Ashwood encouraged. "I need someone who knows the area, can recognize local names, compose complete sentences. Any help you can render would be much appreciated."

She had not expected to be offered a job, much less one with so generous a salary attached to it. If it had come from any other source she would have jumped at the chance. As it was, this one seemed to be bait in the trap. "I'll have to think about it."

"If money's an issue . . ."

"No, it's not that. What you proposed is more than generous. It's only that I'd have to live with Adelle and Steve until I could close up my apartment in Baltimore, if I decided to return here permanently. As it is, I'm an uninvited houseguest."

"Move in here." He smiled at her look of surprise. "Then you could work at your leisure, arrange your hours to satisfy your needs. In fact, it would work better that way. All my papers are here in the library. You'd have free access full-time. I'm surprised I didn't think it from the first."

Jo felt she was being pushed into a very tight corner by a very persuasive man. "I forgot to mention that I've had another job offer."

"Really?" His tone was disbelieving. "You're remarkably in demand."

"Actually, it's translating and answering correspondence for Caleb Gordon."

His smile became triumphant. "Our globe-trotting mechanic. Surely his correspondence can't be that demanding. If you must, then accept both jobs, at least for a trial run. What do you say? You can begin in the morning. That will give me time to set you up before I return to Washington."

Jo smiled for the first time. Any man this pushy would respect no one less forceful. "I agree only to think about your offer, Mr. Ashwood. How long will you be in town?"

"I'm home for a few days now. Then starting next month I'll be in and out. It's an election year, you understand. That, too, convinced me that now is the time to start the book. Of course, you'll have complete privacy most of the summer. The house practically runs itself with Cook and Marilyn to see to any need."

"I couldn't accept so generous an offer." She lowered her gaze. "It might be misunderstood."

"By Brett." He nodded slowly, his brows drawing together over his nose. "Jo, I don't pretend to understand one moment of what occurred between you and Brett earlier today, and I'm not asking for an explanation. It's been a most remarkable day. After years of praying for it, I woke up this morning and found my son on my doorstep." He looked at her with eyes very like his son's. "If there's anything you can do that will keep him here a little longer, you have my blessing."

She stood up stiffly, disappointment arrowing through her. She didn't want to be Mr. Ashwood's bait, or peace offering, for his son. "I can't help you with your son."

He followed her action, not at all ruffled by her animosity. "I'm not asking you to. The job offer stands whether or not Brett ever speaks to me again. Just don't say no. As I've said, the offer to live here is part of the deal. Your cousin and her husband would seem to have their hands full with two small children to care for. I heard from Marilyn about little Sarah's accident last night. Glad the child's going to be fine."

"Yes, we're lucky that it wasn't any more serious."

He reached for her hand and clasped it between both of his. "About the job," he pressed.

Jo hedged, afraid he would detain her indefinitely. "I'll think about it, but I can't make any promises."

"Promises about what?" The querulous tone suggested volumes of supposed intrigue.

Before she could stop herself, Jo glanced at him. He was standing in the doorway, a hand braced on the doorjamb just above head level. Her gaze slipped away but not before she had registered the way the skin was pulled tautly over the bones of his aggressively handsome face. He was still angry. Well, so was she. Damn him, anyway, for being the man she thought she loved, the man she'd come to know as Gus Thornton.

Clutching her purse, she turned away but didn't allow her expression to reveal her feelings as she addressed the father. "I'll think about it, Mr. Ashwood, but I have my doubts."

She turned and walked toward Mr. Ashwood's son without a glance. But she wasn't immune to his proximity as he forced her to pass beneath his extended arm in order to exit the room. The tension between them created intimacy without touching or speaking. She felt the tug of him like a magnet. And the scent of him. And the longing for him that overrode even the purest form of rage. It wasn't until she was out in the hall that she allowed herself to take a deep breath.

Gus waited until Jo had pulled the front door closed behind herself before he demanded of his father, "What the devil do you think you're doing?"

Mr. Ashwood's smile was easy and self-satisfied. "Hiring a personal secretary. Did I mention the book I'm writing? Jo's in need of a job. So I thought—"

"You thought you'd interfere." Anger lent a rough edge to his baritone. "I told you to leave her alone." He lowered his arm from the doorjamb and moved into the room. "I don't want your help, your patronage, your interference, your approval or your opinion in my life."

"I believe you've made that abundantly clear. But I have a question. If you don't want any of those things, then what *do* you want from me?"

Gus ducked his head. "When I figure that out, I'll let you know. Until then, leave Jo Spencer absolutely alone. Got it?"

"What if the young woman decides she wants the job?"

Gus's lips thinned to a line drawn in the sand. "You better hope she doesn't."

Chapter 17

Gus paced up and down the sidewalk before the Spencer house in the darkness. The yellow glow of the streetlight, which had long since come on, cast his shadow as an elongated inverted triangle across the front lawn. Any second now he fully expected a patrol car to pull up alongside him and demand his identification. He was loitering, making a nuisance of himself, but he wasn't going to go anywhere until Jo talked to him.

He had rung the doorbell and been told first that Jo wasn't home and then, after he recognized her voice coming from beyond the door, that she refused to speak to him. He wasn't usually a fool. He didn't usually yell past a homeowner to a guest that she'd better come out before he came in. He didn't usually startle people with his lack of control. It had been a while since he'd made an ass of himself in public. Yet within two minutes of arriving at the Spencers' home he had done all those things.

At least he hadn't barged in. Steve Lawson's restraining hand on his shoulder was probably the reason. The man's level if worried look had calmed his inclination to simply burst in like some macho cowboy and claim his woman.

His woman. He paused to look back at the house, dark now except for the front door light, and smiled. Jo was his woman. It felt right. It sounded right. It was right.

Once he'd been too full of himself to recognize love while lust demanded appeasement. But not this time. This time he knew what he was getting into, had understood only too well where his emotions were carrying him, had even been leery of the intensity of his attraction to Jo. He had warned himself that too much had happened, that the past was like a mine field, that any wrong step would blow to bits any hope of happiness. Well, the worst had happened. The world had blown up in his face. He wasn't certain how badly hurt he was but, curiously, that didn't matter. All that mattered was how Jo felt. In order to gauge that, he had to force her to see him. Any contact, no matter how painful, was better than this frustrated isolation into which she had thrust each of them.

He saw a light he had been watching for nearly fifteen minutes go out on the second floor. Without hesitating he headed in an angled path toward the corner of the veranda. He had learned to live alone, had built the necessary barriers and buffers to make it work. But the crack of Jo's palm across his face three short days ago had been as effective an awakening as Prince Charming's kiss had been for Snow White. He was alert now with all feelings in full operating order. He liked the feeling, was starved for the emotional attachments he had denied himself. Jo Spencer was what he had denied himself. He was as determined as she had once been to possess a love that seemed impossible.

He used the banister as a stepping-stone up to the eave, lifting himself by his arms and then shimmying his hips up onto the roof. The shingles crunched beneath his boots as he quickly crossed the portico over the front door to reach the second window from the left. Finally he knelt before the dark window and rapped on the glass.

The drapes had not been drawn. In the light filtering into the room from the hall, he saw her silhouetted on the bed, her back propped against the headboard. She refused to turn her head, though he knew he must be clearly visible in the streetlight's glare. He rapped louder.

He saw her suddenly jackknife forward and then unfold on her feet by the bed. As she crossed before the open doorway, the hall light made transparent the thin nightgown she wore. He felt himself harden in response to the tempting silhouette of thighs, hips and breasts. By the time she reached the window, his body was humming with desire. It was no random response. With every ounce of his body he yearned only for this obstinate, difficult, yet amazingly passionate woman named Jo Spencer.

She unlatched and raised the window. "Go away! Are you crazy?"

He bent his head so that his words were spoken into the opening. "Let me in, Jo. I need to talk to you."

"No! Go away before I call the police!" Her whispers made her tone all the more urgent, and sexy. "There are children sleeping here!"

"Jo. Don't make me do anything else crazy tonight. Let me in." He swallowed the inclination to bully her again. "Please."

Jo bent down to stare at him. His eyes were two dark wet pools in the meager street-lamp light. He sounded surprisingly desperate, and she wondered if he might actually do something else crazier than climb the roof to her bedroom window. That didn't bear thinking about. Experience had taught her to believe that he would do whatever was necessary to see her. Delaying the inevitable would only further embarrass her and perhaps really frighten her cousins.

She reached for the latch that held the screen in place. Adelle and Steve had given her such strange looks after his appearance at their door. She couldn't explain anything about her relationship with Brett Ashwood without telling them far more than she was ready to. While they didn't ask any questions, their curiosity had swarmed in the air like a cloud of gnats at sunset. Rather than try to watch TV with them, she'd come up to her room to be alone... and think.

"Two minutes. And keep your voice down!" she whispered, as she pushed the screen back so that he could grip and remove it.

But as he lifted the screen free of the hooks that held it in place, she pushed the window higher and then raised a leg over the sill.

"What are you doing?"

"Meeting you in neutral territory," Jo answered. She ducked her head beneath the window frame and scooted her bottom across the ledge to straddle the sill. He reached for her arm, but she pushed him away as she gathered the floor-length skirt of her sleeveless nightgown in one hand and shifted the material across the sill onto the outside of the window. As her bare foot touched the sticky surface of the shingles still warm from a day's worth of summer sunshine, she shifted her weight to that foot and hoisted her other leg over the ledge. With a swivel motion of her hips, she turned to sit on the ledge, both feet poised on toe tips against the roof's surface. As she smoothed the sheer material of her gown down over her knees, she glanced covertly at him. She was glad for the darkness that hid how scandalously thin that covering was.

He had moved a little away from her but was still crouched on the shingled surface, his arms casually encircling his knees. She envied him the flexibility to sit on his haunches. About everything else, she tried to reserve judgment.

Her gaze skittered away, her heart skipping a beat. She couldn't bear to look at his face, couldn't bear the pain, the hurt, the humiliation. She had known—had known!—all along who he was and yet been willing to disbelieve her own eyes. "What do you want?" she asked brusquely.

He was absolutely still, but his voice moved mountains within her. "To see you, hear your voice, be near you."

"It won't work."

"What?"

"Flattery," she replied, seeking refuge in animosity. "The tactic's cheap. You were doing better before you resorted to the commonplace. I don't seduce well."

"Don't you?"

Jo wondered if the streetlight illuminated her expression. She hoped her face was as smooth as glass, frosted glass.

Inside she was bleeding again a little quiet trickle that every thought of him and his betrayal set flowing.

"What did you tell your relatives?" he asked after a few seconds' silence.

Her scant smile was brittle about the edges. So he cared what other people thought. "Don't worry. I have no intention of sharing the intimate details of my life with them."

"Because it's too painful?"

Jo slanted her body away from him and gripped the window frame. "If this is why you came—"

"No." He caught her by the wrist, rising to his feet as he pulled her to him. His free hand reached for and found the inward curve of her slim waist. That's when he realized that her gown was no more than handkerchief-thin cotton that allowed a summer-warmed body to breathe. And breathe she did. The warm tender skin beneath his hand was startlingly alive and desirable.

Jo felt the same jolt of awareness as the heat of his hand penetrated her scanty covering and settled firmly into her skin. She might have been naked for all the protection the gown provided against his touch. She felt the impression of each of his five fingers separately. The heel of his palm rested on the jut of her hipbone. "Tell me what you're feeling, Jo."

She looked away, sensing that this was one argument she didn't dare have with him. "Let me go."

"No." He said it gently, but he might as well have shouted the word because he was pulling her against him. When she stepped back to halt the assault, he suddenly changed tactics, going with her until she felt the clapboards of the side of the house press into her shoulder blades and hips. Trapped.

He leaned forward, resting his brow on hers as he said, "That's not why I came." He rotated his forehead down over hers until their noses touched, and then he canted his head, laying his mouth over hers.

The first touch of his lips was devastatingly effective. Evaporating anger seemed to rise off her mood like mist over a lake at dawn.

"This is why I came," he whispered against her mouth. The play of his words dragged her lips into a more fragile openness. The yielding was unintentional. She hated him, hated what he had done. She despised her own weakness, but she couldn't prevent it from gaining domination over every other feeling.

His hands found her hair. Fingers plowed through the curls to hold her head to his seeking kiss. He shifted his full weight onto her, shoulder pressing shoulder, hip burrowing into hip, as he guided her into deeper kisses and fed her with slow tongue strokes that carried in them the unmistakable motion of lovemaking.

She raised her hands, intending to push him away, yet she found herself holding on instead. She was melting under the persuasion of his kisses, aching where his body molded to hers. For years after he had deserted her, she had dreamed of a moment like this, of freely loving Brett as he loved her back. Her pulse throbbed in her lips, her breasts and deep down at the apex of her thighs. Yet this was not supposed to be happening. She was not supposed to want, to need, to care about how he made her feel. She didn't want to revel in his taste, to marvel at the strength of him, yield to the wicked urge to stretch and purr with pleasure beneath his touch. She had right on her side, pride and decency. It didn't matter that she loved him. It didn't matter that she had loved him for more than half of her life. It couldn't weigh with her that she knew with perfect certainty that she would never again love with this bone-shattering intensity. It couldn't matter. It mustn't matter. But it did.

His hands were moving up and down her body, using the fabric of her gown to rub an erotic massage into the skin beneath. Fight fire with fire, she told herself. If this yielding was inevitable, at least she could take him with her.

Her hands went exploring to take back a little of the control he had so easily wrested from her. He felt hard and tough beneath his clothes. She found his waist was slim but broader than hers, belted by muscle that flared up toward ribs that made faint corrugated impressions easily felt through his shirt. She deftly undid the buttons and spread the material wide, ducking her head to kiss the lightly furred plane of his sternum. She smiled as he made a hissing sound through his teeth. Working quickly before she lost her nerve, she pulled the tail of his shirt from his jeans and then embraced the muscled heat of his back. His skin was hot and slightly moist and plush as velvet. He was kissing her ear, her neck, making deep low sounds of pleasure as his hands found and closed over the fullness of her breasts. When she turned to brush her lips lightly over one flat nipple she felt him shudder. She could move him. That knowledge helped assuage the guilt of desire spilling through her.

The night was suddenly much warmer than before, the temperature in their clinch well beyond simmer. It slicked their skins and made them cling even tighter together. If she were fighting for her emotional life, it was at a price equal to her desire for him.

She traced the bones of his face, reading through her fingertips their exact design. And all the while his mouth fed on hers, giving pleasure while seeking to extract from her the physical stimuli her hands and mouth offered him. She was losing, drowning in his hot desperate embrace, melting under the heat of his hard body. But her naturally stubborn nature balked at total surrender. She reached for his belt buckle, only half aware of where they were and why. She heard what sounded like a murmur of protest as she fumbled with the leather and then tugged at the snap on his waistband. He reached down, grabbing her wrist as she began sliding the zipper down.

For a moment he pulled back from her, his face a study in shadows while the streetlight illuminated her own. "Yes?" He seemed puzzled by the question he asked. But she knew the answer if he didn't. She inched his zipper down farther.

He bent suddenly and picked her up, angling her body feet-first into the open window. Jo slipped from his arms onto the window ledge, ducking her head as she reached for the floor of her bedroom with her feet. He came in quickly behind her, shrugging out of his shirt. And then his arms came around her from behind, his hands cupping her breasts. She felt his lips on her hair behind her ear. "I want you, Jo. I need you. I always have."

Jo closed her eyes and shut down the alarms going off in her head. She knew right from wrong. She understood the difference between reality and illusion. She knew good from bad. She knew it all, yet none of it mattered at this moment. She had to get back a little of her own.

She could feel the tremor of his reaction as she arched her body against the warmth of his. Then he was turning her in his arms, bringing her even closer so that there could be no doubt about the course they were set on, one that she wanted as much as he.

One moment she was pushing her bedroom door closed, the next she was being pressed back onto her bed as he followed her down into the mattress. She was astonished by the avidity of his kisses. He dropped them everywhere, on her cheeks, her chin, her eyes, and ever more deeply and wetly on her mouth. He seemed to drink in her breath. He teased her lips with his tongue.

His hand slid down over her hips, reached below her knee until it found the hem of her gown. He skimmed it up her body quickly, lifting himself off her only long enough to pull it over her head. Crisp chest hair tickled her naked breasts as he bent to her and took one aroused peak in his mouth. She arched against him with a soft sigh. The pleasure was so exquisite, the heat of his mouth so sensitizing, that she nearly moaned aloud.

"Next time, daylight," he whispered in frustration, and she knew that like her, he was using tactile stimulation to feed his fertile imagination.

His actions became more urgent, her hands more bold. Suddenly it wasn't enough to make love. As if by mutual but unspoken agreement, they each realized the desire for a complete, memory-soldered experience that might have to last them a long desolate time.

She registered the exact moment his need became just a shade more desperate than her own. He was chanting her name, his hips making love to her without possession as he reached down into his jeans pocket.

Using more willpower than she had thought she had, she rolled off the bed before he realized what she was going to do. He watched her pick up her gown and slide it over her head and then she moved to the window. Turning back to the bed, she pointed to the open space. "Get out."

He sat up slowly. "What? Why?"

She knotted her arms under her breasts, fighting the urge to back down before it was too late. "You mean, why aren't we going to have sex?"

"For openers, yes." He sounded cautious, uncertain what part he was now playing.

"We never were. I just wanted you to know how it feels to want something so—" She bit her lip to keep back tears that came unexpectedly to sting her eyes. Damn him. Her body was trembling, balking at the need he'd stoked so readily and whose fulfillment she'd snatched away. "I wanted you to experience a loss, disappointment, a hurt. It's the best I could do."

"It's unworthy, Jo."

She lifted her chin. She didn't need him to tell her that. "Also, I wanted to know if I'd been fooling myself."

"Had you?"

She was surprised he didn't ask what she was fooling herself about, until she remembered that he'd just been on the other end of their kisses. He had to know she meant the passion between them. "No," she said miserably.

"Then why?"

"Because now I know why I did what I did before, and I won't be tempted again."

She heard a smile in his voice, though she couldn't see it. "You're wrong. You'll be tempted, like I was tempted. You'll think about us, what we do to each other, about how right it feels, and want that feeling again. I do. Even now." He held out a hand. "Come back to bed."

"No!" She turned her back on him. "I don't want to talk about this any longer. Talking is what got us into trouble in the first place."

"Then let's not talk." He rose from the bed, letting the sheet slide free of his naked body. "Just let me love you."

"No." Jo hunched her shoulders as his hands framed them. If he kissed her again she'd capitulate. "I thought that first time that I was making love with another man. It would have been different if you'd told me the truth."

"Would it?"

Jo no longer knew the answer to that question. Had she really wanted him to be Brett, or was she banking on his being a stranger with Brett's face?

"You say you wouldn't have let Brett anywhere near you," he answered for her. "That you fell for Gus Thornton. *I* am Gus Thornton. It's my legal name. Forget Brett. I have."

"I can't. She broke away from his hands and turned quickly to face him. She kept her gaze well above the level of his navel, for even in the dimness she could tell he was completely naked. "I don't believe you can, either."

"Watch me."

"Your father—"

"Stay away from my father," he said abruptly.

"Why? Because he offered me a job? Why should I care if that bothers you?"

"Because I'm asking you to."

"Not good enough." She was suddenly cold, and trembling harder than before. Why didn't he just go away?

His expression hardened. "Don't make things worse, Jo."

"I didn't start this, but you can't have it your way all the time. This time I think I'll have it mine."

She had marveled before at his ability to remain absolutely motionless. His broad body seemed to hum in the silence. "Does this mean you're going to work for him?"

"It means I'll do exactly as I damn well please!"

She thought she saw him smile. "You do that. So far, it's always worked to my advantage."

Her eyes widened in surprise. "This tonight? It meant nothing."

"It meant everything." He ground the words out softly like velvet over steel gears.

"A hungry man will eat whatever is put before him," she said in defense of her body's reaction to his touch.

"Your hunger has a name, Jo. It's Gus Thornton."

"Sorry. I mistook you for Brett Ashwood."

"Don't." He sounded really angry for the first time since reentering her life. "The name's Thornton," he enunciated, his Australian accent slipping back into place. "It's the only name I answer to."

"Too bad you didn't change your face while you were changing your name," she bit out. "Then I wouldn't have made the same mistake twice."

"Don't fool yourself. I could've changed everything and somehow you would have known the real me. Remember what you said at the cemetery a few days ago? 'I'd know you if you were ninety and bald.' You *knew* me, Jo. The names don't matter." He took a step toward her. "Admit it. I'm in your blood, like a fever."

"There're treatments for diseases like you," she retorted, desperately trying to hold her ground.

She heard him chuckle. "But no cure, Jo. No cure."

She watched as he padded back across the dark room, unable to resist the sight of his long corded thighs and compact buttocks, which she had just been caressing. It made the ache inside her widen. She felt dirty, low, a cheat. She'd never even entertained in her mind the possibility that she'd ever use sex as a weapon. It was something that selfish frigid women did in bad novels about lousy marriages. She'd always thought of sex as something joyful, an intimacy to be shared only in a deeply felt relationship with someone you trusted. She definitely didn't trust this man, whatever he called himself. Nor, after tonight, did she trust herself.

When he had found his jeans and zipped them up, he picked up his shirt and shoes, dangling them off ends of the fingers of one hand as he came toward the window, and her.

He reached out and touched her cheek, his hand remaining even as she flinched. "You've wasted what should have been a good moment between us. I'm aching from the loss but it's a two-edged sword, Jo." He leaned forward and kissed her astonished mouth. "Let's make certain we don't both bleed to death."

She stood by the window and watched until he disappeared on foot beyond the boundary of the street lamp's circle of light. "I don't love him," she whispered when she'd turned back to the narrow empty bed whose sheets gleamed faintly in the dimness. "I can't love him. I can't!"

Chapter 18

Jo placed a head of lettuce in the grocery cart. Stevie, whose infant seat took up a considerable portion of the cart, stopped sucking on a teething biscuit long enough to give her a gummy pink smile. Jo made a funny face that drew a chortle from him before the biscuit found its way back into his mouth.

Jo moved the cart closer to watch Adelle pick over the strawberries. Three days had passed since Brett Ashwood had sneaked in through her bedroom window. Adelle hadn't asked her a single thing about Brett Ashwood, but those unspoken questions had hung like a pall over the household. It was time to break the silence.

"I called Mr. Ashwood this morning and agreed to work for him the rest of the summer. He's offered me a room in his house."

"That isn't necessary," Adelle replied without looking up. "Our house is your home, too. You're welcome to stay with us indefinitely."

"Thanks, but I think circumstances have made things too uncomfortable for both of us."

Adelle glanced up sideways. "You mean because Brett Ashwood has returned."

"Not for long. He lives in Australia," Jo replied as an opening into the conversation they had both been waiting to have.

"That explains the accent," Adelle said, as she dropped a few more berries into her plastic bag.

"He *says* he's changed completely. He's even changed his name. Calls himself Gus Thornton."

"I'll bet Mr. Ashwood is choking on that idea." Adelle picked up an especially juicy-looking berry and bit into it. "If you're asking my opinion, it's this. Do what you think is right."

Jo ran her finger along the top of the milk carton, wiping away the condensation. "You knew I've been seeing him?"

"I knew something has had you in knots since that morning in the cemetery. It wasn't until he showed up at the front door the other night that everything fell into place." Adelle handed her a strawberry and smiled. "You went to Little Rock to see him that first day, didn't you?"

Jo blushed. "Yes. But only because I was afraid that he'd come back to cause trouble for you."

Adelle tightened a twist tie around the top of her bag of strawberries and set it in the cart behind Stevie. "Jo, that argument never made sense. If Brett was the least bit interested in causing trouble he'd not have missed the first opportunity we gave him at the cemetery. As it was, he seemed only a little embarrassed at having been discovered by us. Why else would he have lied about his name?"

Surprised by Adelle's conclusion, Jo said, "If you thought that, why didn't you say something before?"

Adelle reached out to blot biscuit-flecked drool from her son's mouth with a tissue. "You weren't listening to me, remember? Looking back on it now, I think you were just searching for an excuse to see him again."

Jo frowned. "I called myself protecting you."

"You were attracted. Admit it." Adelle pushed the cart into the next aisle, both hands braced on the push bar to keep the loose right front wheel from sending it veering off onto a collision course with a produce case. "Aren't most women attracted to rebels and outlaws of one kind or another?"

Jo didn't answer directly. "I thought you were too much of a lady to think that way."

"Not at all. It's the temptation, the challenge." Adelle began sorting through the onions. "The 'am I woman enough to tame the male savage?' syndrome."

"Was it that way with you and Brett?"

"I suppose so." She dropped her onions into the bag Jo held out. "All during my senior school year, Daddy kept mentioning this young man he'd hired to work part-time. How Brett was so good in the office, really smart, but that he wouldn't trust him around any daughter of his. Naturally, when I came home I made a beeline for Daddy's office. When I saw Brett Ashwood for the first time, it was like he'd been ordered special delivery from Boyfriend Heaven just for me. All that sulky, smart-ass virility wrapped in bad-boy gorgeousness. What girl could ignore a challenge like that?"

"Not many," Jo admitted. She certainly hadn't been immune. If her sleepless night was any indication, she still wasn't. "He thought you were beautiful. He told me so."

Smiling, Adelle pushed the cart a little farther down the aisle. "Any time I could dream up an excuse to visit Daddy's office, I did everything I could think of to attract Brett's eye. Even stuffed shoulder pads into my bra." Her fair skin pinkened. "You should have heard his comments the night he discovered just how much of 'me' was Dacron fiberfill."

Jo grinned. "I told you that wasn't a good idea."

"Easy for you to say, when one of your bras could have been cut up to make four of mine."

Jo's mind edged her back toward the topic. "But Brett was mostly kind to you, wasn't he?"

Adelle shrugged philosophically. "He liked to kiss me and I liked being kissed by him. He'd had enough experience to make it more interesting than anything else going on that summer. We were both bored, couldn't wait to get out of Cedar Bluff. I was going to dance school in New York in the fall. He was going to Harvard. We figured we sort of deserved each other. And he was popular. After three years of boarding school, I was practically a stranger in Cedar Bluff. When I was out with Brett I was accepted." She slanted a glance at her cousin. "I knew I had made the A-list the night we went out to the levee."

"Caleb told me about your levee days just this week." Jo gazed at her cousin strangely. "Why didn't you ever tell me you felt like an outsider? All those conversations we used to have and you never once mentioned it."

"I felt dumb thinking it, much less saying it. Didn't you ever keep secrets?"

Jo nodded slowly, holding her cousin's sky blue gaze. "I had a crush on Brett, too."

Adelle laughed softly. "*That* wasn't a secret, Jo. You practically worshiped him with your eyes. Mother and Dad noticed, too. Your face would light up at every mention of his name. And the way you used to beg me for details of our dates. Sometimes I've thought he'd have been better off waiting for you, you loved him so much."

The statement took Jo's breath away. "I—I didn't think anybody knew how I felt."

Adelle reached out and collected three lemons in one hand. "He once told me he wished he'd married you instead of me."

Jo gripped an avocado she had picked up so tightly her thumb broke through the skin and went into the flesh up to her knuckle. "When did he say that?"

"The few days after we'd brought Zachary home from the hospital. I was still so sick from the anesthesia that I couldn't drag myself out of bed for those middle-of-the-night feedings, remember? You'd offered to feed him at two and five, only Mother wouldn't let you do both because you had finals that week. But you set your alarm, anyway. Brett was impressed by that."

"It was a hateful thing for him to say to you."

"Yes. But, in a way, he was right," Adelle mused thoughtfully. "You were more of a mother to Zachary than I got to be. Later, after the divorce, I used to cry with shame for the way I behaved during that pregnancy. When Sarah came along, I was determined to be the best mother on

God's green earth. I read every book, went to every class on children and childbirth I could find. I know it doesn't make up for the past, but I had to do something."

Jo nodded, fighting some emotional push toward tears. "Was there anyone not damaged by Zachary's death?"

Adelle sighed and gave her head a slight shake. "I think I've been a good mother."

Jo reached out and squeezed Adelle's arm. "Oh, you have been. You have."

Adelle gave Jo a meaningful glance. "Are you still in love with Brett?"

Jo dodged her cousin's eye. "I don't know. I thought he had changed but he hasn't. He lied to me big time. I don't think I can forgive him."

"If you love—"

"Love never solved anything!" Jo turned abruptly away.

"If you'll take a little more advice from an older cousin..." Adelle paused as Jo turned back and nodded her consent. "If you don't want him, then you'd better run like hell, cousin. Time and distance are the only cure for what you've got."

"What makes you think that?" Jo asked sadly. "It didn't work last time." As she disappeared down another aisle, she called back over her shoulder, "I'll pick up the disposable diapers."

"Well, if it isn't Ms. Secret Keeper."

Jo grimaced as she nearly collided with Fawn Gordon's cart. "Hi, Fawn."

Fawn yanked her cart closer to one set of shelves and parked it. As she came toward Jo her eyes were avidly bright. "You knew Brett was in town all along but you didn't say a word, you sly puss."

"He didn't want his presence known about town," Jo replied as she reached down for a plastic-wrapped package of diapers. What the devil was Fawn, of all people, doing in the infant-products aisle?

"I hear he's even trying to make it up with his father." Fawn idly inspected her nail polish. "I suppose the Ashwood inheritance would have something to do with that."

Jo pinned her with a withering look. "Brett Ashwood doesn't need to pander to anyone, not even his father, for his livelihood. He's made a new life for himself in Australia, owns an airline company."

"Really?" Fawn's blue eyes were perfect circles of amazement.

Jo could have kicked herself for revealing so much, but the words of defense had come naturally to her lips. "Look, Fawn, Brett—by the way, he calls himself Gus Thornton now—would like to be left alone."

"Did you say Thornton?" Fawn's expression went blank.

"Yes, the guy on the patio at the country club. That was him."

"I see."

"I hope so. Caleb deserves better than a nagging wife."

"You're absolutely right." To Jo's utter amazement Fawn burst into tears.

"Fawn? Oh, Fawn, I didn't mean to—" Jo reached out to awkwardly pat the woman's shoulder, appalled that something she had said had reduced her to tears. They might never be friends, but she didn't wish her harm. While the other shoppers rubbernecked shamelessly as they passed by, Jo broke open the box of tissues in Fawn's cart and handed her a couple.

"Thank you," Fawn said, her voice swimming in sobs. "It's just that I can't seem to keep a single emotion under control these days."

"These days?" Jo repeated, insight gaining rapidly on her confusion and consternation. "Fawn, would these tears have anything to do with the fact that you're in an aisle filled with baby items?"

Fawn nodded, mascara making black snaky trails on her cheeks. "I just found out this morning, and I don't know the first thing about babies." She gulped back a sob. "I'm no young thing. I'm scared witless, Jo."

Jo grinned. "Caleb must be delighted."

Fawn's mouth formed a tight knot. "He doesn't know."

"Doesn't...? Fawn, have you lost your mind? You've got to tell him immediately."

Injured blue eyes met militant green. "Do you really think he'll react well?"

Jo ditched the first answer that came to mind. "Fawn, Caleb told me this very week that what he wants most in the world is for the two of you to have a child."

The woman's gaze narrowed. "Why would he say that to you?"

"Because I was trying to convince him not to—" Jo did mental gymnastics because this was no time to tell a wife her husband had been thinking of leaving her. "Convince him *to*, that is, make up with you. Remember how hurt he was that you thought he and I were—never mind that. He was saying that he loves you and thinks the two of you would be even happier with a child."

Fawn sniffed back a final tear and reached for her purse. "I never thought I'd want a child," she began, as she pulled out a compact and flipped it open. "Pregnancy seems to be such a messy business."

"It's earthy," Jo returned. The face Fawn made sent her seeking another, better image. "Any woman who's anybody is pregnant these days. Anchorwomen, fortyish movie stars, even corporate CEOs. It's a nineties thing to do."

"I suppose," Fawn murmured past the lipstick she was applying.

"Think of it this way. It's not as though you're a teenage bride with nothing else to do. You've had a career first. That's very chic."

Fawn's expression brightened considerably as she tucked her makeup back into her purse. "You're absolutely right! I've always prided myself on being a modern woman. Just recently I've been seeking a new image for the boutique. Now would be the perfect time to introduce a maternity line. And later, we might go into children's clothing, only designer labels, of course."

On impulse she gripped Jo by the shoulders and brought her in close for a hug. "You're such a dear! I'm glad I told you first. You must come by for dinner sometime."

Jo knew better than to take the invitation personally. Everybody knew Fawn didn't cook. "Go find Caleb, Fawn, before he hears the news on the grapevine."

Too happy to even notice the gentle dig, Fawn cried, "I surely will!" and walked off, leaving her cart.

Jo walked back toward the aisle where she'd left Adelle in bemusement. The child couldn't lose between Fawn's and Caleb's looks. She only hoped that she or he got some other family member's brains. If only her own problems could be solved as easily.

She glanced at her watch. She had promised Mr. Ashwood that she would move in this afternoon. Her bag was packed. The only thing between her and relative peace of mind was Mr. Ashwood's son. She didn't know what he would do when he found out. Curiously, the thought didn't make her entirely unhappy. Somewhere deep inside of her pulsed the outrageous thought that he might again barge into her bedroom and this time she might let him finish what they'd begun. One thing was certain, she mused ruefully, she would never again make the mistake of trying to fight fire with fire where he was concerned. She'd been the one scorched, her banked-down emotional inferno ready to flare at any reference to him.

She recognized him from a distance of the full length of the store. Jo froze, her hand reaching out for the support of a baked-goods rack. He was standing in line with a bag of oranges and a carton of milk cradled in one arm. His dark head was turned away as he chatted with the man in line ahead of him. Her gaze slipped down his back, noting the way his shirt clung to it. He must have been out exercising. Of course he had. That's why he wore skimpy shorts that left yards of hard hairy sculpted leg muscles bare for any woman's roaming eye to peruse. The sight was doing things to her revived body chemistry.

If only she could keep a sturdy grasp on her anger, she'd be in good shape. As it was, she was two heartbeats away from running up to him and flinging her arms around his neck and saying that it had all been a great mistake. She wanted to go back to the morning after the storm when she had believed in him, and loved him. She could only imagine how hard it would be to do that. She knew exactly how much effort it cost her to force herself to turn and walk away from him. If only things were simple.

"I hope this will serve your purpose," Mr. Ashwood said as he gave the bedroom deep consideration. "If you'd like something else or want some of this furniture moved out, only say the word."

"It's perfectly lovely, Mr. Ashwood." Jo eyed the cavernous bedroom in awe. She had forgotten that a house this old would have enormous ceilings and tall windows to match. Yards of lacy window treatments fell from graceful arches. The effect was repeated in the bed hangings. Floral rugs faded by time to soft shades of pastel lay scattered across the highly polished oak flooring. "I feel more like an honored guest than a tenant."

"But you are a guest," he assured her heartily. "Your every comfort will be seen to."

Jo turned to him, her overnight bag still clutched in her hand. "Why me, Mr. Ashwood? And don't say it's because I need a job. This—" she indicated the room with a sweep of her hand "—has nothing to do with the job."

Mr. Ashwood smiled a bit sheepishly. "Let's just say the Ashwoods owe the Spencers more civility than we've shown in the recent past."

"You can't make up for what your son did," she said calmly. "Only he can."

"I know that. But I'm a father." She received his best good-old-boy politician's grin. "You can't blame me for trying."

"He will blame you," she said simply.

She was surprised to see his cocky expression falter. "You think we're making a mistake?"

I certainly am, Jo thought. Brett had flat-out told her to refuse the job. Adelle had told her to run like hell. Good advice in both cases. "What time would you like me to report for work, Mr. Ashwood?"

"Why don't we begin tonight, after dinner? Just the preliminaries, of course. I'd like you to know where everything is. Then tomorrow we can get off to a quick start. In the meantime, please enjoy the amenities of the house. The pool gets too little use these days. When Marilyn's three youngsters aren't splashing about, it stands empty."

An hour later, Jo was reclining by the pool, wondering why she hadn't ever decided to marry money. Money couldn't buy happiness, perhaps, but it certainly made unhappiness comfortable. A swimsuit had been provided, a colorful crushed-ice-filled drink produced without request and even music from the sound system provided the perfect environment for rest and relaxation.

"A person could get used to this," she murmured to herself as she readjusted the borrowed wide-brimmed straw shading her eyes.

"I wouldn't get *too* comfortable, if I were you."

She had heard the low purr of a car engine and the accompanying crunch of tires on gravel a quarter of an hour earlier but had chosen to ignore the implications of the sounds.

She didn't lift her hat, but when she opened her eyes she could see him through the cracks in the open weave of the straw. His face was in shadow, but even a blind man could see he was furious. "I'd have thought you would have worn off that excess adrenaline in the gym."

She saw him blink but it was slow shuttering down, as if he were changing the signal cards behind his eyes. "I asked you not to do this."

"And heaven knows an Ashwood always gets what he asked for, especially from a woman, right?" She couldn't keep the animosity out of her tone, but she wished she could have. She had wanted him to think he had no effect whatsoever on her.

Suddenly the sun was blocked and then she realized he was bending down toward her. She put up both hands to fend off whatever was coming, but he gripped her upper arms and levered her upright on the lounge chair. The hat slipped from her face, leaving her blinking into the light. When her vision cleared, the first thing she saw was his face inches from her own.

"You're driving me crazy," he said softly, every word a grudge.

"Good." She met his golden brown stare with obstinate challenge.

"I'm not a boy anymore," he said carefully between clenched teeth. "I don't like to play games with spoiled little girls."

"Then go away. That should be easy for you. You know all about running."

A spasm of emotion collapsed his anger as he released her. "Right. Brett Ashwood was a low-life coward." He straightened up, seeming even taller than usual as he towered over her. "There's just one thing. You keep confusing me with him. I'm Gus, remember?"

She shrugged elaborately. "Gus. Brett. The man inside is the same."

"Don't ever say that again."

She thought for an instant he might hurt her, though he never moved. The fear that started pumping through her made her even more bold. "What's the matter? Can't you stand a dose of the truth?"

"What truth?"

"That as much as you'd like to think otherwise, you haven't changed. Not where it counts. You didn't have the courage to tell me the truth of who you were. You played games with my feelings, even let me admit things no one else should ever have known. Now that you don't like the outcome, you want to go back to square one, start over. Well, Mr. Gus Thornton, life's not like that. You don't get to start over. You only get to go on. I have."

"Have you?" His tone was like the start of an inquisition, low and silky and unnerving. "You want truth? Let's both be honest. You didn't move on, you moved out of your life. I'm not the only person who ran. Living in Baltimore was tantamount to living in purgatory. You've spent useless years blaming yourself for something that wasn't your fault. If not for me, you'd still be wearing that hair shirt." Though she flinched, he went on. "If you've gotten on with your life, why aren't you married, or at least in a stable relationship? Better yet, why aren't you happy? I'll tell you why. You've wasted the past twelve years waiting for Brett to step back in your life and make you breathe again. You hate me? I don't think so. I think you're starved for the very love you deny."

"Who's talking about love?" Jo shot back, the summer sunshine feeling suddenly like needles driving into her skin.

His smile wasn't pleasant. "You did. The other night. You said you once loved Brett. You thought, hoped, prayed he loved you back. Jo, you were more courageous at sixteen than you are now. You offered Brett everything, in spite of everything. Now you're holding back, afraid."

"Damn straight!" She leapt up from the lounge, practically bumping into him because he refused to yield a step. "Because now I know the cost of loving the wrong man."

That made him smile. Too late she realized that she'd accidentally let down her guard about the single most important fact of their relationship. She did love him. "Don't look so smug. It means nothing. All the heat and hormones are only so much smoke. Like the saying goes, it's too hot not to cool down."

She snatched up her towel, well aware that his gaze had strayed from her face to her body. She felt her nipples stiffen and a frisson of desire. It's only chemistry, she told herself as she turned away, trailing the towel behind her. But the volatile elements were threatening a meltdown.

"I'll be seeing you," he called after her.

Jo didn't turn back, but the explosive expression on her face preempted the maid's inquiry about her afternoon by the pool when they met on the patio.

Chapter 19

"Why French?" Mr. Ashwood asked as the maid replaced their salad plates with the main course.

Jo looked up from contemplating her endive. "I beg your pardon?" Her host had been doing his best to make polite dinner conversation, but seated between father and son she felt like a prisoner being escorted to an execution. To keep her nervousness tamped down, she had deliberately kept her mind on her meal.

"The congressman asked why you studied French in college."

Jo glanced at the man on her left who had spoken. She didn't know what to call him. He didn't respond to his father's use of the name Brett, but neither Mr. Ashwood nor she could call him Gus without stumbling over the name. For his part, he had resorted to using his Australian accent. She turned to the father. "It seemed the antithesis of Cedar Bluff."

"But not very practical."

Jo ignored the son's comment and continued to address the father. "Practicality was low on my list of priorities when I left for college. I wanted to travel, see the world. By my graduation I'd lined up my first job overseas, as an *au pair* in Switzerland. It didn't pay much but the travel opportunities were incredible. I was really sorry to have to cut the experience short."

"What happened?"

His curt tone brought Jo's head around. "Reality, in the form of student loans. The bill for the first payment found me about six weeks into the job. I'd borrowed quite a bit to pay for my education. Suddenly my diploma meant I was thousands of dollars in debt. I came home to find a real job."

"I don't understand." Mr. Ashwood looked amazed. "Didn't your uncle and aunt pay for your education?"

"They offered," Jo answered carefully. "I wouldn't allow it."

"Why not?"

Jo shot her other companion an antagonistic look. "They had done more than enough for me. I owed them more than I could ever repay for taking me and rearing me. I was eighteen, legally an adult."

"And too proud to accept what you considered charity."

"Come now, son," Mr. Ashwood said in a cajoling manner. "Jo's entitled to a little pride." When he turned to her, Jo saw approval in those eyes so like his son's. "I applaud your independent nature. Many young people today can't be forced out of their parents' well-feathered nest. It takes character to make it on your own."

"Something you never thought your own son capable of."

The level of tension in the room cranked up several notches. Jo saw Mr. Ashwood compress his lips into a line, ringed in white from the pressure he exerted. She understood the effort required to control his temper. His son had been as provoking as possible since they'd come down for cocktails an hour ago. She glanced at his son and met a smirk she hadn't seen on his face in twelve years.

He leaned back in his chair like a kid, forcing the front legs off the floor. She nearly corrected him because the antique mahogany chair couldn't be expected to withstand such punishment. Instead, she let him see the disapproval in her expression.

His smirk deepened as he rocked back even farther, daring her to say something. "What kind of job did the French major find in the States?"

"What you'd expect," Jo answered shortly. "I was a salesperson in a department store for two years. After that I worked for a travel agency."

"It was as close as poor little 'Cedar Bluff Jo' could get to seeing the world, right?"

"Something like that," she admitted. Why was he baiting her? What did he hope to accomplish? "It was through those connections that I learned East Coast Air was hiring. Because I had the language qualifications, I was put through months of training and ended up in international security."

"Your flight privileges must have made your dreams a little easier to realize," Mr. Ashwood said kindly.

"You would think so, but I never seemed to find the time to make good use of them."

"Jo coaches a girls' soccer team," Brett interjected. "She doesn't believe in wasting time in frivolous matters, like joyriding."

His reference to the night they had gone dancing brought other more intimate images to mind before she shut them out of her thoughts. "Everybody has to grow up sometime."

"Really? I thought you were too much in love with the past to ever want to move on."

Too often the past week she'd had the urge to slap his face as she had that first day. She rubbed her itching palm on the surface of her napkin until she saw he had noticed her action. She stopped, clenching her fist, and saw his grin widen.

"What brings you back to Cedar Bluff, Jo?" Mr. Ashwood questioned into the palpable silence.

"I was laid off."

The front legs of Gus's chair banged down on the floor as he said, "So, you came home to lick your wounds."

Jo turned a furious expression on him. "I came home to be with people I care about and who care about me."

His eyes were bright with amusement. "You came home to hide."

Jo blinked back the fury that singed her eyes. "At least I came home as Jo Spencer, *Mr.* Thornton."

They both started at the sound of Mr. Ashwood's laughter. "Children, children. Dinner is getting cold. Suppose we suspend the fireworks to enjoy Cook's pecan chicken."

Jo picked up her utensils, but in her mind's eye the vision she carved with the sharp edge of her knife was a buzzard named Brett Ashwood.

She had been looking forward to this meal, the first she was to share with Mr. Ashwood as his houseguest. In trade for the black dress she'd left with Adelle, her cousin had insisted she accept a skirt of several layers of floating chiffon printed in shades of gold and brown and black. By adding a black silk blouse, gold belt and earrings she had dressed it up. She was glad she had gone to the extra trouble when she came down to find Mr. Ashwood in suit and tie. The aperitif he suggested of Midori, a melon liquor, and soda was zesty and refreshing. Just the thing for a summer evening. He was a perfect host, polished but easygoing, a master of small talk. The dining room table was set with damask linen, imported crystal and silverware so heavy and ornate that she knew it was part of the family heritage. She had just relaxed in expectation of a pleasant evening when the third—uninvited—member of the party joined them.

Jo glanced sideways at the man who wore a black T-shirt and well-worn jeans to a formal dinner. She half expected him to prop his boots up on the table. His stiffly waved hair stood on end in places from the blast from an open car window. He hadn't even bothered to shave. What he had done was go from charming to boorish without even pausing at dull. No, the one thing Brett-Gus Thornton-Ashwood wasn't and that was dull. Even now, as angry as she was, she couldn't ignore the fact that he sat less than three feet away. Even his obnoxiousness was sexy. Not that she would admit it under torture.

Gus might as well have been eating sawdust for all the attention he paid to the taste of the excellent meal. He'd never been more angry with a woman. What was worse, he couldn't think of anything else but her. He couldn't understand it. After all that had been said, after the way she knew he felt about his father. In spite of the way he felt about her and he knew she felt about him, she had done this. Moving into his father's house was equivalent to siding with the enemy. He felt betrayed by her.

He slid a sideways look at her and her mouth snagged his interest. It was moist and full, more tempting than whatever he was consuming at the moment. He wanted to reach over, scoop a hand behind her head and drag that mouth under his. He wanted to lick away every trace of hostility, replace the flavor of the meal with her delicious taste. He wanted to bury his tongue in her warm wet mouth and hear her sigh in response. But since he couldn't do any of those things, he wanted to make her as miserable as he felt.

"I'm leaving in the morning."

Jo's gaze swerved sharply in his father's direction as the flat statement resounded inside her head. She saw Mr. Ashwood's expression fall as hers must have. *He was leaving.*

Mr. Ashwood recovered first. His practiced smile returned. "You can't. You've just arrived." He looked encouragingly at Jo, but she couldn't think of a thing to say that wouldn't have betrayed her own feelings. "I'm expecting your mother in the morning," he added after a brief hesitation.

His son shrugged, his face closed against all expression of emotion. "I told her yesterday that I wasn't going to be in town long enough to make a trip worthwhile."

"But since she's coming..." Jo began.

"I've got an appointment in Fort Worth," he cut in, not even glancing her way. "I'm buying airplane parts to be shipped back *home*. I've got a flight *home* from Dallas the next day. Like everybody else, I have a life—and a *home*—to get back to."

Every mention of the word "home" acted like a hammer blow to his father's composure. "Surely, Brett," he began, only to stop as his son's expression darkened. "All right. Have it your way. Gus."

Jo saw the pain using that name caused him and wanted to throttle his son for forcing the concession. She laid down her silver and half turned in her chair to face their tormentor. "If this is for my benefit, you can stop."

He held her stare for a long moment. "This has absolutely nothing to do with you. It's a father-son matter. Now, if you'll excuse us."

Jo gasped softly at his curt dismissal.

"Son!"

But Jo was rising to her feet. "No, that's all right. I've had enough." More than enough. She felt slightly sick. She turned an anguished expression to her host. "Thank you for the lovely dinner. Next time, perhaps, the company will have improved."

She got as far as the hall before anger set her heart pumping more evenly. It had taken every ounce of her nerve to walk out of the room while her heart seemed arrested in its action. She had been angry, could have withstood every potshot he took at her, but she couldn't bear the beaten-down look in his father's face. She knew the source of rancor between them, remembered how haunted the young Brett had sometimes looked after a session with his father. In those days she had always sided with him. But that was over. He was no longer a son tied to his father's will by need and circumstance. He was a strong, successful man of independent means. If he wanted his father's approval, he had it. Even she could see the changes in Mr. Ashwood, how eager he was to please. What Gus had been doing in the dining room was beneath the dignity of the man he had become. Why was he behaving so boorishly? So viciously?

When the door opened behind her, she spun around. He came in at a fast clip, his face dark as thunder. He had no right to be angry, she thought. She did, and she was.

She stepped into his path. "That was unforgivable! To hurt your father when he's trying to reconcile—" She caught him by the arm as he continued past her. "Oh, no you don't." She tugged on his arm to bring him around to face her. "You're not leaving until you explain to me just what you're trying to do."

His eyes were as hard as agate as he shrugged off her hand. "I'm just being what everybody expected." He leaned into her, forcing her back a step into the wall. "What *some* people wanted me to be. The old Brett. Arrogant, selfish—"

"Boring," Jo interjected, lifting her face to meet the challenge in his gaze.

"Boring?" He said the word as though it had a taste he could savor. "I don't think so." He reached up and flattened a hand on the wall behind her. "I think you're fascinated."

"Think again."

He followed her progress along the wall as she tried to elude him. "The old Brett took what he wanted, isn't that what you told me?"

Jo halted as his other hand met the wall at her waist level, blocking her path. "I don't remember what I said."

"I do. I remember every word." He inclined his body closer. "I remember how jealous you were because Brett took your cousin into the boathouse while you had to sit and wait and listen and dream that it was you he was screwing."

"Don't be vulgar." She wished her tone had been more crushing. It sounded like a whisper for clemency.

"Why not? Wasn't Brett a son of a bitch?" He leaned in until she could see her daunted expression as twin reflections in his eyes. "Isn't that what intrigued you? If he'd touched you here." He laid his hand on the upper curve of her left breast. "Would you have brushed his hand away?"

"Of course," she answered, but didn't accompany the words with action. His little finger slid down over the crest of her breast and her nipple sprang instantly to life. The look of triumph in his eyes was hard to endure.

"If he'd kissed you, forced his tongue down your throat, would you have run away?"

"I'm not afraid of you." But she was unable to decide whether she feared most that he would or wouldn't kiss her. Which would be worse, to give in or struggle? Conflicting emotions eliminated any possibility of coming up with the right answer.

"Let's see if that's true."

His lips settled over hers with possession in mind. He sealed their mouths together in a deep absorbing kiss. Jo braced her hands palm flat on the wall on either side of her thighs. She wouldn't give in to his display of physical dominance. He took her face in both his hands, licking at the barrier of her teeth. "Stop this," she hissed as her hands curled into fists.

Sensing her resolve to simply endure, he switched tactics. He lifted his head fractionally and bit gently into her lower lip. Her murmur of protest pleased him. He sucked her sensitive lip into his mouth, the gentle tugging action eliciting a sigh this time. The next sweep of his tongue found access to her mouth. She tasted wonderful, better than he could keep in mind when he was away from her. Warm and wet and spiced with excitement, her mouth offered everything he could want from a kiss. Tilting his pelvis against her lower belly, he let her know the power she had to arouse him.

Jo brought her hands up to clutch his waist, giving up the pretense that she didn't want his hungry kisses or the touch of his body. She wanted it all and more. She wanted to love him, to know him intimately, to learn his body and then relearn it, to have the leisure to lie with him after lovemaking and know that he would be there always. She wanted to trace the pattern of his chest hair, to follow it down into denser brush and explore what made them gloriously and delightfully different. She wanted to know him better than she knew herself, to kiss the scars and heal the pain. To make him happy.

A noise at the far end of the hall brought back reality. They pulled apart, breaths coming quickly between parted lips. Both heads turned guiltily in the direction of voices as a figure crossed the back end of the hall and disappeared. Finally there was no excuse not to look at each other.

They gazed deeply into one another's eyes, each gauging the effect of the last moments on the other's temper and powers of persuasion.

Feeling the most vulnerable, Jo licked her lips free of the taste of his kiss and said, "What now?"

"Dammit, Jo," he muttered and ducked his head to claim her lips in a hard kiss. When he lifted his head, his face was flushed. "You play with my head, Jo. I can't leave like this. Come home with me."

"Where?" she whispered in disbelief.

He buried his head in the curve of her neck. "Come to Queensland. Let's start over. Come see what I've built there. Get to know me as I am when I'm away from all this."

His words should have been the very ones a woman in love wanted to hear. They lacked only one thing. "You're asking me to come halfway around the world with you. For what?"

He frowned. "For this." He touched her low. "And because I need you."

"You hardly know me," she answered, making up excuses to defend herself against the powerful persuasion of her own needs.

He smiled. "I will. Better each day."

"What if you don't like what you discover?" His roguish grin made her add a little breathlessly. "I mean about Jo Spencer the person."

He searched her face. "Why are you making this difficult?"

"Because it is." He was touching her again, his fingers curved along the column of her neck as his thumb lazily stroked her jawline just below her left ear. Did he know what he was doing to her? How could he not? "You don't live just down the road a piece. It will take my entire life's savings to follow you."

His expression cleared. "My treat. I'm not rich but I'm not poor, or didn't you dare hope?"

She looked away from his sexy smile. She needed to concentrate as never before in her life. "It's not about money. I don't know you very well. We could find we don't have enough in common to have a future."

He lifted her face with a hand under her chin. "I distinctly remember you saying that you don't like being thought of as a coward."

Jo stared up into his ruggedly handsome face, wondering why he didn't just say the words that would persuade her to come with him. She wasn't going to ask. She thought she knew the answer. She was part of his past, a past he hated and had wanted to remain buried. Because of her, he'd had to dig it up and sift through it again. Though he might not want to admit it, every time he looked at her, he'd be reminded of that past. If he didn't deal with it here, she knew there'd come a day when she'd have to deal with it in his new world, and that she might lose.

"Maybe I am a coward, after all. I can't just let go of everything in my life on a gamble." She rested a hand on his cheek, willing him to say something, anything that would reassure her about the depth and endurance of his feelings. "Stay here a little longer. Your father—"

He pulled back from her by degrees, as though the parting were a painful leaving of something of himself behind. When he had levered fully away from her, he straightened up. "Is that your answer?"

"What answer?"

"No. Is that your answer? No?"

"I don't think..." she began in confusion.

"Just answer the question."

His tone of voice gigged her temper. "It's not a fair question."

"Coward?"

"No. But in the past few days so many things have changed in my life. Things that I thought I knew about the past were wrong, things that nearly ruined my life. I'm not ready to just walk away. Neither should you. Your father is trying..."

He turned away abruptly.

She didn't know what else to say. She couldn't know to what degree his father had hurt him. Maybe reconciliation was impossible. Yet she'd seen Mr. Ashwood's face when his son announced that he was leaving. He'd been like a man watching from shore as a loved one drowned. Suddenly she was tired of fighting, of trying to figure it all out. "What do you want me to do?"

He turned, his face full of hope. "Come with me. Never look back."

"What about Adelle and Steve and the kids?"

"What about them?"

"Are you asking me never to contact them? Never see them?"

He spread his arms wide. "Can't we settle this later?"

"You can't be serious." Astonishment colored every syllable. "You can't expect me to give up my family just because you can't make peace with yours?"

"That's not what I said."

The great weight of sorrow dragged at her. "But it's what you are going to continue to do."

"Twelve years ago my father disowned me. That day I rejected him, as well. There's no turning back." His voice became lower, softer, more persuasive. "We'll be enough for each other."

She felt suddenly chilled by his coldheartedness. This was a side of him she had never before seen. "What if we had a fight, said things we regretted? Would you turn your back on me forever?"

"Don't make up stories to frighten yourself with," he said impatiently.

"I would forgive someone I loved anything." *I already have, because I love you.*

"Then maybe you are the stronger of us." His voice sounded weary. "I'm not brave enough to find out if there's anything left between my father and me. The wrong answer..."

She put up a hand to stop him as he took a step toward her.

"Don't throw away the best damn thing that's ever happened to either of us," he said angrily. "We've waited half our lives to be together. We're alike, you and I. We couldn't wait to get out of Cedar Bluff. This place is a ghost town of nothing but bad memories for both of us. Let it go. We'll be together. Nothing else matters."

Round and round, the question always seemed to come back to what he wasn't saying. *Do you love me?* She couldn't ask him without it sounding like a plea for feelings he obviously didn't want to voice. Or didn't trust.

"You're wrong. You have a family. You have the option of tossing it away. Mine was taken from me—no options offered. If they were alive nothing could force me to turn my back on them permanently. That's the difference between us."

She turned and hurried away, hoping that he wouldn't come after her, touch her, make her take back those painful but heartfelt words.

He didn't.

Gus sat by the poolside in the dark with his head in his hands. He felt like a man who'd been a victim of a hit-and-run. He didn't know what had hit him or why. But suddenly his life had veered off course and he'd been struck by circumstances beyond his control.

He'd never begged anybody for anything in his life. And that's what Jo had wanted, for him to beg her to come with him. It went against the grain. Everything he had done these past dozen years had been done to prevent him from ever needing to beg anything of anyone. Independence had been his salvation. Now the one person he wanted in his life expected him to beg. He didn't know how.

"Mind if I join you?"

He looked up at the sound of his father's voice. The yard was dark. The glow of fireflies twinkled in the nearby bushes, flanking the brighter glow of his father's cigar.

"I thought you gave up smoking years ago." His voice was harsh with disapproval.

Mr. Ashwood took the tobacco out of his mouth. "I don't inhale."

When his son didn't say anything else, he sat down heavily on the lounge chair next to him and balanced his elbows on his knees. "You love Jo, don't you?"

"So what?"

"Why don't you tell her?"

Gus stared resentfully at his father's silhouette. "What makes you think I haven't?"

"Have you?"

He turned his head away.

Mr. Ashwood tapped the ash off the end of his cigar into a nearby pot of moss roses. "You'd changed. Yes. I could see that the moment our eyes met on the porch a few mornings ago. 'My son's become a man.' That was my first thought."

"Don't try to soft-soap me. I'm not a registered voter."

"I wouldn't presume to tell you what to do. Only there's a very unhappy young lady in the guest room crying her eyes out."

Gus winced. "I asked her to come with me."

"And she refused?" His father's amazed tone grated.

"She says she's not willing to cut herself off from everything and everybody else in her life."

"She's a wise young woman."

Gus swiveled his head around, his tone belligerent. "Why? Because she doesn't trust me to love her enough to make up for all the rest?"

"Because she's smart enough to know no one can successfully run from the past. I'd wager it's not the distance that frightens her. It's that you want her to go into exile."

"Did she say that?"

"I haven't spoken with her. It seems to me she knows what she wants. That's to be with you. You just need to convince her that it's what you want, too."

"I haven't got time to court her," he said shortly, not really wanting to talk to him about Jo. "I'm expected at home. I've been away too long as it is. The months in the hospital—"

"What months in hospital?"

Gus met his father's startled gaze through the dimness. "I nearly died in a plane crash last year."

"My God!"

His father's fading cry surprised him. "Sorry if I startled you. To be honest, I didn't think after all this time it would matter to you much one way or the other."

"You nearly died and I didn't know, might never have known. It matters."

The silence between them stretched out as cricket chirps filled up the night.

"Your last words to me were 'You're no son of mine.'"

He saw his father's shadow rock. "I—I remember." The gruff edge of emotion surprised Gus. "I remember how you looked. Young, lanky, but defiant as hell. I told myself you'd be back, that you were just reacting to your son's death. You'd get over your rage and come home. Your mother believed me for nearly three months. After that, I thought I'd lose her, too. She filed for divorce."

"Because of me?"

"Partially. It made me take a long, hard look at things." He glanced at his son. "I don't like failure. I don't like losing. I'd failed you. I was able to persuade her to remain. I just kept thinking you'd come home, too, and that we'd start over."

"You don't know your power to persuade. I believed you'd disowned me. I legally changed my name."

He heard his father sigh like a dying man, a low shuddering breath of resignation. "No wonder you hated me."

"I did. And I'm good at hating. I used that anger to prod and push and force me to survive. And then I used it to help me succeed."

"Ashwoods always succeed," his father said with a returning glimmer of his old boastful self. "I never doubted you as much as I doubted me. Seeing you stumble was the most frightening experience of my life."

"You should have had more faith in me."

"I learned to."

"When?"

"After you left. I set about getting to know the son I'd been too busy to pay attention to. You want to know the name of your teachers? I can recite them all, kindergarten through twelfth grade. Test me."

"I believe you. But what good was that to you?"

"They knew you, Brett, and that was enough for me."

For the next two hours Gus listened to his father talk, offering an occasional glimpse into the past twelve years. It wasn't easy to offer anything of himself. He'd spent too long in another life to think of himself as Brett Ashwood again. But it was a beginning—sometimes boastful, tentative, truculent—but a beginning of a healing process.

"So, what are you going to do about Jo?" his father asked as they started back toward the house.

"I don't think there's anything I can do now." Gus rubbed his temples. "She said some things that made sense, dammit."

"She's waited a long time for you. I'd be willing to bet she can be patient a little longer."

He turned to his father and said before he could reconsider, "Will you look after her, keep her here until I sort out a few things?"

"I don't think anybody could keep Jo Spencer where she doesn't want to be. But something tells me she'll stick around awhile."

Chapter 20

Jo pulled a red pen from the brass pencil holder and struck through a sentence on the sheet of paper lying on the desk before her. As her eyes continued down the page, she absently gnawed the pen tip. It had been a long time since she had been required to write in French, and correspondence was especially tricky. Caleb's praise notwithstanding, she doubted her efforts were much above the most rudimentary communication.

"I thought you'd be finished for the day."

Jo looked up with a smile for the man standing in the doorway. "Hello, Mr. Ashwood. We were expecting you. I was just correcting a letter I'd written earlier." She rose from the deep leather wing chair she had been occupying most of the day. "Did you want to get to your desk?"

"No, no. I'm glad to be out from under pressing business for a change. Summer weeks in Washington are the longest. I thought August would never arrive."

Jo bent to collect her papers. "Things have been going very well here. I hope you'll have time to read my preliminary outlines of your material, now that you're home."

"I've already done that." He nodded at her glance of surprise. "You're quite talented. Have you thought of writing a book yourself?"

Jo laughed. "No. I wouldn't have anything to say. But I'm pleased you're happy with the results. There are days when I feel like an imposter. Sitting beside the pool and working in swimsuit and sunglasses all day, I feel I should be paying you."

"You earn your wages, my dear. You're the only person on my staff who can decipher my penmanship. My secretary on the Hill doesn't even try anymore. Insists I carry a minirecorder to make my notes on."

"That might be a good idea for this book. You're at your best on paper when it sounds like you're talking to the reader. The voice is casual, friendly, like someone you know well."

"My editor agrees."

"You've shown my work to your editor?" Jo offered him a nervous smile. "What did she or he say? Did they like it?"

He laughed. "Jo, you sound like a real writer. *He* said the book has the potential to be a major political bio. It does have a nice down-to-earth quality. Thanks to your judicious editing, I sound almost as clever as I'd like to think I am."

Satisfied, Jo plucked up her purse and water glass from the desk. "I think I'll do a few laps before dinner. I left your personal correspondence in its usual place."

He walked over and picked from the pile three blue envelopes with an Australian address. He tore them open and scanned each one before pocketing them with a satisfied smile. "Brett has become quite the letter writer. I believe I have you to thank for that."

Jo turned back from the door with a frown. "Why would you think that?"

"You did talk to him about me, didn't you?"

She looked down, pretending to fumble with her papers. Privately she was delighted by Gus's gesture, though it hadn't affected things between them. "Maybe I did mention something."

"Thank you. As letters go, they aren't much—three or four lines at most. And, stubborn man that he is, he signs them Gus Thornton. But his mother savors them like chocolates. I'll get these to her first thing. What do you think of his new postal service idea?"

Jo's brows rose. "I wouldn't know."

"He does write you?"

She nodded once. "I don't read them."

He studied the young woman before him. She was dressed in white shorts and a turquoise T-shirt that made her curls seem afire. With her open face, tanned bare legs and firm supple body, she would certainly be attractive to his son. But he knew it was more than that. During the weeks of his association with Jo Spencer, she had proved to be as smart, sensitive and incisive as any member of his trusted staff. He had half a mind to ask her to come to Washington with him, but so far Brett's interests had prevented him from doing that. If, however, by fall his hotheaded son hadn't made a decisive move, he would ask her.

Jo waited until his gaze moved away. "There is something I'd like you to do for me, if you don't mind."

"Name it."

"The next time you correspond with your son, would you ask him to stop writing me?"

He noticed she had a death grip on her papers. He didn't need to be a veteran in delving into the motives of others to figure out what was wrong. "Don't you think you should find out what's in those letters before you send him that message?"

Jo shook her head. How could she explain her feelings when she barely understood them herself? All she knew was that he had left without saying, "I love you." She didn't want that intimate declaration to come in the form of a letter. Yet anything less from him would be too painful to read.

"That's a rather hard line to take."

"I don't mean to embroil you in my personal matters. If you'd rather not send the message, I understand."

"No, it's not that I mind. In fact, I'd pay for the plane ticket myself, if I thought you'd go out there."

Jo checked a smile. "That's very kind of you."

He slipped his hands into his pockets, frowning a little as he chose his words. "I'm going to be perfectly frank with you. My son loves you. And I want him to have what he wants. You're just what he needs." He saw Jo's lower lip begin to tremble. "What's wrong?"

Jo shook her head slightly, embarrassed by her reaction. "You say he loves me with such confidence while he's never said those words to me."

"Why, the young fool!"

"Exactly." Jo composed her expression. She had no desire to spill her unhappiness over onto him. "But it's his loss. Now, if you will excuse me, I need to copy this letter and get it over to Caleb to sign."

He admired her poise. He respected her intelligence. But, looking at her slightly drawn face, he thought she was about as muleheaded a young woman as he'd ever met. "I've been meaning to ask about this business of holding down a second job. I hope Caleb's not working you too hard."

Jo grinned. "Not at all. Of course he seemed to think that because I speak French I should know German, Italian and Arabic, as well. As he says, foreign languages all sound pretty much the same to him."

The congressman shared her amusement. "What do you do about the other correspondence?"

"I have a system. The Arabic goes to the greengrocer, Mr. Akbar. The Italian is translated by the shoemaker, Mr. Barrarotto. The German is done for me by Mrs. Rhuel, the librarian."

"I like resourceful people. Will I see you at dinner?"

"Of course."

When she was gone, Mr. Ashwood sat back in the leather wing chair she had abandoned and contemplated the view from the window behind him. What he had in mind was going to require some orchestrating. He couldn't send her Down Under because she wouldn't go. He couldn't summon his son home because he wouldn't come. It was a puzzlement.

As he swung back around, his gaze lit on one of the letters Jo had been working on for Caleb Gordon that she must have overlooked. The letterhead read MAITLAND MO-

TORS, MELBOURNE, VICTORIA, AUSTRALIA. Smiling like the devil himself, he reached for his phone.

"How can I?"

"Well, I certainly can't go along in my condition."

Jo chuckled as Fawn patted her belly. Though three and a half months along, Fawn still possessed a stomach flatter than that of many unpregnant women. They were sitting on Fawn's front porch while Fawn practiced deep-breathing exercises. "I don't see the problem. Let Caleb go alone."

Fawn practically choked on an inhalation. "You can't be serious. I've seen those commercials, miles and miles of sunny beaches and miles of slim young bodies showing practically all God gave them. Blondes, every one of them." She touched her own hair, which had been styled into a softer, more touchable look. Even her signature red fingernail polish had been traded for seashell pink. Fawn was making motherhood a serious fashion statement. "Caleb has a weakness for blondes."

"Then get a travel release from your doctor. It's early enough in your pregnancy to travel."

Fawn drew herself up indignantly. "I don't want my baby on foreign soil. He's going to be an American. I want him eating only American food and breathing only American air."

Jo didn't even attempt to countermand that statement with logic. Fawn, the mother-to-be, was operating on a level of understanding all her own. "Then let Caleb go alone. He's been overseas a dozen times before."

"But I've never been pregnant before," Fawn challenged.

That non sequitur left Jo scrambling for new ground. "Okay, consider this. Caleb's never been a father-to-be before. He's so proud I doubt he even knows there's another woman on the planet besides you right now."

"That won't keep women from noticing *him*. The man needs protection."

Jo stared at her. It wasn't like Fawn to encourage Caleb's association with any other woman, herself included. All Jo could figure was that this was Fawn's way of trying to prove her trust after the accusations she'd made against her at the beginning of the summer. "From what he said originally, he wasn't all that hot to go in the first place. Maybe you can get him to stay home."

Fawn began to pout. "I thought you were my friend. I thought when you took the job Caleb offered you, it was a sign of peace."

"I appreciate the job, Fawn, but—"

"There are limits to your loyalty. Is that it?"

Jo sighed in exasperation. "I give up."

"Does that mean you'll go?"

"It means I'll think about it. Though, for the life of me, I can't imagine what good I can be to Caleb, standing in the desert watching cars churn up dust while I fry in the heat."

"You can translate," Fawn suggested.

"Oh, for the love of Mike! Australians speak English, Fawn."

"Not very well, at least according to Caleb, not so a *normal* person can understand them."

Jo took away with her the distinct impression that she had been manipulated. She just didn't know for what purpose.

Perhaps I don't want to know. In her heart of hearts, she had secretly jumped at this chance to go to Australia when it first came up. At the very least, it was a place she had always wanted to visit. She didn't even dare dwell on the other, much more enticing, reason for wanting to go there.

Of course, she reminded herself, visiting Melbourne wasn't exactly landing in Gus Thornton's backyard. He lived more than fifteen hundred miles to the north. She wouldn't have to sneak in and out of the country to avoid him. The chances of running into him were akin to spying a friend who lived in Dallas on the streets of Boston. No, the chances of running into him were about nil. Unless she wrote him.

"No." Jo shook her head as she rang her cousin's doorbell. She had some pride. That's why she had avoided reading his letters, which would have weakened her resolve. She wasn't going to beg him to see her again. He had left her. He would have to come back to her...if he came back at all.

She had made a few other decisions about her life. One was that as much as she liked Mr. Ashwood and the work she was doing for him, she was going to leave Cedar Bluff. As the weeks passed, the town had been gradually closing in on her. Despite having grown up here, she felt like a stranger in many ways. The rhythm of life was too different, too soothing. She was restless and bored and vaguely unsatisfied. So many things reminded her of Brett and what had been. Everything else reminded her of Gus and what might have been. As much as she hated to admit it, he had been right about her hiding from life. She just didn't know what she was going to do next. If a visit Down Under was tempting fate, then so be it.

"You're right on time," Adelle greeted her when she'd opened her front door. "I've set out the jars for Stevie's supper. Sarah's already had her bath. The pizza has been ordered. Should arrive any minute. Are you sure you don't mind sitting?"

"Not at all," Jo assured her as she followed her cousin into the living room. As harrowing as the night of Sarah's accidental poisoning had been, it had become the turning point in her relationship with Adelle's children. She was no longer afraid to be alone with them. "By the way, the dress looks fabulous on you."

Adelle turned and gave her a tentative smile, running a hand over her lycra-covered hip. "You really think so? It's not too much for a business party?"

Jo gave her cousin an approving once-over. "You'll knock them dead. Steve should make senior partner on your style alone."

"It really is a fun dress. Thanks. Now, you know where diapers, pajamas and storybooks are?"

Jo nodded, reaching down to hug Sarah who came barreling toward her with a squeal of "Aunt Jo!" and locked on to her at knee level.

"Where's your soccer ball?" Sarah questioned enthusiastically. "We're supposed to have a lesson. You promised."

"Tomorrow, after breakfast," Jo replied. "Tonight it's a Disney video and game of Candyland."

"But...in...the...morning..." Sarah spun out.

"Yes, in the morning." Jo gave her an extra squeeze. "Now where's Stevie?"

"In his playpen. He pulled up today. Mom says he'll be walking before we know it." Sarah rolled her eyes. "Then there'll be the devil to pay."

Sarah's adult phrasing made both mother and aunt smile.

As Sarah returned to her TV viewing, Adelle gave her cousin an appraising look. "Well? Have you decided?"

Jo didn't have to ask what she was referring to. "I suppose the whole town knows. Yes, I'm going."

"Are you going to write him?"

Jo shook her head. "No, and I'm going to extract a promise from Mr. Ashwood that he won't contact his son, either. I'm not going there for that."

"It's an awfully long way to go *not* to see him."

"If he wants to see me, he knows where to find me."

Adelle didn't say anything else, but the look she gave Jo left her with the distinct impression that she wasn't fooled by Jo's cavalier tone of voice.

Later, after the children were in bed, Jo drifted back into the family room and perused the shelves for reading material. When her eyes lit on Adelle's wedding album stuck far back in one corner, she pulled it out and sat down cross-legged on the floor to look at it. It wasn't until she opened the cover that she realized this wasn't Adelle and Steve's wedding album, but Adelle and Brett's.

She had forgotten that both families had insisted on the full regalia of a happy marriage. There had been formal invitations, a bridal shower Adelle had been too ill to attend and a wedding reception at the country club.

With a sense of anticipation, she lifted the lacy flyleaf. The first picture was of the bride and her maids of honor.

Jo bent over it to peer closely at the faces. Adelle's natural willowiness had made it easy for her to wear a gown with a nipped-in waist despite the fact that she was more than three months along. The gown was elaborately laced and beaded, the veil an antique. She looked, at first glance, like a society-page dream. Yet as Jo's gaze searched the ghostly pale face shining out from the picture, she wondered if any other bride had ever looked so overwhelmed by her raiment?

Her scrutiny slid sideways. Standing next to her cousin in a gown of royal blue was a young girl with bright red hair and an expression of bruised unhappiness. Jo sucked in a breath of surprise. She'd never noticed that before. No wonder Adelle had always suspected that she was in love with Brett. The camera hadn't lied in this case. She'd felt as miserable as she'd looked.

Finally, she turned the page.

Brett Ashwood wore a tuxedo. She remembered thinking at the time that he was the most handsome, fearless person in the world. Now her jaw dropped. The Brett who stared back at her from the picture looked incredibly young and vulnerable. The smirk that had become a permanent fixture on his face in those days yielded to her inspection now the truth of what it was—a mask of protection against harsh realities that he could neither prevent nor avoid.

As she gazed at the sullen young man in the picture, trying to reconstruct her feelings for him, eyes of tawny gold as warm and stimulating as a sip of Jack Daniel's black label superimposed themselves over the picture before her. Those eyes held a history the boy in the album could not yet conceive of. The face that assembled itself in her mind's eye was stronger yet, strangely, more compassionate than its leaner counterpart. The proud expression marked a self-determined man. She remembered tracing with a fingertip the arch of those brows, lingering over the scar that made a permanent crescent moon above his left eye.

His nonchalant sexiness had made her feel both female and desirable. It was a fact of life, not a lure for self-gratification. He'd been an unselfish lover, something she couldn't judge but suspected that the Brett in the picture under her fingertips had not been. Yet the foundation of the man he had become was there even then. Nineteen-year-old Brett hadn't taken advantage of her when she'd all but climbed on him. He'd said they should wait.

Twelve years had been an incredibly lonely wait.

Jo turned page after page, seeking something that, seemingly, had evaporated. The boy of her bittersweet memory was not contained in this volume. Gradually it came to her that the Brett of her fantasies might well never have existed. He was her first hard crush, but not her first love. How could he have been when he wasn't free to return her feelings? No one had ever returned her feelings the way a certain Australian who called himself Gus Thornton had.

Jo shut the book and hugged it to her chest, eyes closed. Perusing it had been like rereading a favorite story from childhood, only to discover that memory and time had embroidered the tale far beyond the words actually written.

With a pang of longing as intense as physical pain, she understood now what he had been trying to tell her before he left. By holding on to memories, she was denying the experience of twelve years of both their lives.

If he had betrayed their past, she had betrayed their future.

The man who had appeared in her life two months ago was the one she had fallen in love with. Coincidence notwithstanding, he was distinct from the boy whose images lay captured within these pages. And that was good.

Jo rose, then put the book back in its tucked-away spot. "What now?"

"I thought Australia was the land of sunshine, beaches and desert Outback. What the hell kinda weather is this?"

Jo silently echoed Caleb's rude assessment of the climate. The tourist propaganda had assured the unsuspecting that the continent was balmy year-round. Dressed in a walking-shorts suit, silk T-shirt and sandals, she was wholly unprepared for the antarctic breeze that nearly swept her off her feet upon stepping out of Melbourne's International Airport at Tullamarine. It was August, after all.

"A bit of southern blow, that's all," their host assured them with a sharpster's smile. "Not to worry. It's nearly spring. Two or three months off, at most."

That's when the full impact of their location hit her. The seasons were reversed. Directly opposite August on the calendar was *February*.

During the next three days, Jo had many chances to grow to appreciate the Aussie partiality for understatement and self-deprecating humor. She'd quickly become one of the boys after Caleb explained she wasn't his "Sheila" but an employee. Fawn had nothing to worry about, Jo decided. These men seemed to prefer strictly male company.

In fact, she quickly came to realize that there was no reason for her to be here at all. Their hosts, wealthy sheep-station owners with the resources to indulge their passion for fast cars, were kind and cordial, but Caleb preferred to hang out with the mechanics, and where he went, she went.

They took her everywhere. She went to the garage where she listened for hours on end to discussions about "revolutionary" breakthroughs in auto mechanics that might as well have been in Swahili for what she understood of them. At night they retired to a favorite pub where she learned the hard way that Aussie beers were larger and more potent than anything this side of Ozark moonshine. One afternoon she sat through a "football" game that made the American sport seem, by contrast, as civilized as lawn croquet. It wasn't so much the blood as the missing teeth that had left her queasy.

After three days she could "G'day" with the best of them, but she was ready to go home. Despite her resolve not to, she couldn't keep thoughts of Gus Thornton out of her mind. Everything she saw and did made her wonder if he had been there, done that. The third evening she nearly gave in to the impulse to call and tell him where she was until she realized that she didn't know how to contact him. She hadn't even brought his address, in order to resist the very temptation she now wanted to indulge.

She'd been through it dozens of times in her mind. It wasn't a cowardly streak that had kept her from contacting him before now. She'd read his letters, finally, and had been both heartened and disappointed by them. He harangued then cajoled her about her feelings but never once did he write the three little words that would have sent her hurtling toward the nearest phone. Now she didn't even need that.

That night she cried herself to sleep.

In spite of her increasing misery there were things that required her skills as a translator, as Caleb would say. She learned quickly to interpret the phrase "not a trauma" as a sure sign of trouble. It was said after Caleb had already agreed to follow the test car north to the testing grounds south of Broken Hill and then realized what it meant to drive on the left. Well, sort of.

"Seems like folks in this country don't take sides at all. Just drive right smack damn down the middle!" Caleb exclaimed after one particularly close call.

Looking for her heart, which had been left stunned in the intersection, Jo firmly closed her eyes and prayed. If she died, she didn't want to see it coming. If she lived, she didn't want to know the exact number of times she nearly didn't make it.

Driving north with Caleb did have its advantages. Acting as navigator kept her mind off Gus during the day. After the frigid temperatures of Melbourne, which looked and felt more like London than the South Pacific, the daytime temperatures steadily rose with the mileage. But that brought other concerns. One that gave her pause was the NRMA regulations manual they were handed when their destination was made known at a tourist shop at the border of New South Wales. It included statements like "The driver... should have a reasonable knowledge of running repairs," "A well-equipped first-aid kit, four and a half liters of drinking water per person, food and a reserve drum of petrol are essentials" and "Your proposed itinerary should be known so that, if necessary, a search could be made more easily."

"Not to worry," a companion assured them as he took off without any of the above. Jo began to worry with a vengeance.

When survival wasn't on her mind, Gus Thornton was.

Now, after nursing an aching heart through the Outback, she was certain of only one thing. She would never again risk losing for the sake of pride the man she loved. She'd wasted nearly half her life doing just that. She had learned from her mistakes. As soon as she got home she was going to make the first step. If he didn't take the second one...

"Not a trauma," she told herself. But she didn't believe it, even when she was the one saying it.

Three long dusty days after leaving Melbourne, they arrived at their destination. At least that's what the map said. The dirt track they had followed was at times nearly covered by drifting red dust. At least the color was familiar, a close kin to Arkansas river mud. The village was little more than a sheep station, including half a dozen buildings with corrugated roofs. Here, her lack of winter clothing was not a problem. Eternal summer reigned—without the compensation of air-conditioning. The experimental car they didn't want seen put through its paces was stored in a shed and uncovered in preparation for the following day's test.

The intricacies of mosquito netting were explained, with good reason. By morning Jo was ready to get on with another kind of Outback experience. What didn't bite sang.

She found Caleb, alone for a change, hunched over a breakfast of eggs, lamb chops and a stack of toast half a foot high.

"I want to go home," she said without preamble. "Now. Today."

"'Fraid we're stuck here a few more days," Caleb answered with an easy shrug.

She dropped into a chair beside him. "What do you mean, stuck?"

He smiled at her, and she couldn't help noticing that the sharp desert light did wonders for his elegant features. "Seems we forgot something. We're waiting for reinforcements."

"What sort of reinforcements?" Jo asked doubtfully and sipped the tea she was handed.

"We need a certain caliber tool that must be flown in from Sydney," Caleb answered, then loudly slurped the contents of his cup.

"Not coffee. Tea," Jo said in answer to his retch of surprise.

"Damn sheep whiz!" he muttered under his breath.

Jo took another sip, trying to accept the earlier assurances of their host that drinking hot liquid in this heat would cool her off. But with perspiration already sliding down her forehead at 8:00 a.m., she would need some time to adjust to the idea. "When will this tool arrive?"

"Any day." The fact that he didn't meet her eye wasn't encouraging. "Why are you all of a sudden in such an all-fired hurry to go home?"

"I'm plainly not needed here. I'm wasting my time and your money." *And delaying the start of my new life.*

"You should settle down, relax. Hang around a few days. Get a tan."

"Caleb?" she said ominously, as she leaned toward him. "Is there something I should know about this tool? Like, for instance, that it has yet to arrive in Sydney on a slow boat from China?"

"Not to worry," he quipped.

Jo groaned.

"I tell you what?" He grinned at her scowling face when she glanced up from the breakfast plate that had been set before her. "You can hitch a ride back to civilization with the feller who brings in the tool. Fair enough?"

Jo scanned his face for assurance. "Fair enough. If it's soon."

By noon, the general quiet of the station was disturbed by the low but steadily growing hum of an engine, an airplane engine, to be exact.

Jo went out into the brassy heat of the day with the rest of their party to watch the landing. There wasn't really an airstrip, just a pounded strip of flat earth beyond the holding pens.

The pilot executed a sweeping turn over their heads and waggled his wings before straightening out and coming in for a quick smooth landing.

Jo hung back a little as the others rushed out to greet him. Something didn't feel quite right. The moment he opened the door she knew what it was.

He stepped out into the sun, aviator glasses reflecting silver light, looking remarkably refreshed in khaki shorts and shirt.

Caleb stepped up to greet him, pumping his hand enthusiastically. "About time. Figured you'd gotten lost."

Jo turned and marched away. She knew now why Caleb had been so glib at breakfast. He'd set her up. Gus Thornton had arrived!

Chapter 21

She knew she was being a coward. She knew she couldn't hide much longer. She knew she should take the initiative, grab the bull by the horns, roll the dice and take a chance on fate.

She just couldn't.

Frozen in indecision, she sat on her bunk staring out the open door toward the horizon, where the red earth met azure sky in so definite a delineation that it made her eyes water.

Gus Thornton was in the next room.

She could hear the drone of male voices and the occasional outbreak of laughter coming from the pub room.

Perhaps he hadn't seen her.

Of course he had. If, on the odd chance, he'd been blinded by the sun, then Caleb's cry of "Hey, Jo! Look who's here" would have clinched it.

So why hadn't he come looking for her?

Maybe he didn't want to come looking for her. Maybe this was some sort of wild coincidence. Maybe it was a cosmic joke. Maybe it was synchronicity.

"And maybe pigs fly!"

Caleb had sent for him. After some thought it seemed to her that Mr. Ashwood must be behind this. How else would Caleb know how to contact Gus? Collusion certainly explained Fawn's strange eagerness to have her come along on this trip. The only question left was the big one. Did Gus know she was here before he arrived, or was he feeling as awkward and angry as she was?

Muttering in self-disgust, Jo unfolded her bare legs and rose from the cot. Then, with a sigh of despair, she sank down again onto the thin mattress.

He'd looked awfully good climbing out of that plane.

He was a little tanner, a shade leaner. No doubt he had been more active since his return to work. No more holidays fishing on the bayou or dancing on the patio of a country club. Even though she had turned away at once, she had, like a die-hard fan satisfied with the merest glimpse of her idol, noticed a dozen other tiny changes. Like the fact that his limp had improved.

The shift in direction of voices drifting in on the breeze made her jump. She slipped back out of sight of the door just as they rounded the outside corner of the building, heading for the shed where the experimental car was being kept.

Her eyes narrowed as she watched Caleb slap Gus familiarly on the back. She rose once more to her feet. No random chance had brought Gus here. Caleb was responsible. Perhaps Mr. Ashwood hadn't broken the letter of his promise, but it hadn't prevented him from contacting someone else who could then contact his son. Mr. Ashwood was nothing less than deceitful.

A few other less ladylike thoughts dashed through her mind as Jo grabbed her brush and dragged it through her curls. It seemed that nobody could be trusted.

Anger was a good antidote for indecision. The last thing she wanted was for Gus to think that she was waiting with bated breath for him to condescend to visit her. Damn him!

She put on lipstick, changed into a fresh blouse and shorts before going out toward the shed. The best defense was a good offense. She only hoped she remembered the game.

"There you are," Caleb greeted her as she entered the shed. "Wondered what happened to you, Jo."

Jo smiled in the general direction of the men gathered around the engine of what looked like a rocket turned on its side with four wheels attached. "I was tired. Took a nap."

"You missed lunch." His reproach sounded as if she'd breached one of the Commandments.

"It's too hot to eat." She carefully avoided looking at Gus, who stood beside him. Let him speak first.

"Aren't you going to say hello to Gus?" Caleb encouraged, like an eager kid.

"I was wondering the same about him," Jo answered smoothly. She turned her head fractionally in his direction. "Hello, Gus."

"G'day, Jo." The sound of his voice, the accent he'd used to seduce her, made her quiver inside. "You're looking well."

She heard one of the mechanics murmur, "She *knows* him."

"Figures," answered another. "Lucky bloke."

She saw Caleb's glance swing between Gus and herself in the first calculating gesture she'd ever seen him make. Yes, he was definitely one of the culprits. "I was just saying how you said you wanted to get away for a few days. Gus has offered to show you the sights."

Jo could have shrieked in frustration. She didn't want them forced together by circumstance. Didn't anyone understand that? Their moment of meeting wasn't supposed to happen in hundred-degree-plus heat and before a nosy audience of mechanics. "I'm not here to sightsee," she said carefully. "I'm here to trans—to assist you."

Caleb held up a racket wrench. "Like you said at breakfast, does it look like I need you now?"

Six pairs of male eyes watched her in amusement, waiting for her reply. "Okay, so I'm as useful here as a fifth wheel. But I don't want a guided tour. I want...oh, I don't know." Fury made her skin feel hot. "I'll muck about on my own."

"What's the matter, Ms. Spencer? Lost your nerve?"

She turned an indignant expression on the man she'd almost despaired of seeing again. Now that he was before her, all she could think about was that maybe he didn't want to be here. She wasn't going to grovel. "It's not the offer, Mr. Thornton. It's the company."

His eyes wrinkled at the corners. "What if I asked you very nicely?"

She tucked her chin in, resisted the teasing lights in his eyes. "What if you did?"

"Would you say yes?"

"Why don't you ask and find out?"

One of the mechanics let out a low whistle.

Smiling, he leaned across the hood toward her. "Will you allow me to show you a bit of my adopted homeland, Ms. Spencer?"

"Why?"

"Let's just say I've a special interest in your reaction."

Jo could feel the curiosity of those in the shed mounting. "When do you want to leave?"

"Now."

"Now?"

"Unless you've got something better to do."

"No." Jo let the syllable fill the space of a dozen questions she wouldn't ask before strangers. "I'll just get my things."

"I'll help you." He turned and stuck out a hand to Caleb. "See you in a few days."

She didn't wait to hear their exchange, but the mechanics' grousing came clearly to her ears.

"Why is it the American always gets the girl?"

"Don't you watch movies?"

"What about *Crocodile Dundee*?"

"What about him? You saying you got a *knife* that big?"

The ribald laughter made her smile despite herself. Her humor didn't last. As Gus Thornton fell into step beside her, she found it took her whole effort of concentration just to breathe. She couldn't be flip and easygoing with him. She loved him, and she didn't know the first thing about how he now felt about her at this point.

She stopped short in the full sunshine, halfway across the yard. "Look, there's no need—"

He touched her shoulder and gently urged her on. "Can we do this later, somewhere less conspicuous?" he asked coolly.

She glared up at him. "Right. Later." She turned and walked on while he angled off in another direction.

She collected her things quickly and hauled them out to where the plane sat on the treeless arid earth.

He was there ahead of her, lounging against the wing with arms and ankles crossed. "You ready for the adventure of your life?"

The question was so loaded that she didn't know quite how to answer it. "Let's begin with you getting me up and down in one piece."

He grinned at her. "Going up and down with you is my favorite daydream."

The remark tightened the growing knot in her stomach. If he thought she was coming with him for a fling— "What?"

He was tugging on the corner of her bag. "I said, aren't you going to let me stow your luggage?"

She released the handle but not before his hand brushed hers. He looked at her strangely as she backed away from him. "Are you all right?"

"Touchy. Must be the heat," she said, and turned toward the door of the plane.

She was amazed to see him store her bag in the wing of the plane. Once inside, she understood why that was necessary. There were exactly six seats, one on either side of the row, and no place to put luggage.

He nudged her from behind when she stopped at the rear seat. "Come up front and get the full effect." His hand pressed her right hip just below her waist. Warmth flooded her lower body. She wondered if the touch affected him as much as it did her. Afraid to turn and look into his face, she moved forward quickly and settled in the copilot's seat.

The takeoff was literally breathtaking. The swooping effect of leaving the ground made Jo gasp. Suddenly the rusty red earth was gone. Only brilliant blue sky filled the cockpit window. The pressure of gravity pushed her deep in her seat while the wind soughed past. As the ground continued to fall away, so did her worries.

"This must be how eagles feel," she enthused, smiling her pleasure as the small plane executed a sharp banking turn.

"Would you like to fly it?"

Jo turned a disbelieving look to him as they leveled off. "I couldn't."

"Sure you can." He released the control wheel and leaned back. "Take the control. Gently."

Jo stared a second at the wheel in front of her before grabbing hold. The vibration of the engines filled her hands, making the plane seem like a living thing. "Oooh," she breathed in pleasure, even as sweat popped out on her brow.

"Not so tight. You know how to drive. That's all this is."

Jo shot him a quick sidelong glance. "There are a few other options up here. Up and down, for instance."

He laughed, and the sound of it was more pleasant to her than the experience of flying.

"It's easy. Just follow my directions," he began, leaning closer to her but not touching the wheel.

For the next fifteen minutes he led her through a series of easy maneuvers meant to enhance her confidence in her ability to control the plane. Though she listened intently, she was equally aware of his warm breath brushing her cheek, of his lean fingers pointing out various controls or guiding her hand with the deft touch she'd experienced on her body. His voice was little more than a purr, low and confidence inspiring.

When he finally took back the controls, Jo slumped down in her seat and shut her eyes. "I can't believe I actually did that!"

"You've the makings of a first-class bush pilot. I suspect you've all kinds of talents." He sent her a warm glance. "You just need the chance to explore them."

She met his gaze a little shyly. "Thank you."

He shook his head. "It's this country. It's so immense. It's what you can do that counts out here. And there're plenty of chances to do pretty much whatever you're brave enough to dare."

"That's why you love it here?"

He nodded. "It's where I grew up."

She could appreciate that sentiment. "Won't you ever go back?"

"To the States?" He turned to her, his expression perfectly serious. "Not to live permanently."

She digested this before she said, "What is your home like?"

She saw the near side of his mouth curve upward. "Would you like to see it?"

"Yes."

They flew for hours, stopping briefly to refuel. It was nearly dark when he began his descent into what seemed another world. She saw strips of green land and in the distance the pleated folds of mountains and then it all disappeared. She had already learned that night came quickly in this country. One moment the sky would shimmer with the glorious colors of late afternoon. The next it had dimmed to night shades of purple. In the time it took to make a pass and land, darkness fell. She knew how familiar he was with the approach by the way he scarcely looked for landmarks and followed a single small beacon to the ground.

She saw a house in the distance as they deplaned, but when two men approached them out of the night, he motioned for her to wait by the plane as he went ahead to greet them.

Alarm touched her spine. They were absolutely alone, without protection or aid. She couldn't tell in the darkness what the men looked like, but she finally heard Gus say in a beleaguered tone, "Time enough tomorrow, mates. Tomorrow."

She heard laughter, the raucous kind that punctuated pub noises late at night, and then they turned away.

As he came back toward her, she suddenly realized the significance of her situation. It was dark. She wouldn't be going back to Caleb tonight. More than that, she was alone with a man whose motives were far from clear. He hadn't said anything significant on their journey, keeping their conversation light and the subjects neutral. She had concurred. The tension between them didn't need any encouragement.

When he reached her, he lifted a hand and touched her cheek with the back of his fingers. "Tired?"

"Hm."

"Hungry?"

"Yes."

He leaned close and brushed warm dry lips across her cheek. "I think I can handle both needs."

He took her hand and led her away from the plane. "What about my bag?"

"Later," he said softly, his fingers increasing their grip as he drew her along behind him.

The house lights looked especially welcoming, considering they were the only lights in the area. Tall trees formed skeletal sentinels against the night sky. Their lean, towering presences seemed exotic even in the dark.

He led her up the steps and across the deep porch to the door, which he opened for her. The main room was simply furnished but neat, with lace curtains at the floor-to-ceiling windows and fine old carpets scattered across the polished floor.

Jo turned to him, smiling. "It's lovely. Who lives here with you?"

"No one." He didn't smile in answer to hers. "You could change that."

The unexpected statement took her off guard, and she turned away to touch a nearby cherrywood table. As her fingers played over the polished surface, she reached for a light tone. "How did Caleb know you were in Australia?"

"He's always known."

She turned back in amazement. "You mean he knew you were going around as Gus Thornton and never once slipped up and told Fawn? I can't believe it!"

"Caleb has untold depths." He smiled. "I wasn't willing to talk to my father for many years, but I did want to know what was going on. Caleb's kept me informed over the years. He's been a right mate." He sobered. "He got you to come here."

Jo digested this information before saying, "I think your father might have had something to do with it, too."

"I wouldn't be surprised."

His calm reply amazed her. "That doesn't bother you?"

"Not the way it once would have. Not since it brought you to me."

Jo's gaze slithered away from the penetrating eyes watching her. "Why did you go back to Cedar Bluff?"

"I told you the truth. My doctor had ordered a long rest. The accident had made me believe I was mortal. The instinct to go home took over."

"And that day in the cemetery?" She had to see his face. She lifted a wary gaze to meet his. "Why were you there?"

He was smiling. "I had come into town to see Caleb. His shop is just a block from the cemetery. He was the one who pointed out Adelle's car turning into the gates. I was curious, so I crossed the street and climbed the levee to sneak a peak at her."

"What would you have done if Adelle had been alone?"

"I can't answer that. No, I think I can." He walked over and poured liquid from a pitcher into two glasses. "I'd have spoken to her, if she'd allowed it." He extended a glass to her. "You were right. I'd been running too long. I thought I was moving ahead, but I was still trying to outstrip the past."

She watched him with serious eyes as she took a sip. It was water, clear and fresh and cool. He must have a housekeeper, she thought absently. She watched him drink, enjoying the simple spectacle of his swallowing. Dear Lord, she loved him. "What did you think when you saw me?"

He set his empty glass aside. "That you were the most alive person I'd ever seen. That I envied your zest for life." He moved in close, reached up to lift a strand of hair from her brow. His fingers lingered to trace the smooth curve of her brow. "And that I wanted that joy for myself, wanted you."

She couldn't look anywhere but into his warmly lit eyes. "Then why the pretense?"

His forefinger traced an erotic pattern down her cheek to her chin, skimming the tender skin. "I wasn't prepared for my feelings. I didn't know what your life was like. You could have been married with half a dozen kids."

Jo trembled as his thumb grazed her lower lip. "And later, after you knew all about me?"

"I didn't know what I wanted."

She spoke so softly that he guessed more than heard her words. "And do you know now?"

"I knew two months ago but it scared the hell out of me." His expression altered, the glib cockiness giving way to an open vulnerability. "I love you, Jo. I know now I always have."

Jo smiled feeling every doubt, every regret fall away. "If you love me..."

In answer he bent and briefly touched his lips to hers. Even as he moved away he changed his mind and kissed her a second, longer time. When he lifted his face from hers his eyes were half closed. "I've been waiting to do that ever since I left Cedar Bluff."

"Then why didn't you come back?"

"Pride? Stupidity? Insanity?"

"I choose door number two."

His laughter was like water on parched earth; she drank it in gratefully. "You had me shanghaied!"

"I swear I didn't. It wasn't until Caleb called from Melbourne that I even knew you were in the country. I warned him that you'd be furious when you realized what he'd done."

"I was. I am." She blushed. "No, I'm not." She reached up to stroke his face. "I'm ashamed that Caleb had more sense than the two of us put together. I'm sorry for what I said about you running from your life. I can see you have a life, a very good life, here."

"You could, too, Jo. I could make you love it here as much as I do. You've got the spirit and stubbornness to make it work for you."

She frowned. "Sounds like you're praising a mule."

This time he gathered her close when he kissed her. And she embraced him in return because there wasn't any place on earth for her but here. She had been a stranger in her own life for too long. Home was here, in his arms, in his kiss, in the promise of their bodies to create a future more secure than any past either of them had ever known.

He found with his lips the pulse points at her temples, the throb of blood in her lower lip, the beat of life in the arch of her neck. She pressed herself into his hard warmth, luxuriating in his masculinity. Their kisses spun out as their hunger fed on itself. Each tried to get closer to the other. Clothing drifted to the floor and then they followed it, stretching out on the carpet with faded cabbage roses.

He pulled her over on top of him, wrapping her within his arms and legs. His kisses deepened, his harder, tougher body demanding the compliance of her softer self. He found the clasp of her bra and removed it. Then he rolled her over on her back, nuzzling and suckling her until she gasped with pleasure.

He reached down, found where her secret river flowed and whispered words of delight into her ear.

"Let me, Jo. Yes, good. Good. You like that? Yes, I can tell you do. That's right. You move so well, so sexily. Take the pleasure, Jo. Make it yours. For you. All for you."

Mindless, drowning in sensation, Jo gave up to his touch, dimly aware by his words and actions that he enjoyed her pleasure, exulted in his ability to please her. He drank in her breaths, his tongue matching the rhythm of his fingers. Suddenly she was shuddering deep inside, her breath little choppy gasps as sensations too intense to be purely pleasant undulated through her. She grasped his shoulders, her body arching against his as she whispered his name over and over.

As she subsided with a whimper of release, he nibbled her earlobe. "Jo. Jo, you make me hard as rock."

Then, incredibly, his hand slipped away and he levered his chest off her by supporting himself by his arms.

Jo's eyes flew open and met the dogged determination in his golden depths. "I seem to remember that last time it was you who pulled away early."

"You're not going . . . ?"

His chuckle was profane. "Not for heaven or hell. I just wanted you to have a taste of what you missed last time."

"You're incorrigible."

"As long as you realize that." He bent his head and kissed her so thoroughly that she moaned when he broke it off. "Jo, we've wasted enough time, don't you think? I can't live without you. I can't wait to tuck you into my bed and love you until I can't move."

She looked up into his passion-darkened eyes. Joy and love pumped through her. "For how long?"

"How about forever?"

"Is that a proposal?"

"It's a vow."

* * * * *

HE'S AN

AMERICAN HERO

He's a man's man, and every woman's dream. Strong, sensitive and so irresistible—he's an American Hero.

For April: KEEPER, by Patricia Gardner Evans: From the moment Cleese Starrett encountered Laurel Drew fishing in his river, he was hooked. But reeling in this lovely lady might prove harder than he thought.

For May: MICHAEL'S FATHER, by Dallas Schulze: Kel Bryan needed a housekeeper—fast. And Megan Roarke did more than fit the bill; she fit snugly into his open arms. Then she told him her news....

For June: SIMPLE GIFTS, by Kathleen Korbel: For too long Rock O'Connor had fought the good fight to no avail. Then Lee Kendall entered his jaded world, her zest for life rekindling his former passion—as well as a new one.

AMERICAN HEROES: Men who give all they've got for their country, their work—the women they love.

Only from

Fifty red-blooded, white-hot, true-blue hunks
from every State in the Union!

Look for MEN MADE IN AMERICA! Written by some
of our most popular authors, these stories feature fifty
of the strongest, sexiest men, each from a different state
in the union!

Two titles available every other month at your favorite
retail outlet.

In April, look for:

LOVE BY PROXY by Diana Palmer (Illinois)
POSSIBLES by Lass Small (Indiana)

In May, look for:

KISS YESTERDAY GOODBYE by Leigh Michaels (Iowa)
A TIME TO KEEP by Curtiss Ann Matlock (Kansas)

You won't be able to resist MEN MADE IN AMERICA!

continues...

Once again Rachel Lee invites readers to explore the wild Western terrain of Conard County, Wyoming, to meet the men and women whose lives unfold on the land they hold dear—and whose loves touch our hearts with their searing intensity. Join this award-winning author as she reaches the POINT OF NO RETURN, IM #566, coming to you in May.

For years, Marge Tate had safeguarded her painful secret from her husband, Nate. Then the past caught up with her in the guise of a youthful stranger, signaling an end to her silence—and perhaps the end to her fairy-tale marriage.... Look for their story, only from Silhouette Intimate Moments.

ROMANTIC TRADITIONS continues in April with Carla Cassidy's sexy spin on the amnesia plot line in TRY TO REMEMBER (IM #560).

"Jane Smith's" memory had vanished, so when Frank Longford offered her a safe haven and a strong shoulder, she accepted. Then the nightmares began, with memory proving scarier than amnesia, as Jane began to fear losing the one man she truly loved.

As always, **ROMANTIC TRADITIONS** doesn't stop there! July will feature Barbara Faith's DESERT MAN, which spotlights the sheikh story line. And future months hold more exciting twists on classic plot lines from some of your favorite authors, so don't miss them— only in **INTIMATE MOMENTS** ™ *Silhouette*®